CW00481034

SOUL CATCHERS

Also by Tony Moyle

'How to Survive the Afterlife' Series

Book 1 - THE LIMPET SYNDROME
Book 2 - SOUL CATCHERS
Book 3 - DEAD ENDS

The 'Dr. Ally Oldfield Series'

THE END OF THE WORLD IS NIGH

Sign up to the newsletter
www.tonymoyle.com/contact/

SOUL CATCHERS

TONY MOYLE

First Published: November 2017

ISBN 9781980380269

Limbo Publishing a brand of In-Sell Ltd
53 The Sands
Ashington, West Sussex RH20 3LQ

www.tonymoyle.com

Cover design by Lucas Media

For Tom, Amelie and Laure

*"Simply said, you put up with me,
although I have no idea why." T.M.*

soul

/ˈsəʊl/

noun

noun: **soul**; plural noun: **souls**

    1: the spiritual or immaterial part of a human being or animal, regarded as being immortal

    2: emotional or intellectual energy or intensity, especially as revealed in a work of art or an artistic performance.

catcher

/ˈkatʃə/

noun

noun: **catcher**; plural noun: **catchers**

    1: a person or thing that catches

Notes from Book 1 - The Limpet Syndrome

(Note: Contains spoilers)

John Hewson thinks he's ordinary. He doesn't trust scientists, isn't particularly religious and has no interest in politics. That's until his death changes his views on all of them. In Limbo, a massive metal sphere in the heart of the Earth's crust, his soul is about to be put on trial. It's the fate all neutral souls have to endure and he doesn't understand any of it. The Arbiter, an impossibly ancient figure called Laslow Kreicher, decides that John's fate is destined to be a hot one.

John's soul is drawn to Hell where Mr. Brimstone, a three-foot-high demon constructed from molten rock, proposes John's only chance of redemption. He must return to Earth to recover two souls that have succumbed to the Limpet Syndrome, an unexplained form of reincarnation. The souls belong to Sandy Logan, an old friend and the Minister for Homeland Security, and his incompetent accomplice, Ian 'Cher' Noble. They must be returned before the summer solstice when their presence could fracture the Universe.

Sandy Logan lives a double life, torn between a thirst for power and his secret passion for animal rights. When a bomb kills three government scientists, the Prime Minister, Byron T. Casey, wants to know why Sandy's department has no answers. Byron is nervous that this recent development will disrupt the production of Emorfed, a drug designed to subdue humanity.

Sandy and Ian go to the Tavistock Institute to confront Violet Stokes, a co-conspirator whom Sandy must hand over to the government. Instead they discover hundreds of caged pigeons being used to test Emorfed. When Ian forgets to adjust his watch due to the switch to British Summer Time their bomb detonates an hour earlier than planned, killing them and the pigeons. Agent 15, a ruthless killer with a secret OCD problem, manifested in the need to open and close every door three times, is sent to protect Emorfed.

Sandy wakes in darkness surrounded by a smooth, round prison, escaping only to be confronted by a huge pigeon. Unsure how, he's clear that he, too, is a pigeon, taking the revelation better than his friend Ian, who has also suffered the same predicament. John is sent back to Earth to possess the inconspicuous Edward Reece, but poor navigation directs him inside Nash Stevens, the lead singer of a famous rock band. Nash, a renowned womaniser and compulsive addict has recently slept with the Prime Minister's seventeen-year-old daughter, Faith, making John's possession even trickier.

Influenced by John's need to find answers, Nash is arrested on a flight to Geneva and thrown into prison on the orders of Byron. They're released a month later by Laslow Kreicher who reveals his knowledge of the Limpet Syndrome. John concludes that Sandy and Ian have been reincarnated as pigeons, but when he presses Laslow for more answers he grows violent, callously slaughtering the jail wardens.

Sandy starts to reconnect with the memorics of his former life and his determination to remain on Earth. At the forty-fourth attempt they master the art of flight and take off for London followed by a large swarm of the pigeons instinctively devoted to their protection.

Even though Nash is the prime suspect in a massacre, John convinces him to sell his story to Fiona Foster, a small-time journalist who has revealed secrets about Tavistock. Agent 15 reveals to Byron that Sandy is 'not alive, but not dead either', and an unexplained link between Sandy and Nash. Byron recruits his daughter to find Nash and reveal the link. Yearning for action, and egged on by John who is captivated by Faith's beauty and his own loneliness, Nash allows Faith entry. She discovers the link but is forced to relinquish it by Agent 15.

Ian, dispatched by Sandy, describes the dangers of the Emorfed plot to Violet. Nash and John then locate Ian and explain that his existence is threatening the Universe. Determined to make up for his earlier incompetence, Ian escapes, pursued by Nash and Agent 15, until his stupidity drives him to his death and his soul is returned to Hell.

John is forced out of Nash's body by an exorcism, but determined to remain with Nash, and motivated to stop the oppression of Emorfed, he unknowingly enacts the Limpet Syndrome. An unidentified voice indicates John's choices and casts doubt on his deal with the Devil. He explains how John can possess without being noticed and his ability to use the Limpet Syndrome once more. Returned to Hell, John discovers that the other souls around him emit emotions of hope. When he confronts Brimstone about the experience and the deal that they have struck, he gets no answers. John deliberates about who to possess next – Violet, Agent 15 or Byron.

At Trafalgar Square, Violet identifies Sandy, before both are captured by Agent 15. Byron meets Agent 15 to task him to take Emorfed to the water treatment plant, where it will be added to the water supply two days prior to a general election. Byron, the only one who recognises Sandy, reveals himself to be John Hewson possessing Byron's body. Determined to double-cross the Devil and save himself, he tells Sandy how they can stop Emorfed. John is devastated to discover that Faith is being held as a guinea pig to test Emorfed, robbing her of her emotions and vitality.

John conducts a TV broadcast where video footage, taken by Sandy, reveals the Emorfed plot against the British people. He steps down as Prime Minister, one day before the election and two days before the solstice. John reveals himself and seeks Nash's help to get a plane to Switzerland. Agent 15, whom John framed for the Emorfed plot, is waiting for them. When he threatens to kill him, John explains that only Byron will die. The pursuing pigeons and Nash come to John's rescue.

When they fail to find the entrance to Limbo, John knows he must kill Sandy to return his soul. Unable to murder, the mountains vent their disapproval and they fall through the Earth's mantel onto Limbo. John attempts to reverse the polarity and send Sandy to Heaven, but Laslow appears to stop them 'playing God'.

Laslow reveals that John's mission is a façade. It was always about getting him, not Sandy, to this spot at this moment. Realising the comparisons between Laslow's influence over him and John's own oppression of Byron, he is overcome by anger and doubt, shooting Sandy to regain control. As the solstice approaches, Laslow reveals that it was he who originally killed John. Laslow shoots Byron and uses the power of the solstice to heal his dead body.

John is dragged before Asmodeus, the guardian of Hell, and is shocked to find that Sandy's soul has returned, concluding that there is no Heaven and explaining the human need for the Limpet Syndrome to survive. His spirit is placed in an enclosed cell with only his guilt for company. As he struggles with the voices in his head he recalls his one last chance to use the Limpet Syndrome, one chance to put things right. When Brimstone is presented with John's empty cell, the only clue is the inscription, 'Remember Newton's third', burnt onto the side. John is gone, but not for good.

CHAPTER ONE

FROM GRAVE TO CRADLE

The tombstones stood to attention, row upon row, some faded and forgotten, some gleaming with life, as if the body inside had barely stopped breathing. Many of the inscriptions were illegible, the words appropriately faded for a long-forgotten occupant. Who would be coming to visit these ramshackle and broken monuments now? The living had no connection or memory to once-vibrant and meaningful lives. Their friends, family and descendants had long since passed on, or forgotten that these ghostly figures had actually been born in the first place. Such is the fading quality of the circle of life.

A lone finger traced the words on a cold, black stone, etched with gold font, pronouncing in just four lines a life that had consumed several decades. This grave was somewhat fresher than the others. No rough, lichen-encrusted words for these fingers. Only the deep cuts of a chisel left more than a decade before these hands became the first to follow it.

As the conflicting elements of old stone met young hand, the clean, unblemished finger made out a letter J. Slowly it traced out an O, his other hand leaping forward with excitement to assist in the discovery. The second hand found an H and with an anxious anticipation it hesitated. This was the grave that the boy had been searching for all his life. Across continents he'd travelled to quench the curiosity living in him since his very first memories. He opened his eyes once more and placed his right index finger against the final letter, N.

Even though he could see the headstone as clearly as he could see the sandals on his feet, only the feel of the word made the experience tangible. The sensation of touching an object with a genuine connection to someone that you have spent so long searching for. Decades after being buried deep beneath your feet has no impact on how much you love someone. The passage of time doesn't stop you missing them or removing the harbouring resentment that things could have been so different.

Aching from the cramp that had settled in his knees, he shuffled his position, brushing his long, black hair from his eyes where tears were noticeable only by their absence. This was not a visit of sorrow. What was the use of tears if he could no longer influence the result? This was merely a pilgrimage that had taken him across distant countries and wide oceans to an image indented in his consciousness for as long as he could remember. The image that now lay in front of him may well have been the first picture that had ever entered his mind. Impossible as it sounded, this gravestone was his oldest memory. Certainly it had brought him to this spot and driven away eleven years of dreaming.

His eyes settled once more on the black marble. In a vase at the bottom drooped a simple collection of wilted daffodils well past their replacement date. The ceramic pot had long since dried out in the scorching summer heat, unable to scurry for the shade of the nearby trees. The sight of these miserable flowers seemed to prompt the boy. Reaching inside his green satchel, he removed his own offering. Emptying the daffodils from their parched grave, he planted a single white yarrow flower in their place.

Sacrificing his last mouthful of water, he emptied the plastic bottle into the vase. His thirst was secondary to hers. The white flower appeared to grow in its new home as it drew up the liquid through its stem. The offering was purely symbolic. There were plenty of stories surrounding this simple little flower. Its rumoured ability to heal the sick would be utterly redundant in the face of a twelve-year-old corpse with several feet of soil between it and them.

Not for the first time the world was ignoring him. The loneliness of the single mourner at peace amongst the lonely. How long had he been here? The sun was already seeking refuge behind the trees, waiting for the next region of the Earth to hitch-hike into view before continuing its tireless, unwavering duty. He had done what he wanted to do, so why was he waiting? There were plenty more jobs to complete. As the only current visitor in a cemetery overflowing with history, somehow he felt his presence was keeping the dead alive, just for a while at least. The moment he stood up and left, John Hewson would cease to be again, all deeds and achievements lost amongst the graves with only the vegetation for company, the only organisms willing to live permanently amongst the dead.

"The nerve of it. How dare you come here?"

Above the boy's right shoulder the voice had appeared, unannounced and unwelcome. Calmly he flicked the black, sleek hair from his eyes again in an attempt to look more presentable and less hoodlum. Even as he stood up the woman's demeanour projected her five-foot frame like an eagle extending its wingspan, rendering his six feet of height meaningless. She was never going to know, but this wasn't the first time she had made him feel this small. David Gonzalez was about to be put on the spot with one of the last people he wanted to be tested against.

"What have you been doing this time?" said the woman, prodding a firm finger in his direction with one hand whilst the other clutched a collection of freshly cut daffodils.

"I'm sorry but I don't know what you mean," replied David.

The boy's Latino accent complemented his natural olive skin, which had been reinforced by the unseasonably hot British summer. It wasn't uncommon for a boy to look such a way in this part of the world. But in the eyes of this woman, her prejudices said foreign, and for foreign read trouble.

"You've been putting graffiti on my son's grave again, haven't you? Well, now I've caught you. I'm going to ring the police right now. That'll put a stop to it."

David doubted the notion, but wasn't prepared to find out if the police had anything better to do.

"Don't do that," he said serenely. "I really haven't written anything on John's grave. I don't think there *is* any graffiti, and if I had do you think I would be standing here talking about it?"

It wasn't usual for these toe-rags, as she saw them, to hang around. Normally they turned on their heels as soon as she confronted them. "No graffiti! Obviously you haven't been looking very hard, have you?"

Her prodding finger turned into a grasp, pulling him by one skinny arm to the rear of the tombstone. Daffodils directed David's gaze to an inscription carved into the back of the stone. It was understandable how he'd missed it, the backs of gravestones being one of the most unobserved objects in the known Universe.

There are many odd activities that people participate in for *fun*: plane spotting, collecting engine serial numbers, and even finding visions of Jesus in bits of burnt toast. But to his knowledge there was no association for spotting anomalies on the back of tombstones. David was about to become their first and only member, because what he found on the back of this one was particularly fascinating.

It wasn't just what was written that drew his attention. These markings were no rush job piece of graffiti. With skill and artistry the work had to be delivered with the same care and patience as the chisel that had carved the front: each letter in line with the next, straight and even. Each one bold and sharp, shouting for attention, desperate not to be missed. This wasn't vandalism, it was clearly a four-word message for someone.

'GOD PROTECTS THE KING'

David read it again, although there was absolutely no need. Anyone interested in cemeteries could be forgiven for making assumptions and guesses to the words eroded back to the grain whilst in search of a distant relative. There was no such assumption needed here. The words looked as fresh as ink just pressed out of a fountain pen. What they meant was anyone's guess, but he wanted so much to understand. The words circled around in his mind, each one examined for clues, failing to meet a connection to the one that followed it.

The woman, surprised that the sight of the words had not forced a remorseful confession from the boy, doubted her own initial conviction of his culpability. "Are you saying this wasn't you?"

"No. I had no part in it," he replied, still unable to take his eyes from those four words. "I don't think it's graffiti, though. It's not the sort of thing that graffiti artists write. I'm no expert but I think they go with things like 'no ball games' or 'Chazza was 'ere', or occasionally just a poorly painted representation of the male reproductive organ."

"If someone damages my son's grave, then it's definitely got malicious intent," she said.

"This must have taken hours. When did it first appear?"

"Last week. I always visit once a week and it was here then."

"Do you have any idea what it means?" asked David politely, attempting to stay on her better side, to which he felt he was starting to drift.

"I didn't give it any thought. I just thought it was meaningless vandalism. They won't allow my son to rest. He was persecuted in life and now they are persecuting him in death."

The old woman was desperate to maintain the true story of her son's existence with the same resolve as she protected him in life. Unable to perpetuate the façade, her initial stature of strength relented and was replaced by the true frailty of age. Her bones struggled to gain permission to stoop down and place the daffodils next to David's white flower, and were then completely refused permission to return.

"Do you like my flower?" David asked casually, as her arthritically ravaged body forced her to kneel in quiet prayer.

"Yes, although daffodils were his favourite."

David had no recollection of John's horticultural preferences but there seemed little point in challenging such an irrelevance. There were so many other details that might not be how he was told them. Maybe he wouldn't get another opportunity.

"What was he like?" asked David calmly.

"He was a shy boy. Spent much of his free time on his own reading books or drawing elaborate, fantastical scenes that he'd pluck from his imagination. Although he didn't find it easy to mix with others he was always there for you if you needed him. Sometimes when you least expected it. I remember when he was in his twenties I was taken into hospital with suspected meningitis. No one told him what had happened but somehow he sensed that I was in need of his support. There he was on the ward within hours of my first set of tests. He was very much like his father in that respect."

"I read that his father died in the Falklands War?"

Mrs. Hewson paused for a moment, glancing up into the sky forlornly to give herself inspiration or the courage to answer.

"Yes. He was a hero, posthumously decorated, I might add. Saved many lives. Amazing man, he was. Affected John his whole life not having him around."

"It must have been very hard for both of you."

"More than you could imagine," she said, but pulling herself from the conversation as if reminded of the fact that this eleven-year-old foreigner was not really worthy of the information. "If you're not here making trouble, then why are you taking so much interest in my son's grave? You can't even have known him, you're far too young."

"Sometimes I feel I know him better than I know myself," replied David dreamily, "in a manner of speaking."

"What rubbish," the old woman replied scornfully. "Youth. They think they understand life and emotion. You can't possibly know my son. What are you, seventeen?"

"You're right, I can't say I have ever understood emotion. I'm younger than seventeen, though, I'm only eleven."

"Eleven! You're about six feet tall."

David had always been big. He'd weighed twelve pounds at birth and passed four feet in height before he was five. It might have been explained apart from the fact that his parents were so tiny. His father, a Chilean llama herder, had barely threatened five feet six inches, and his mother wouldn't have looked out of place at a pixie convention. His size had always been an advantage, until today that was.

"How can someone born a year after my son's death have any interest in him? I knew you were up to no good, even if your demeanour suggests otherwise. Maybe you're just a good actor?"

The vitality returned to her legs and with piston-like reflexes out sprang her pointing finger. David wasn't a good actor. At the best of times silence was all he could muster, and at the worst of times he had a tendency to reveal the truth in a heartbeat. He couldn't explain his inability to lie: it appeared to be as much a constant in his life as his abnormal size. He had, though, developed the ability to offer alternative facts that were true but not the truth. Certainly the truth would not be wise now.

"I'm studying law in London on a scholarship. I'm working on old cases, unsolved fatalities. The circumstances of your son's death intrigue me. I wanted to get close to him as part of my research."

None of this information was incorrect, even if there was far more that David failed to reveal. Along with his physical size, his intellectual capabilities had developed just as quickly. In some ways he was even more advanced than the multinational teenagers who made up his classmates. The college had done everything in their power to block his entrance, fearful that an eleven-year-old, a fact unavoidably laid out on his birth certificate, might bring undue publicity. Once David's entrance exams results broke records they were powerless to stop him.

The college archives gave access to information unavailable outside of the library computers. Not that he needed to review the case at all: he knew the circumstances better than anyone.

"What do you mean it intrigues you?" asked Mrs. Hewson.

"It just seems so unlikely that he would die from that type of road traffic accident."

"What are you talking about? It wasn't a road traffic accident. He was murdered. Are you sure you've got the right John Hewson?" replied Mrs. Hewson, instantly correcting him, the case weighing heavily on her soul.

"Yes, believe me, this is the right John," replied David unnecessarily pointing at the headstone. "Are you sure you're not mistaken?"

"Of course I'm sure. I lost my only child: you never move on from that," explained Mrs. Hewson, again doubting the boy's stated purpose. "Surely you must have known that if you've reviewed the case?"

"Well, yes, of course. I have reviewed it, but it's a difficult case. A lot of details are missing in those files," replied David, again revealing the truth of the actual files that he'd added to his own experiences of the case.

"There certainly was a lot missing. They never found the weapon and more importantly no one was ever successfully prosecuted."

"What weapon?"

"A gun."

"No, that can't be right," responded David matter-of-factly.

"I can tell you it was, because I found him. He sustained a single shot to the heart. The coroner said he'd been hit at close range and died instantly. He must have been lying there a few hours when I found him. He was all alone and I couldn't save him. I promised I would always be there for him. I just couldn't protect him," she said, wiping the tears and mascara combination from her cheek.

She turned away to prevent a perfect stranger seeing her well with tears, as fresh now as they were that day twelve years ago. The natural reaction in these circumstances should have been for David to reach out and comfort the woman. But it wasn't the oddness of the situation that deterred him, it was a total lack of desire to do so. To him, the thought of hugging someone was uncomfortable, an alien reaction to something incomprehensible. Anyway, he was too busy dealing with his own confusion. How could she be right?

"Did they ever find anyone?" he asked, far more insensitively than any other human being would.

"They identified one suspect, but they never found him."

"How did they identify him?" asked David.

"They had some CCTV footage of all the people who went in and out of the flat on that morning. A shady-looking old man had entered the building in the hours before the shooting. He didn't even use the security system."

"I'm not sure I understand," replied David.

"He was just *in* the building. He didn't go through the front door to enter or exit the place. He wasn't there when they searched the property either. One minute he's there and the next he's not," she tried to explain, although he could see that she really wasn't able to.

"How do they know it was him, then?"

"He wanted us to know."

"How?"

"He took time to stop and talk to the CCTV camera as if delivering a confession."

"What did he say?"

"He said, 'How many times have I killed you now, John?' It made no sense."

"What did you say he looked like?" prompted David.

"Very old, all skin and bone really, wore a pinstriped suit as old and tatty as his own features. I'll never forget the way he grinned into the camera, as if he wanted us to recognise him. It was as if he wanted us to know who he was, but with an arrogance that told us we would never catch him."

David thought back to the inscription on the grave. Could it have been Laslow that placed it there? Laslow's endless control over John's actions now seemed to be pursuing David. Was there nowhere to hide, nowhere that was safe? If he was to complete the tasks that had been set for him, he wouldn't be unopposed. Someone was watching.

"Did he say anything else?" asked David, hoping for more clues to this bizarre change to his understanding.

"Just one other thing. 'See you next time'. We never did find out what he meant. How would he see John again after he'd already killed him? We just ignored it after a while as irrelevant. Look at me, going on about something that happened years ago to someone young enough to be my own grandson whom I've never met before," Mrs. Hewson mumbled to herself. "I don't even know your name."

CHAPTER TWO

THE COUNCIL OF CREATURES

"The more observant of you will notice that I'm wearing my compassionate face today, but be under no illusions, I'm quite prepared to break out the malevolent one if I don't get the answers I want to hear," announced Asmodeus to the congregation.

The demons squirmed nervously in the jewel-encrusted thrones that circled the large stone table at the very centre of level twelve. Like guilty schoolchildren they attempted a pose that neither demonstrated direct eye contact with their master, nor made it apparent they were avoiding it. No one wanted to be the one who looked the most eager or least reluctant to be asked the first question. None of them pulled the look off with any aplomb.

Occasionally a hand would shoot under the table in an attempt to put one of their peers off their stride, a foolish endeavour when you consider most of these creatures had their own unique anatomies more than likely to cause the antagonist varying degrees of pain. Following his attempt to prod Mr. Volts in the thigh, Mr. Graphite's hand leapt into the air along with a muffled yelp.

Asmodeus glared at him. "Are you starting us off, then, Mr. Graphite. Come on, don't be shy: share the joke with the group."

Mr. Graphite's eyes sank to the ground as if gravity had been turned off in a phenomenon solely isolated to the vicinity of his face.

Asmodeus had metamorphosed back into his most comfortable form. The angelic white robe, with its bold, bright sheen, may not have appeared as hideous as his three-headed guise but it had a more influencing quality. It had the ability to lull people and creatures alike into a sense of ease, lowering their defences and removing their fear. The demons knew all too well that this trickery was an attempt to get them to lower their guard.

"Perhaps you think what has happened here is in some way acceptable. That once in a while someone will beat us. THEY WILL NOT!" he bellowed as his fist hit the table and his composure was momentarily broken.

The demons all nodded furiously in agreement.

He pointed to the only chair around the table that was empty. The demons, sensing sudden reprieve, glanced over to the throne that Asmodeus was currently pointing towards. "Why don't we start with you?"

"I don't think he's there," whispered one of the demons to his neighbour.

"Yes I am," came the indignant response from the empty seat.

"Mr. Virus, can you offer any words of enlightenment on what has happened here?" demanded Asmodeus.

After a pause, Asmodeus acknowledged the shake of Mr. Virus's head, which only he appeared to witness, and his stare moved back to the ensemble. Again the demons reset their default positions to *not wanting to be noticed*, brief relief replaced by palpable anxiety.

"It's a good job that I am here and not the Devil himself. Imagine what malice he would be smiting out on you in these circumstances. Imagine what mood he'll be in when I tell him."

A congregation of heads sagged onto their chins.

"What I want to know most of all, and I'm happy to hear any mere nugget of wisdom or outlandish conspiracy theory that you care to offer, is how the hell did John Hewson, an insignificant no one, get out of that prison?"

Their attentions were drawn in the direction of John's empty metal box, still lying open, broken and empty on the red, dusty floor.

"I think I can offer some opinions on it," came a gurgled voice from the far side of the table.

The council of creatures had not been assembled for such an eternity: very few could remember any of the correct protocols. It was the only time that all the senior demons, responsible for one department or function of Hell, gathered to debate or solve a problem. The last time they had been summoned, the Devil himself had chaired it. That debate had focused on what to do with the rumoured appearance of the Son of God. On that occasion the atmosphere had been quite jovial, more akin to a trivial board meeting with an agenda to discuss nothing more vital than which stationery they should order or who should be chosen to organise the annual fun run.

They had all voted unanimously in favour of the motion put forward at that meeting. The Devil would descend to Earth to deal with any minor inconvenience these rumours might cause. Consequently it was the last time that any of the demons had seen him in the flesh. It was also the last time all but one of the group had heard this current voice.

The slithering body of ooze transformed its shape in its seat, unable to comfortably confine itself to such a foreign object. If there was any demon who created trepidation on an equal scale to Asmodeus, then it was him.

"Primordial, welcome back," said Asmodeus, his tone softened in recognition of his own respect. "Perhaps you can show this useless bunch of imbeciles why you are held in such high regard?"

"There is only one way that John could have escaped from his vessol," he croaked. "The Limpet Syndrome is the only explanation."

"So, the human condition for survival rears its head once again. One day soon we will need to deal with that condition for good. The Limpet Syndrome only explains how he escaped the vessol: it does not explain how he escaped the cask itself," said Asmodeus.

"Not if it was his first time, no," replied Primordial, "but if it was his second time, then it is possible."

"Explain," demanded Asmodeus, seemingly blind to anyone other than Primordial, to the great assuagement of the others.

"Nobody knows the true origins of the Limpet Syndrome itself, but what we can speculate, from what we have been delivered in the forms that live in my domain, is that it is a purely rational condition. No one with faith in religion, unless they know the truth, can trigger it. It's a subliminal reaction to avoid what their subconsciousness cannot fathom – essentially a way of avoiding the only possible final destination, Hell. We have no way of knowing how it evolved, although all of us around this table know *why* it evolved."

Now united in a sense of solidarity, the group nodded in agreement, hanging onto Primordial's words like children listening to an engaging fairy tale, anxious and eager to discover the ending.

"What we do know is what constitutes the soul. The soul has the capacity for three equal properties: the good, the bad and the neutral. These three parts are rarely in balance and have a potential mass of twenty-one grams, or, to put it another way, three multiples of seven, two numbers purposefully symbolic. I believe that the Limpet Syndrome is neither an easy nor a painless process. It fights the pull of the fifth force, a force far more powerful than the bonds that hold the soul together. The energy required to resist such a force must have some consequences. I suspect it is the same consequence that Emorfed has on the shadow souls that you have seen come here."

"Are you suggesting that part of the soul is sheared away in the process of the Limpet Syndrome?" enquired Asmodeus.

"Indeed. Although I think this is only the case when the soul doesn't have its own body. When it does, the body is the by-product," replied Primordial.

"As interesting as this turn of events is, I'm still unclear how this has helped John escape from what used to be one of the most secure places in the Universe."

"I think I can offer a view on that one," came a voice from what appeared to be a second unoccupied chair. In order to be fully audible, Brimstone clambered onto his throne so that he was now at the same height as his seated peers.

"Ah, Mr. Brimstone, I wondered when you might add to this debate," said Asmodeus. "Please enlighten me."

"If what Primordial has said is correct, and I am certainly not going to argue with him, then what I saw in the Soul Catcher at the time of John's escape may hold the answer."

The table's attention shifted to the bubbling stone figure standing on his tiptoes, scorching the precious metals contained within his chair. Some were watching purely to see if he would melt it and fall through; others were interested in what might come out of his mouth.

"Whilst I was being summoned pointlessly back and forth to level twelve to explain John's disappearance, a foreign object of no identity entered the Soul Catcher. When I finally returned, it was gone."

"And?" said Asmodeus a little underwhelmed.

"Stay with me. I'm building up to it. If part of John's soul had already been splintered from him in the weeks prior to his escape, then it is feasible that that fragment returned unrecognised. Unrecognised because no one was expecting it, least of all the Soul Catcher."

"How could part of his soul have remained on Earth unnoticed, even if he did pull off the Limpet Syndrome?" cried Asmodeus disparagingly.

"Has anyone been known to enact the Limpet Syndrome whilst they were possessing another human?" replied Brimstone.

The room fell silent as they considered the revelation.

"If they have, none have ever got back here at least," replied Primordial. "I would guess that whichever part of John's soul was removed when he experienced the Limpet Syndrome first time would stay with the human host until it was released from him."

"What about the writing on the side of the cask?" Asmodeus added, walking across to the metal box to be sure that it was still there. "Did anyone ask Newton what it means?"

"I did, sir," replied Mr. Silica excitedly, wanting to separate himself from his cowering colleagues.

"What did he say?" enquired Asmodeus.

"He wasn't very compliant at first, but once I explained the dichotomy between his work on gravity and Einstein's theory of relativity, he said that was torture enough. He explained that Newton's third law was based on every force having an equal and opposite force."

"What you do to me will be done to you with the same intensity!" exclaimed Asmodeus. "John thinks he can rewrite his story. He wants revenge, then. If only he knew who his revenge should be aimed at. So many people have done him wrong. John Hewson versus the Universe. I still can't figure out how he wrote the inscription, though."

"I think that might be the easiest part of this mystery," replied Primordial. "The soul is made of memory and feelings. If revenge was his last emotion before he achieved the Limpet Syndrome, then it might have been imprinted in the metal. As one part of his soul was drawn from Earth it attracted the other part of his soul through the walls of the box. The neutral part of his soul would have been left behind. Almost invisible it waited inside until we opened the box and it departed completely undetected. This theory is dependent, though, on the positive part of his soul leaving John after the first Limpet Syndrome. Which would make sense, as revenge is a purely negative emotion."

"There's only one person who can answer that question for certain. Laslow was the only person who met John at different times before he came back here. He'll know whether his attitude changed at all," replied Asmodeus. "Let's bring him down."

Asmodeus clicked his fingers and two demons at the far end of the table immediately leapt to their feet and started to work at the winch directly below one of the dark black metal boxes that floated on the edge of space high above their heads. The thick, metal chain clinked and clanked through its crank as it struggled to descend to the floor. It nestled quietly on the surface of level twelve and the demons went to work.

The sound of a billion atoms being wrenched apart tore through Hell. Even the creatures on level zero raised their heads. All due to a single touch of a demon's finger on the outside of the metal box. No trace of metal was left and all that remained was the pale and withered form of a vessol flattened to the floor.

There were no signs of life. The plastic of the vessol had become wrinkled and worn as if the soul inside was being pressed in by its prosthetic exoskeleton.

Without the slightest degree of sympathy, the two demons carried the corpse and threw it down on the huge, round table in front of Asmodeus. With a twisted smile and a strong hand he lifted the wretched figure by the hair, raising Laslow's head up to his eyeline.

"Wake up, Laslow. You're a lucky lad. It appears you've been granted a brief holiday from your everlasting insanity."

"No more pain. I beg you," mumbled Laslow.

"Only now does he regret the folly of deals with Satan. If you feel there is nothing more that we can do to hurt you, you are wrong, Laslow. I need answers and I will get them."

Laslow's eyes widened, revealing two pitch-black irises devoid of character that not even the light could escape. All-consuming black holes that once witnessed the pureness of beauty and the bitterness of sorrow now saw nothing but despair.

"When you last saw John Hewson, had his demeanour changed at all?" Asmodeus demanded.

"I was promised a second chance."

"Were you indeed? Maybe you shouldn't have accepted his deal, then," replied Asmodeus.

"I had no choice but to accept his deal. He said it was the only way to save her."

"Now that won't do, Laslow. I did say I wanted answers and there are far more agonising ways for me to get them from you than asking nicely."

"It's so difficult to tell: the Devil's shadow was on me always. After three hundred years in his company I had little control over my senses. My body was his to use at his leisure," complained Laslow.

Asmodeus raised a fist to strike him, but in one final act of self-preservation Laslow summoned up his last memories.

"My recollections are that John became far angrier towards the end. He became bitter and twisted when he acknowledged how things had been played out against him."

"Excellent. That wasn't hard, was it?" Asmodeus replied. "Put him back where he came from."

"Kill me, I'd rather be dead," pleaded Laslow.

"But you are dead, my pathetic, plastic friend. Anything else would be too good for you."

"You have what you wanted from me!" screamed Laslow.

His voice diminished as he was carted off into the distance, dragged by his long, straggly nylon hair.

"That suggests the positive part went first, which explains why we never saw it here," declared Primordial. "It had nowhere else to go but into its host."

"All this fails to explain where all the parts of him are now!" shouted Asmodeus, losing his patience. "Where is the little shit?"

"After he disappeared we scanned the area to detect his soul. All we found was energy that seemed to belong to him," replied Brimstone. "That energy could have been the fragments of his soul, although I think the neutral part returned to Earth."

"How could he return there? We'd be able to see him if he was possessing someone?" spat Asmodeus, directing much of his anger at Brimstone, convinced that he in some way was partly responsible for John's escape.

"That's not the only way to get back down there, I'm afraid. He could have gone for an unborn, then his soul would effectively become part of a new person. John Hewson would cease to exist, at least to us."

"Who told him about that?"

"I did," replied Brimstone. "You have to remember I had no way of knowing that any of this would happen. Plus, he's an inquisitive little git."

"Why didn't you just give him the manual and a set of keys?" shouted one of the demons who was concealed by the crowd and happy that the flack was being aimed elsewhere.

"Are you saying that there is no way of knowing which unborn he has gone into?" raged Asmodeus.

"Not unless he reveals himself to us. If the Newton reference is anything to go on, I expect he will when he's ready. Remember his soul is now purely neutral. The Devil can no longer speak to him and neither can…" He paused and nodded knowingly. "The other side."

"Doesn't give us much of an advantage, though, does it?" spat Asmodeus.

Brimstone was feeling the heat. Being made of molten rock meant he was hot most of the time. But it was nothing to the heat of the searing accusations that were increasingly building up around him. The whole council seemed to have decided to gang up in collective finger-pointing, safety in numbers always being a safer place than out on a limb. If he wasn't careful he was in danger of being dragged off for a week with Laslow in the darkest, most depressive holiday chalet in history.

"I disagree," replied Brimstone. He knew he could only make his situation better rather than worse. "I think we have a double advantage. If 'neutral John' has gone back to Earth, answer me this: who helped him reverse the Soul Catcher and press all the buttons?"

The demons developed unique expressions on their faces that only the unique fear of an unanswerable question can have on a group of delegates fighting for their own personal reputations. They searched their brains for the answer, at the same time hoping someone else might have the wrong one before them. After Brimstone had allowed the silence to make him look far more intelligent than anyone else, and cooled the hot stares that had been bubbling his skin, he answered.

"It's quite simple, really. Only one part of John is accounted for, so the two other parts of his soul must be here. *Good* and *Bad* John, if you will, are somewhere in Hell. They must have fused together when the positive part encouraged the negative part to pass through the metal cube. I'm guessing that *Good/Bad* John helped the other John get home. He probably got inside a vessol so that he could operate the controls. He has seen the Soul Catcher with me a number of times before: it wouldn't take much to work it out."

"Ok, I want every part of this place searched: find me both of them, and when I say now I do actually mean you've already found them. One last question, Brimstone, you said we would have an advantage: I don't quite see how," asked Asmodeus.

"If we can find *Good/Bad* John, the John with all the hatred, all the anger, all the cunning, all the bitterness, we could make him go back and find… um…John. Who better to find John, than John?"

CHAPTER THREE

HOLLOW MAN

David Gonzalez had never found dreams easy. Sleep was the only time when he experienced anything remotely close to an emotion. During waking hours he was the most stable and rational eleven-year-old you'd ever meet. Come to think of it, he made most adults look childish. Sleep was different. Sleep took away his ability to reason and apply logic. This complete lack of control allowed his dreams to run wild with imagination and colour in a way that his normal conscious self would never allow.

This morning he woke in the same conditions as he always did. The bedsheets were wet from the profuse sweating that seeped from every pore of his body. It was accompanied with a scream he'd learnt to instinctively muffle in case his flatmates came on a cavalry charge to see who was attempting to assault him. This pattern was replicated every night for as long as he could remember. The dreams were not all the same, but they had the same themes and qualities to them. At least until tonight.

Tonight a new dream had been added to the roster of repeats he got used to taping night after night. And like all the others, this dream featured John Hewson. That's not to say that David was in the dreams with John, but more that he was acting John's part with the aptitude of an Equity cardholder.

Sometimes he played the part of John as he was crumpled against a postbox in a car waiting for an eventual fireball. Occasionally he played John standing in a metallic sphere facing the barrel of a gun that was aimed at him by a decrepit old man.

Once in a while he was walking in a field of white grass with a red sun beating down on him through a translucent barrier where blue, electric clouds attempted to break through to meet him. In that scene he was at his most comfortable, but the scene never lasted long enough for him to enjoy it. That was the dream he had the least first-hand knowledge of, like it was trying to encourage him to imagine rather than remember.

David picked up the folder and pen that he kept on his bedside table in order to quickly document any new findings before they ran from his waking moments. The new dream had been released, kicking and screaming, from his subconscious by the recent and unexpected meeting with John's mother. Tonight he'd played John as a bullet travelled through his heart and he'd hit the floor of an apartment. Although clearly dead in the dream, David experienced the out-of-body experience of climbing out of the body and following the shooter.

If the story that John's mother told him was genuine, there had to be some record of it inside him, even if it had been buried deep down in what was left of his soul. There would be no emotions left to associate with it, but there would definitely be fact. There was, after all, nothing else in his head anymore. Where the rest of his capacity to feel was he could only guess.

Once a few of the details had been beautifully scribbled down and catalogued in order to obtain easy access in future, he flicked through to the first page. The first page of any book is always the most important. It's the launch pad for the reader to decide whether the combined contents of the following pages are likely to be entertaining or informative. The first page of this book was neither. All that existed on it was a list entitled at the top, 'Newton's Third'.

David always had an unbending drive to make things right, even though it was often difficult for him to be certain as to what 'right' looked like. Lacking the emotions to feel or recognise pity, righteousness, fear, anger or empathy meant that you had a unique view on the subject of right and wrong. His desire to put things right was, in his mind, logical. Unjust deeds had been carried out and they must be undone. David ran his finger down the list to double-check that everyone that should appear was accounted for.

- Laslow
- Hell in general (those demons particularly)
- Donovan King
- Victor Serpo/Agent 15
- Baltazaar? (undecided)
- Faith
- John Hewson

Which item should he work on first? There were at least some of the entries on the list that he didn't have any clear plan for. But there was certainly one that he could start with. One name had just revisited him in his most recent dream, and it was the single most important name on the list: Laslow.

Eleven years had gone by with this single name constantly flooding his mind. This time nothing would stop him. Well, other than only being eleven, having a zero track record of assassination and Laslow probably being the most dangerous person to walk the planet, that is. Still the algorithms in his brain had done the calculations and he liked the odds.

*****

Sandy Logan was many things depending on whom you asked. If you were going to accurately document all of them, you'd need the world's most comprehensive thesaurus. Distinguished observers, and even some family members, would immediately offer 'bastard'. Some might say 'clever'. and just a few people might even refer to him as 'clever bastard'. Sneaky, devious, corrupt, ambitious, intelligent, single-minded would all potentially make an appearance. These words more than adequately described the deceased former Minister for Homeland Security.

Yet there was one word that you'd never hear associated with him, even if you asked every single person ever to have had the displeasure to meet him. That word was 'slow'. His mind was as sharp now as ever and could outrun any adversarial intellect. Of course, outside the confines of level zero all of these descriptors were lost in history and only one word was most appropriate. Pigeon.

Not the only pigeon, though. Unlike all the other creatures that occupied this lowest level of Hell there were two of them. Level zero was like a warped version of Noah's ark. In this version a drunken Noah had decided to kill one of every species because he was pissed off with all the rain and sea. The animals went in one by one, hurrah 'hic' hurrah.

Pigeon or not, he'd lost none of the speed of thought or instinct that had been evident in his human existence. Much had happened since his meeting with John on level twelve when Asmodeus had confirmed what he'd already suspected. John had tried his best, but there never had been any other destination than where he was now. Even more significantly he'd worked out why. To him it was obvious, and if he could he was going to use it to his advantage.

Ever since he'd been consigned to the relative paradise of level zero he'd taken to exploring. The most sparsely populated of all the levels in Hell, it had the equivalent population density of Greenland. Under the stagnant lake of the level above, the land stretched out for mile after mile through desert, around forest, over ocean, and across swamps right up to what Sandy called the window. The window was a vast opening that looked out on space to reveal the workings of the Universe. Where others would simply be captivated by its magnificent grandeur, he had keener eyes.

Sandy was an expert at reading between the lines in order to spot opportunities no one else could see. It was this talent for exploiting the information available to him that made him both brilliant and extremely dangerous. Ian, on the other hand, was only one of those things and it didn't begin with the letter 'b'.

Armed with his unique ability for creating catastrophe, Ian could be extremely dangerous in a vacuum. A Harvard University team with a decent-sized grant could spend years trying to understand it and still be none the wiser. What's more, the two of them were once again coupled together like two incompatible train coaches, a spanking brand new high-speed locomotive next to a knackered old coal truck.

"I really did imagine it would be worse than this, but it's not so bad really," said Ian, attempting to stimulate conversation when it was clear that Sandy was not the least bit interested.

Sandy's concentration was fixed on the activities that were continuing at a constant rate on the other side of the window. A steady stream of blue electricity was coagulating on the other side of the translucent barrier, desperately fighting to get in, whilst in the other direction a less intense, almost dulled, light blue gas seeped away from Hell into the Universe.

"I mean I wouldn't have chosen to spend the afterlife as a bird, but I think we got off lightly compared to what I've heard goes on upstairs," continued Ian.

"Shhussh," chirped Sandy, the words whistling through the valve of his fake body.

"Why do you spend so much time down here, Sandy? I know it's a good view but I've sort of got used to it now."

"You amaze me, Ian, and not in a good way," replied Sandy, realising that the peace he sought was the one thing he was unlikely to receive.

"It's just a view, though. It's always going to be there, isn't it?"

"It's not the view I'm interested in, it's what's going on in the scene. I bet when you used to go to an art gallery you'd look at a painting and say, 'It's a screaming man, move on!' Sometimes you have to look deeper."

"Ok. I'll look harder," replied Ian, genuinely trying to observe more than what he saw, but actually only seeing exactly that. "What am I looking for exactly?"

"Opportunities," replied Sandy.

"What do they look like?"

"It's not like looking for a star, Ian. They don't come in shape form. An opportunity can be a gap as much as it might be an object. It could be a sound or a taste or something that doesn't even exist."

"Right," replied Ian, with one of the stock responses he used when he actually didn't understand. "But why are you looking for them?"

"Because that's what intelligent beings do. They don't just switch it on and off. If you must know, I'm looking for a way out," said Sandy.

"Then you're looking in the wrong direction. The trapdoor to level one is in that direction," he replied, pointing to a pale white, plastic wing in the opposite direction.

"Not an exit, a way out. They're different. Do you know I thought it was enough that you were the stupidest person I'd ever met on Planet Earth, but in the short time we have been here I've discovered that you appear to be the most intellectually challenged person anywhere, at anytime, in any Universe. It'd be worth an award if it wasn't so depressing."

"A trophy or a medal?" asked Ian excitedly.

"It also makes me the most unfortunate person in history," he said to himself. "Maybe that's my punishment. Sandy, welcome to Hell, we were going to place you somewhere really nasty but when we saw you were friends with Ian, we all took a vote and agreed you'd suffered enough!"

"How many times can I say I'm sorry?"

"Many, many more times…"

"Sorry."

"…and that will still never be enough. One day I hope you regret your actions rather than just apologising for them. Look, this is not the time. I've come up with a theory about how this place works and I need to find a like-minded creature with an IQ greater than nine to debate it with."

"What sort of theory is that, then?" asked Ian.

"I said greater than nine, Ian, not lower."

"Suit yourself, I was only playing along. I have other plans tonight, anyway, so I'd better set off."

Level one wasn't even close to being like the other levels in Hell. In many ways it was the equivalent of an open prison. Inmates came and went as they pleased, under the proviso they played nice with the guard, didn't kill anyone, and made sure they were tucked up securely in bed by lights out. And even then the creatures had their vast habitats rather than any prison cells. There was only one guard and no one had ever been brave or stupid enough to break his rules. Although Primordial was rarely seen, everyone knew he had the habit and ability to turn up almost anywhere at anytime.

This unique freedom meant the animals of the various habitats were in constant contact, with little fear of contravention. A lack of punishment or confinement made death here bearable. An initial lack of planning or guidelines for managing reincarnates meant they were pretty much left to their own devices. So far a thousand or more Earth years had passed and the 'days since last incident board' was still stuck on nought.

"What do you mean you have other plans?" asked Sandy, drawn away from his observations of the window for the first time.

"There's going to be a 'pass over' party," replied Ian.

"A what?"

"Well, apparently when a soul is totally worn out it leaves the vessol and returns to the Universe. They call it a pass over. Down here they celebrate it like a funeral."

"Interesting. What time does it start?"

"Hard to say. No one really knows. Everyone just collects in the region where the creature is and waits for it to happen. By all accounts Paul's been looking dodgy for several weeks now," said Ian.

"Who's Paul?"

"He's one of level zero's oldest residents and a soon-to-be extinct dolphin," replied Ian.

"Perfect," said Sandy. "Dolphins have a much higher IQ than you. Let's go."

CHAPTER FOUR

NUMBER TWELVE

The crack in the Alps, that first emerged over a decade ago, was quite the tourist attraction. Gone were the days when small groups of plimsoll-wearing Chinese punters were only interested in the panorama of vast, ancient glaciers. That was so nineteenth-century. Now an hour's walk from the Jungfrau visitor centre was a huge crater that allowed the paying public a view into the Earth. When the sun was out you could see a metallic sphere at the bottom of the thousand-metre drop.

To aid the view, and protect from any mishaps, they'd already constructed a viewing platform. It had absolutely nothing to do with making money. It was purely coincidence that you had to pay five euros for the privilege of looking into a hole. Sadly for David they'd not yet finished the extension of the railway line that would lead right up to it.

Retracing steps that John had taken on the longest day many years previously, he made his way through the snow and up the slight incline. He'd booked onto the last available time slot and, unlike the others in his group, he was well prepared not to return with them. A huge backpack, brimming with bulges and lumps, was carried with the ease of a husky pulling a sledge. He made light work of the journey, eager to reach the viewing platform even before his guide could.

Several minutes before anyone else, the lanky frame of a young Latino boy leant over the metal barrier to take in the full scale of the void. There it was, just how he remembered it. As the sun started to set over the mountains, a shimmering, metallic slope glinted up at him from the heart of the Alps. If his eyes weren't deceiving him there was even a scattered wooden door panel, once part of a hillside retreat, stuck in the very top.

"I see your legs are stronger than mine and I work here," said a man in a red and black Jungfrau-embroidered jacket.

"I grew up in the mountains," replied David. "I'm used to much higher peaks than this one."

"Gather in the rest of you."

He gestured to the half a dozen stragglers making their way onto the platform out of breath.

"Will this take long?" asked David. "I'm keen to get on."

"Now that we are all here I can start with the tour. Welcome to one of the greatest wonders of our natural world, the heart of the mountain. Some one thousand metres below you is a discovery that is still a mystery to mankind. A dozen years ago a seismic event split this valley open to reveal an object that still baffles all scientific experts."

Although many expeditions over the last decade had made attempts to solve the mystery of the sphere, none had succeeded. Separate parties of mountaineers and scientists had climbed down to the strange, metallic dome, but none had figured out what it was or why it was there. The first group attempted to take a sample. They failed but took the opportunity to name the substance.

"The metal of the dome has been given the name Celestium. It has never before been detected on Earth, or any place of human exploration. It's a completely new substance. There are many theories as to why it's there. Some experts believe it is a by-product formed through volcanic activity, and some believe it's an alien spaceship," he said with a laugh. "Some mountaineers have claimed to have witnessed blue energy being drawn to the sphere or seeping from it. One has even suggested the sphere contains Heaven itself. Mountaineers, though, are known to get rather caught up in their own stories, and I for one have never seen the blue gas for myself. Anyway, please take a moment to look around before we make our descent back to the visitor centre."

A number of complex and lengthy zoom lenses were immediately added to cameras to capture the best shot. David didn't need zooms: he was planning to get up close and personal with it later.

"Excuse me," he asked the guide. "Why did the scientists fail to discover more about it?"

"Good question. As much as they've tried it has not been possible to remove a sample. Every time they attempt to extract one the whole structure becomes as solid as the rock beneath your feet. Yet when they move away from it, the structure continues to flow freely in front of them like a liquid."

"Interesting. Maybe scientists called it Celestium because not everything can be understood by physics?"

"You may be right," replied the guide.

"Anyway, an excellent tour but I'm going to make my way back. You'll only slow me down," said David.

He had no intention of returning to the sanctuary and warmth of the corporate-coloured coffee kiosk and overpriced gift shop. As he retreated out of sight of the group he made a detour in order to double-back on himself. As darkness fell and the rest of the group were well on their way back to home base, David returned to the platform. Unpacking his oversized rucksack he unfurled a parasail and prepared for launch.

Just as he'd seen fellow enthusiasts do throughout the day, he ran a few steps and felt the sail catch the wind. Unlike the others, who enjoyed the rush of floating effortlessly past the north face of the Eiger, a cliff that had taken decades and countless lives to successfully climb, he spiralled into the chasm, winding like a screw cutting through a cork. Finally he came to rest where metal sphere met jagged stone.

David was grateful that the scientists who had gone before him had only attempted to remove a sample and hadn't yet had the foresight to attempt entry. After all, they didn't know what was inside. Gently he submerged a hand and the metal consumed it just as his soul remembered. Without fear of failure he walked confidently through the wall.

It was a trip that David's body had never made, even though his soul was more than used to it. Pushing his skinny, muscular body further through the liquid, he crossed his fingers, hoping the end would come soon. After several minutes he burst through the other end of the wall of metal and with a squelch it wobbled back into place as if nothing had disturbed it. The scene in front of him was not as he imagined it.

Limbo had always had a dimly lit quality to it. Normally that came from four gigantic pyres that jutted from the sides like the points of a compass. Whether they were still there, unlit, was unclear, as only one source of light was obvious. Like a Navy squadron on shore leave, a trickle of blue, electric gas was marching erratically from a point to his left down the smooth surfaces and up to the white funnel, only visible from the light emitting from the line of souls.

Torch in hand, he made his way carefully down to the centre. David felt no anxiety for this change in his expectations. Everything had an explanation even if the evidence was currently unavailable. It wasn't arrogance that drove him either, even though many in the past had accused him of it. In his short life he'd appeared to demonstrate a level of bravery far bolder than any of his peers. As long as he was able to calculate the odds of success against failure he did so without flinching. This lack of empathy had not endeared him to children his own age. Plus he was over five feet by the age of six, which definitely hadn't helped in making friends. They called him Goliat, Spanish for 'Goliath', a smart biblical reference for a bunch of nursery schoolkids.

David questioned everything. The main one on his lips right now was: where is everybody? Limbo was hardly a place of great human density, but on every other occasion there were at least some people around. Now there was no one. Unless you counted the line of souls being fed into the white funnel like a never-ending sausage machine. There were no trials for these souls. The line was unbroken from the metal wall to the white cone, and when each popped and crackled their energy underneath it, they were immediately sucked up and away. As he shone his torch up at the funnel he found the answer to where some of the people were.

Nailed to the cone by his feet and outstretched hands was a withered skeleton hanging upside down. Pinstriped material hung limply to its frame to confirm its identity. It had always been David's intention to kill Laslow. Now someone had beaten him to it. This intention was not brimming with emotional intent, it was just how David's mind worked. The deed had to be completed and the fact someone else already had was enough for him. Who had done it didn't bother him. It didn't intrigue him how he died. Why he'd been killed was far more interesting. He removed his writing pad and slowly drew a line through Laslow's name.

Although Laslow's demise had been a surprise, what he found at the base of the white funnel certainly wasn't. The lever that John tried to switch from 'negative' to 'positive' in order to redirect Sandy's soul was now set permanently to 'negative'. It wasn't a shock because he knew that all souls went in one direction. He just didn't know why yet. It was the big, elephant-sized unanswered question. If this situation had always been the case, why had John been put through his mock trial all those years ago? The only thing to do was to retrace John's very first steps in this peculiar place.

Doing his best to avoid the unpredictable movement of the souls as they bobbed apprehensively down the stairs that led to the centre, he located their entry point into the sphere. There was no obvious door to allow them out, they just seeped through like the water from a faulty washing machine. He knew that the waiting room was on the other side but before he ploughed his way through the liquid, something caught his attention.

A build-up of electricity was forming a pocket like a boil on the surface of the Celestium. The cyst-like bulge struggled to burst the outer membrane of the metal as it repeatedly attempted to break through. Whatever this thing was it had managed to stem the flow of any other souls into Limbo. David watched intently to see which foreign object would be the first to buckle under the pressure. The build-up of intensity was too much for the wall and finally a dark blue cloud of electricity breached its prison.

There was no question it was a soul, although it shared none of the conformity that went with the thousands that were marching their way to their unknown doom. This soul was much less stable. It attempted to break itself in half as it wrestled with some internal conflict. The only noise an unclothed soul made came from the crackle of the electrical charges that occasionally discharged from the storm-like structure of its body. Not this soul. This one moaned as if the emotions it was constructed from were rebelling against its own existence.

As it charged forward, quite unprepared to wait in line, it met its first opposition. The line of souls waited patiently for the one in front to move forward, having learnt through experience not to push in case it had the misfortune of coming into contact with another. The dark blue soul let out a screech of pressure and, without warning, approached and then consumed the soul directly in front of it. As the electric blue particles of its foe disappeared inside it, David was certain he heard a deep belching noise.

The commotion was not lost on the souls in the queue. One by one, as if ordered by an extrasensory memo, they moved rapidly to one side, leaving a clear path all the way down to the centre. Its cloudy chest pushed out like an alpha male, the mutation roared its approval and marched down the steps to a guard of honour. It sneered at the masses as it floated past them. From his position at the wall, David struggled to see it reach the bottom, but he certainly heard it. The psycho soul let out what can only be described as a war cry as it leapt in the air and was shot through the funnel en route to the farthest reaches of the Universe.

After a brief pause to see whether the anomaly was likely to return, the collective souls returned to their queue. Was that what he thought it was? In his analytical way of thinking there was no other explanation for it. He continued on his original path, making mental notes of his experience to be jotted down in his notebook when the light was more acceptable. Once more he pushed through the metal.

On the other side of the wall the waiting room was empty except for the line of souls, some scattered pamphlets and an open door into the next room. It was the same picture in the Tailor's room. Apparently you just couldn't get the staff these days. The wardrobe, where John had first picked out a body for himself, was tightly shut. With no one to clothe them, the souls showed no interest in it, bundling past one another to be the first to make it to the waiting room. What was the hurry? Did they really have no idea what they were getting themselves into?

David opened the wardrobe and confidently strode inside. Two lines of prosthetic bodies hung on hooks down either side. They were tattier and more worn than he remembered them, as if the lack of an internal occupant for company had in some way damaged their quality. As he moved nonchalantly down the line, far further than John had done, the flaccid bodysuits swayed with the breeze from his movement. All but one. One of the bodies seemed much thicker and fuller than the rest and its feet weren't hanging in the air.

"I know a prosthetic body when I see one. I've been inside a few after all, and you are not one," he said to the body whose eyes were firmly shut.

"Go away," it whispered from the corner of its mouth.

"You're not fooling anyone, you know," replied David. "I know who you are."

"No, you don't. I'm not available, pick a different body and be on your way."

"Clerk, what are you doing here?"

The Clerk opened one eye, expecting to see someone he recognised but perplexed and confused that he didn't. "Who are you?"

"It's a good question, I'll tell you when I figure it out. What are you hiding from?"

"I'm not hiding…I'm…resting."

"Pull the other one," said David.

"There's nothing to see here."

"Yes there is! There's a mass of souls swimming in and out of Limbo like a chaotic eight-year-old's birthday party. There's no Tailor, no court and no order. What happened?"

"Hold on. How did you get in here? You're not a soul, you're wearing a real body and everything."

"I have a personal interest in this place. Let's just say I know where the exits are. Now what say we stop messing around in a wardrobe like a couple of naughty teenagers and take this conversation outside?"

The Clerk shook off his poor acting and nodded in agreement. As he moved slowly through each room he appeared on edge. All the confidence and energy that once flowed effortlessly through him, part of a job that he seemed to both enjoy and excel at, had gone. The hair on his head had receded more than the twelve years should have reasonably expected, and there were marks of violence across his arms and face. Once back in the waiting room, he sank into a plastic seat.

"What happened here?" asked David once it appeared that the Clerk's pulse rate had returned to an acceptable level.

"He killed everyone. Everyone except me, that is."

"Who did?"

"Well, Lucifer, of course. No one had any idea that he was here."

"Lucifer was here?"

"Yes, it appears he always had been. He was possessing Laslow's body all the time," said the Clerk. "But now he has one all to himself."

"What do you mean?"

"When John Hewson brought the fat guy down here some twelve years ago at the pinnacle of the solstice, he removed John and healed the fat guy. Once he'd removed both souls from the body he was able to pass from Laslow into it. It wasn't good for Laslow, or the rest of us."

"No, I saw that. I found Laslow's corpse nailed to the funnel."

"Once he'd killed Laslow, he went after the rest of us."

"Byron is the Devil," said David under his breath.

"So you know him, then, the fat man?"

"I'm aware of his work."

"His back catalogue is nothing to what he's capable of now, let me tell you. His body is renewed and he walks the Earth undetected, looking for you."

"So now that Satan has acquired a younger body he is less conspicuous," said David. "Hold on, what do you mean looking for 'you'?"

"We all knew that you were the last of the twelve: we just didn't know we were already in the endgame. There's only one way you could be here. Only the twelve can enter here as you have done."

The number twelve was ever-present in David's mind. That number had been assigned to him in a past life by a still unidentified man during a rather unpleasant exorcism. It was the level number in Hell where he'd been incarcerated for part of his afterlife. It was the number he was being assigned again. If he was the twelfth it also meant that there had been eleven others.

"I'm a little tired of riddles. What is this place really?" asked David.

"Well, this is Limbo of course."

"But it's not the one you described to John Hewson, is it?"

"No. It hasn't worked like that for a while and certainly doesn't now. Things have changed over the last millennium."

"How do you mean?"

"It was all so simple in the beginning. The soul has always had three nodes. One negative, one neutral and one positive. In the olden days the spread of religion meant that almost all souls ended up at one end or the other of the polarity scale. The process was easy. Negative ones went to Hell and positive ones to Heaven. Then things changed. People stopped believing. They started to think for themselves."

"That's not a bad thing, is it? You can't force people to believe in gods, even if it's hard for me to argue against it at the moment."

"You have to remember there is a constant war for control over belief. There has always been genuine concern that a third way would open up. A neutral way."

"A neutral way? How would that work?" asked David, looking more confused than he was used to doing.

"What if a paradise for non-believers developed and all the Universe's energies were pulled towards it? A place where souls didn't need gods, only themselves. Neither Hell nor Heaven would survive."

"Is that even feasible?"

"Oh yes. There have always been homes for positive and negative souls, why not one in between? Why do you think they built Limbo in the first place?"

"Are you saying that God built this place to enable him to polarise neutral souls to positive, even though those souls wanted to go elsewhere."

"Don't just blame God. Satan was also keen to stop any neutral souls."

"They just can't help meddling with human willpower, can they?"

"Parents generally think that way, I'm afraid," replied the Clerk.

"What has all this got to do with me?"

"This place was always built as a court to deal with that neutral threat. If you have a court, you need staff. We assigned lawyers to prosecute and defend from both Heaven and Hell. But all courts need twelve objective men and women."

"Jurors. Where did you get them from?"

"Well, they had to be balanced, so we recruited the first twelve neutral souls that came here to us. Who better to decide on the fate of their kind than the neutrals themselves? They would listen to the evidence and make a decision, on the balance of probability, as to the best final destination. Objective, unemotional but with the capability of reaching all three parts of their soul at the same time."

"And I was one of them. Why don't I remember?" asked David.

"Because your soul has been through so many bodies it has written over the memories like recording over an old videotape."

"I might be wrong. My mind isn't as connected as it used to be, but I don't recall any jurors at John's trial."

"Well, by then they weren't needed. Things changed about a thousand years ago. Since the dawn of time Heaven and Hell have been at war. To win, each side has always searched for some advantage over the other. Whether barring souls from entering Heaven was part of that, who knows?"

"What happened to the twelve?"

"There was nothing for them to do. They were recycled. You're the only one left."

"What does that mean?"

"It means we are in the endgame. You do realise that your presence here on Earth threatens the very existence of the Universe?"

"How gullible do you think I am?" said David.

CHAPTER FIVE

PASS OVER

The demons had never been so busy. On top of the never-ending assault by human souls on their unique part of space, they had some organisational problem-solving to manage. Just like any complex business, Hell had its protocols, policies and structures. The problem was that some of them didn't work very well, particularly when something unexpected occurred. When you're 'too big to fail' you sometimes had to rethink how you did things. Evolution stops for no one.

Every demon had an opinion as to how things should be done, especially the ones closest to the bottom of the organogram and furthest removed from the most difficult decisions. The right course of action always seemed so easy when you were at the bottom of the pile. The most common complaints from the worker demons related to the perceived overcomplexity of how results were delivered. Surely it was easy. The patients came in, they were diagnosed, treated and finally discharged, quite literally on that last point. What was difficult about that?

The answer, of course, was always volume. There were just too many 'patients' being admitted. Yet they never increased the resources or allocated more staff to cope with it? The answer to the increasing volume was always efficiency savings. Do more with less, period. That was all very easy to say if you were management. But you try laundering souls when two prongs of your pitchfork have fallen off and they refuse to make you a new one.

There were of course many bosses. Every time efficiency savings reared its ugly head it coincided with a new and even more complex restructure. How many subcommittees, trusts, executive boards and team pods were needed? Apparently, it was one hundred and fourteen. Although that was the last time Brimstone had counted them and a lot can happen in a morning. He couldn't remember how many of these groups he was part of so, he just went to all of them and waited to see if he was kicked out.

On top of the everyday trauma that came from running Hell, they were dealing with several exceptions with no offer of overtime, assistance, or a morale-boosting thank-you note. Brimstone was contemplating the formation of the first outer planetary union movement when he heard his name mentioned in the meeting for the first time.

"Do we have to do these things over the telepathy phone?" replied Brimstone as he rocked backwards and forwards in his chair, his vision trapped behind his eyelids. "I do find it hard to concentrate when I'm not in the room with everyone else."

"It's difficult for everyone to be in the same time zone, let alone the same place," replied Asmodeus aggressively. "Your update please, Brimstone."

"Well, we're still searching for John's remaining parts. There isn't much news really, other than…" A loud bang stopped Brimstone's answer for which he was most thankful, as it was boring even him.

"Sorry, that was me. Someone slammed the door to my office."

"Mr. Bitumen, you need to make sure that you put your 'on call' sign up. How many times do I have to tell you? It's clearly stated in the policy document," said Asmodeus.

"Sorry," came a whispered remorseful response.

"Mr. Brimstone, continue."

"We've scanned most of the levels from twelve down and there are no signs of him so far. My team is currently working the lower levels as we speak."

"It's not good enough. Can I remind you *who* is listening in on this call. You must work harder. We can't allow John to make a fool of... Is someone snoring? Who is it?"

It was always the same with telepathy conferences. No one really paid much attention because no one really knew why they were there in the first place. The organiser always invited everyone, to protect themselves from any lack of communication down the line. It was another example of an efficiency saving that looked good on paper but never really delivered. Just because all demons had the capacity to tune in to the telepathy network, it didn't guarantee their undivided concentration. As no one admitted to having passed out, the conversation continued.

"Demons, if we can all just stay upright and conscious for a few more minutes we might get through our agenda," demanded Asmodeus.

A series of muffled groans didn't offer much hope.

"The final piece of news I have is the most concerning," said Asmodeus. "As you all know, we received two 'shadow' souls in this domain as a result of them having Emorfed in their systems. It was anticipated that this would be the end of it. We were wrong. Over recent time a series of these shadows have arrived here and occupied the Soul Catcher. This can mean only one thing. Emorfed has not been eradicated."

"How can that be?"

"Protocols, people! When you talk you have to say your name first so we know who it is," said Asmodeus.

"Sorry it's Mr. Fungus. How can that be?" he repeated.

"That's better. We are still investigating but it would seem clear that either there was a batch left over or someone has a new supply."

"Brimstone," said Brimstone following the rules to the letter. "We have found a way of removing them from the Soul Catcher, but if we don't stop them we're going to run out of places to store them. There are only a limited number of vases that we can produce and if they escape they could just pollute the whole place."

"I'm aware of that, Brimstone, which is why we have commissioned Mr. Silica to create a new stock of vases for us."

"There's only so much of me to go around, sir," replied Silica. "I'm already down a belt size."

"And we all appreciate your sacrifice. We just can't wait around idly for these shadows to arrive. We must stop them at source."

"Leave that to me," came a distant voice that very few of them recognised.

"He didn't use the protocol," replied Mr. Fungus indignantly.

*****

Sandy hated beach holidays with a passion. Where was the fun in sitting down on a pile of sand being slowly fricasseed by solar rays before marinating yourself in dodgy sangria and exuberant dancing? It was a holiday for the unstimulated. If you're going to waste money on a holiday you might as well spend two weeks working in a builder's yard and save all the jetlag. A holiday for Sandy had to involve exploration of either location or the mind. As he congregated with some of the other creatures on the shores of the ocean biome, he was able to do both.

A pass over event on level zero was much rarer than on the ten other occupied levels of Hell. Whereas the process above was exaggerated by the constant 'room service' offered by the demons that patrolled their own personal sections, here life was a lot more patient. In truth, not even Primordial knew what the consequences were of allowing a spent soul from a reincarnate to escape back into the Universe. Maybe they'd come back again? As long as they stayed here no damage was done.

The lack of external punishment did have a downside. It meant there wasn't a huge amount to do. Boredom was a formidable enemy. Most of the animals responded by sleeping or pretending to hunt. Occasionally Zoe, the resident lion, would catch up with Arthur the buffalo and get overexcited. Once Primordial found them being propelled around the savannah by the force of Arthur's soul escaping his butt with Zoe's jaws still attached. The whole 'acting like an animal' was thoroughly discouraged. There were no statues on level one, so any instinct that Ian had to shit on one were gladly removed.

A pass over filled the time. The animals, insects and birds had descended on the beach like a pilgrimage. Everyone had set up their own version of camp and were protecting it, like a German holidaymaker protects a towel, to get the best possible vantage point when the curtain finally fell. Some of them had been there so long they acted like unofficial programme sellers for the event.

"I remember when we first got here," said Jeff the lizard to the aardvark sitting in the area next to him.

"Well, you weren't here first. I've been here ages," replied Cyril, lying back in the sand with his four legs in the air.

"Ok, it's not a competition. Do you remember the last pass over we went to? It was for the leopard, wasn't it? That pass over was so loud I left a little bit deaf."

"Yeah, that was a good gig. The light show was pretty amazing."

"Shame about the sound, though. The acoustics in the jungle just aren't as good as they are out here. How many times have you seen it?" asked the lizard.

"This is my eleventh now."

"I've seen way more than that," boasted the lizard. "It was way better in the old days. The crowds weren't so big. It was more intimate."

"I really don't like the superficial fans that come now, just because it's popular," said the aardvark.

None of this attention seemed to have the slightest impact on the star of the show. Puffed out and knackered, Paul lay a short way out to sea contemplating how big the audience might get before the end came. Certainly there weren't many missing. A few 'old-timers' who weren't far from the end themselves, and had seen it happen way more than eleven times, had taken a rain check. As first-timers it was all new to Sandy and Ian, and they weren't quite sure what the etiquette was.

"You can't stand there," bellowed Jeff to the newly landed pigeon. "You're blocking the view. Find your own spot."

"Keep your scales on, I'm not stopping," replied Sandy.

"That's what they all say. Before I know it you'll be making a nest and spending the whole event jumping up and down in front of me."

"Look, I'm really not staying. When do you think it'll start?" asked Sandy.

"Should be soon: Paul hasn't moved for a couple of days now. When Valerie went she didn't move for about three days but she wasn't in water at the time so it was harder to notice. Anyway don't change the subject, bugger off!"

"What right do you have to sit here?" said Sandy, purposely looking to make trouble.

"What right do I have?!" replied Jeff, his scales changing colour in line with his mood. "I've been following these events for years and you come along

60

on the first occasion and think you own the place. First come first served, and I was definitely here first."

"The good thing about being a pigeon is you don't need to sit on the beach to get a good view," said Sandy, rising from the ground with a hop and a flap.

"Show-off," said Jeff.

Sandy wasn't particularly interested in rubbernecking with these glorified ambulance chasers. It was information he needed, not entertainment. Although Sandy had perfected flight, no amount of practice was ever going to help him float. Instead he landed gently on the dolphin's back. Its vessol was frayed and damaged as if the plastic body itself was decomposing in anticipation of the demise of the soul within.

"Think it's funny, do you?" huffed Paul. "Just come to mock the dying, have you?"

"No, not at all. I'm not here to watch you die. I wanted to talk to you," replied Sandy.

"Well, I'm a bit busy to talk. Apparently I'm passing on, or at least that's what the crowd is expecting. Why don't you just fly back to the beach and join the hordes?"

"It's a bit crowded, to be honest, and I really was more interested in finding out how you were feeling."

"How would you be feeling if everyone was watching you? It's like someone bursting in on you when you're trying to have a dump but a thousand times worse. So much for resting in peace."

Sandy felt a flicker of an emotion that he didn't recognise. It was such a long time since this particular emotion had made any sort of appearance, having been kidnapped by its more dominant siblings, selfishness and insensitivity, many years ago. Now guilt, last seen when he was about nine years old, was rushing headlong for his mouth without so much as a restraining belt.

"I'm sorry," said Sandy, bewildered that the word came out at all. "I just wanted to ask your opinion."

"You want what? My opinion!"

"Yes," replied Sandy.

"You do know how a pass over works, don't you?"

"Not really but I'm not here for that. I need information."

"You're quite strange for a pigeon."

"Thank you," replied Sandy to the compliment. "How old are you, Paul, if you don't mind me asking?"

"It's hard to say. No one gives you a calendar when you get here. I know I was one of the first to arrive. I think there were a couple of dozen before me."

"And how many of those early arrivals have you seen 'pass on', as it were?"

"A few now. Li Xeng the rat was one of the first to go. That was quite an event. It never gets better than the first time."

"I have a theory about this whole passing-on process. I wanted to know what you thought about it. After all, dolphins are extremely intelligent creatures."

"Well, I'm a dolphin now but I used to be a bricklayer."

"Were you a clever bricklayer?"

"Not especially."

"Ok," replied Sandy, uncertain quite how to proceed. "Still, I'm going to ask your opinion anyway. I've watched the gases coming in and out of Hell for ages now. I know that the blue gases coming in are souls destined for one of the levels. But I think the stuff being leaked out is the result of the passing on process."

"Well, anyone could tell you that, bricklayer or not."

"That's not the clever bit. When a soul is in Hell it is cleansed from its memories and emotions. Purged of it sins. Which means the bit that is left can't have any. But it's still part of the soul."

"Ok, what's your point? I was busy trying to die, you know."

"Well, back on Earth there was a substance called Emorfed that did the same thing. It removed all the emotions from the soul. It looks the same as the gas leaving Hell and it's definitely not man-made. What if they are one and the same thing?"

"Interesting theory. I wish I gave a shit, to be honest. The bloke that brought me here would be more interested in it than me," replied Paul.

It never entered Sandy's mind that for every creature currently occupying their own piece of personal coastline, each had been captured and brought to Hell on the endeavours of someone like John. Perhaps they were all double-crossed in exactly the same way as he had been. Promised what could never be delivered. He'd seen plenty of metal boxes floating in the air above level twelve. Maybe Paul's minder was amongst them?

"Paul, tell me about the person who brought you here."

"Do I have to? I'm quite shagged out, you know."

"It's important. There aren't many old-timers left."

"Alright, as long as you promise to leave me in peace."

"I promise."

"Interesting guy. Very opinionated and self-righteous. It was as if he was always trying to help me get away, like he knew what was really happening. He seemed frustrated, unable to see the truth for himself, even though he suspected it existed somewhere within him."

"What was his name?"

"Matthew, I think. It was a long time ago."

"Paul, there's one more thing I need to know. Then I promise I'll fly back to the beach. Has any creature ever escaped from level zero?"

"No, why would they want to? If you have to be in Hell, this is the best place to be. You're not likely to find many of those creatures over there that even want to."

"Maybe they just haven't had a leader to show them the way yet. I can tell you, as you won't be here for long, it is my aim to escape. In fact it's my intention to take over the management of the whole place."

"Ok, crazy pigeon. Clearly you've not met a demon called Primordial before."

"What harm can a pile of mud do? I wish you all the best, Paul. It's time I started to recruit an army," he said, casting his mind to the build-up of creatures waiting for Paul's big moment.

Sandy lifted gently off the dolphin's back, not wanting to accelerate the recycling process. He wasn't convinced from his conversation that Paul's demise was likely to come anytime soon. Which gave him plenty of opportunities to talk to the eager bystanders. Who would be willing to join him?

Back on the beach a squabble had broken out and it was no surprise to find out who was in the centre of it. In a circle of animals stood Ian, lacking a few plastic feathers and sporting a ping-pong-sized lump on his forehead. At the other end of the circle, only visible from Sandy's viewpoint in the sky, was some sort of rodent. Even if he was thirty percent bigger than most rodents, he still didn't compare to Ian's stature, and yet he was kicking the pigeon's arse. Sandy landed directly between them.

"What's going on here?"

"This rat nicked my space," whimpered Ian from a position on the ground where he'd collapsed in a heap.

"Rat!..*cough*...shrew, you idiot...bite me...come on, fight...arse...I'll take you all on," replied the rodent. "Damn it...are you alright...? I'm awfully sorry I hit you...stupid bird."

It was impossible to keep an eye on the rodent's movements because they never stayed in one place. Every third second he shook his head as if a fly was constantly bothering him. He coughed regularly to clear his throat and struggled to deliver a coherent sentence. The vessol he wore was equally volatile.

Little blue sparks crackled out of the seams and on every occasion his mood changed to mimic his body.

"What's your problem?" asked Sandy.

"Nothing…I want to kill Ian…biscuits…hug him. No, I don't…shut up, you," screamed the shrew insanely.

"How do you know his name is Ian? How is that possible?" said Sandy, analysing the strange creature further.

"I brought him to Hell…and he deserved it… tosser…I will feel the guilt forever…forgive me."

"John!" said Sandy. "Is that you?"

Out in the ocean Paul answered the question with what sounded decidedly like a fart. It started slowly, wheezing from his body with the momentum of an old plumbing system cranking into action. The plastic body, where Sandy had been standing moments earlier, started to buckle and expand. Gas burst from the valve in his throat like an overboiled kettle.

Distracted by the fight, the crowd stampeded furiously back to their original positions. Watching avidly from the sidelines, they collectively hushed each other for the event that many had been waiting on for weeks. If the fight had been an unexpected support act, this was the main event. After it finished they'd all be forced to go back to the dens, nests and caves until the next one.

Sandy hovered over the beach in order to maintain a view without blocking anyone else's. If his theory was right, this was the closest he was going to get to see it. An almighty crack disturbed the air and a BOOM flooded in from the sea. Paul's ripped vessol quickly took in water and sank below the waves. A trace of wispy, blue gas hung above the shoreline momentarily, before floating unhurried into the sky.

CHAPTER SIX

THE SERPO CLINIC

In a valley to the south-east of Calgary, clinging to the mountainside with all the precision of a tightrope walker in a circus, sat a vast spruce wood cabin. A place of solitude hidden from the normal bustle of everyday life: all around it was peaceful. Huge pine trees camouflaged its existence from all but those who knew how to find it. A crown of snowy white peaks kept both the world and its troubles at bay. This place was designed with secrecy at its very core.

Log cabins weren't exactly a rarity in the Canadian wilderness and barely any of the people who lived in this beautiful desolation had noticed this one's arrival. After all, it was customary for them to be placed where it seemed both illogical and impossible to build one. There were several reasons why this one had appeared.

This was no ordinary retreat for the rich classes keen to escape the trappings of nearby metropolises in order to reconnect with the isolationism of nature. This was no ski lodge for those in search of a five-star pampering where every whim is extended. This building was the Serpo Clinic, the world's first and only location for the practice of psychothanasia. As with euthanasia, Canada was one of the few countries in the world that would allow it.

There are, of course, many places in the world that offer refuge from the mind. Rehab clinics are two a penny in most First World countries. They charge inordinate fees in order to cure people from the ailments that course around their brains. Many of these conditions are serious, and the work that is done to treat them necessary. For every dedicated practice there are also those that house wayward celebrities who feel it necessary to take regular trips to keep up their reputations and the public's sympathy.

The Serpo Clinic was very different. It didn't purport to offer healing from chemical imbalances, substance addiction or celebrity breakdowns. It offered to remove mental health problems completely and permanently. 'Soulicide not suicide' was the message on its branding and television campaigns. Where euthanasia helped the body to die, psychothanasia helped the soul to die. And they weren't short of applicants.

"Your first patient is here," came the call from the receptionist to the phone in treatment room seven.

"Send him in."

Treatment room seven was the room set aside for consultations. It lacked the medical rigmarole that accompanies so many other examination rooms. A huge log fire roared in a hearth, surrounded by thick animal rugs from beasts that should have been rampaging through the local scenery. Instead their lives had been cut short so that some rich dude could feel reassured that his money was being well spent. A sofa of red velvet, capable of seating nine patients at a time, stretched along the centre of the room. The high ceilings above it advertised the mountains through large glass panes to all who sat below. In a large, one-seater leather chair sat a tall, blond man dressed in a white turtleneck jumper and a pair of blue corduroy trousers.

"Mr. Bouchard, welcome to the Serpo Clinic. Please take a seat," said the man, pointing towards the overproportioned sofa that had the unique characteristic of swallowing most who sat there.

"Thank you," replied Mr. Bouchard nervously.

"My name is Victor Serpo. Please try to make yourself comfortable, this is not a job interview."

"I am a little nervous."

"Really no need. Nothing will be decided today, Mr. Bouchard. This conversation is simply to ensure that you are of sound mind and clear motive to receive the treatment that we offer here. There are some routine questions that I must ask to establish that, of course."

"Of course," replied Mr. Bouchard as his plump body sank a little further into the red velvet.

"What is your full name?"

"Antoine Roland Bouchard."

"Age?"

"Fifty-seven."

"What is your profession?"

"I'm the CEO of a large multinational oil company."

"And how much do you earn a year?" asked Victor pointedly, twiddling his pen in order to capture the number of noughts in the answer.

"Is that necessary?" replied Antoine. "I have already paid my deposit."

"It's an important part of the consultation. After you go through our therapy your ability to earn and work will cease, and therefore we must be certain you leave your family in a sound financial position."

This was the explanation that Victor always gave because the real reason was far less palatable. The price was never fixed. It was always dependent on the candidate.

"Three and a half million dollars a year, excluding bonuses and share options, of course."

"Of course," said Victor, trying to stop his eyes overreacting. "And what is the reason for applying for treatment here?"

"I can no longer live with myself."

"None of our clients can," replied Victor. "What are the specific reasons for that?"

"Just over a year ago one of my company's oil tankers ran aground off the coast of Brazil. Several of the crew were killed in the blaze and the damage to the environment was considerable."

"What's that got to do with you? You're just the boss, you can't be held responsible for that."

"But I do feel responsible. I made decisions that put profits in front of safety. My thirst for money clouded my judgement and drove my greed."

"Well, you'll get over it. I don't think it calls for such drastic action."

"In three weeks' time I will face accusations of corporate manslaughter in an American court. I will be found guilty, yet the guilt I feel is a scar that I already carry," said Antoine, as he started to blub like an oversensitive actor delivering a Shakespearian monologue.

Victor was unmoved, "So you're telling me you're a coward. You want to run from the chaos you've created?"

"No, I just want peace from my guilt."

"Don't worry, Antoine, it was not a criticism. We love cowards. They're some of our best clients. Cheats, criminals, con artists, the bereaved, the mentally unstable, disgraced public figures – we love them all. We are the last bastion for the desperate and depraved. Your last and only friend, for a fee of course."

"Is it painful, what you do here?"

"Not for you, it isn't. It's a simple procedure no more complicated than taking an aspirin. Within minutes of taking it you will feel nothing at all. No more guilt. In fact no pain at all from the emotions in your mind or body."

"Will I still be able to have sex?"

"I'm sorry, is that important given you're likely to be spending a fair amount of time locked up in a cell?"

"I'm not banged up yet."

"And sadly, if you forgive the pun, you won't ever be banged up after taking our therapy. Not in a consenting way at least. You can have sex, of course, but you'll have no desire to. What have you told your family about this?"

"They are aware. Clearly if I go to jail they'd rather not see me suffer," replied Antoine.

"That's understandable. After all, they haven't done anything wrong, have they? They will need to sign our contract, though, to demonstrate their willingness to let you participate."

"That shouldn't be a problem."

"Ok. Well, I have enough information for the time being. Take this prescription to the receptionist and she will arrange a time for the therapy to be administered. The total fee will be two hundred and fifty thousand dollars, which must be paid upfront and we don't take PayPal."

Mr. Bouchard made several attempts to extricate himself from the sofa with little joy. Eventually, Victor came to his assistance. Victor's fragile movement showed none of the strength and vitality a younger version of himself once had. His current mannerisms showed a man struggling to live in a changing body some distance from the powerful man at the peak of his influence. There had been no such change in his outlook, though. As he guided Antoine across the uncluttered space of treatment room seven he stopped before reaching the door.

"It was good to meet you, Antoine. I would show you out, but I don't really do doors."

As Antoine left he traded places with a woman coming in the other direction. Long, auburn hair flowing down to her shoulders, she learnt forward and gave Victor a kiss on the lips. She floated into the room like a puck on an air hockey table, sitting elegantly on the sofa that had given Antoine so much difficulty. The Versace suit hugged her body like a lizard's skin. It had once felt so alien against her body compared to the lab coat that she'd spent so many years wearing to work. But that was then and Dr.

Trent's circumstances had improved exponentially in the past decade.

"How did the interview go?" she asked, removing a minuscule laptop computer from her handbag.

"Good, I think he's a win for sure. Strange little man but fucking loaded so I jacked the price up a little."

"Well, that's good. Sales have been pretty strong, two million dollars so far this quarter."

Since the clinic had opened three years ago the total number of patients treated had increased rapidly in each quarter, which was good because their investors had demanded ever-greater returns. Strangely, corporate types never wanted less, always more. 'We think you've had an excellent quarter and you've worked really hard, so as a reward we thought you should have a break. Let's go for twenty-five percentage less next quarter.' Never going to happen. Unknown to the Serpo Clinic's investors, the profits would not continue forever. But by then, Victor would be richer than any of them.

Although the clinic currently made good money it had not always been the case. Victor had started with nothing. In fact, nothing was an overstatement. Out of work and lacking the protections his last profession gave him, he'd been forced into hiding. The only element of his past life that he kept was his name. Not the one he used most often. Victor Serpo, not Agent 15, was his real name and almost no one knew it. Those that did – Byron, Dominic Lightower, John Hewson and Sandy Logan – were no longer a threat.

Byron hadn't been seen since the days after the last election. Dominic had been arrested and sentenced to life imprisonment for treason against the state, although many had called for the death penalty. In truth he didn't know where John and Sandy were, although there was a boatload of evidence to suggest they could have been dead the first time he'd had dealings with them. There wasn't a lot he could do. Pigeons he could track. The undead not so much. The final person who knew who the real Victor Serpo was now sat opposite: his current partner, in both business and life, Emma Trent. In many ways it was her actions that allowed them to live in their current opulent surroundings.

"Are we on target, then, Emma?" asked Victor.

"We are, although it won't last forever."

"How are the stock levels looking?"

"At this rate we'll run out in a year and a half. That's at current levels of candidates, a rate that is going up all the time."

"Any luck with replication?"

"None. Over a decade I have been working on the formulation. I have more scientists than ever, including some of the best and most brilliant ones, and still we search in the dark. This substance is just beyond current human knowledge. It just depends how far in front it is."

"Well, it is what it is. We must continue with the small amount we have left and be prepared to retire this time next year. We have enough money," said Victor, lacking any great concern.

"It's not just about the money. Don't you want to know what this stuff is? Aren't you curious to unlock its mysteries?"

"Not in the slightest. It makes me money and that's it. The money gives me the opportunity to get back some of what was stolen from me. That's all I really care about."

Why didn't he want to know? Emma was infatuated with knowing. You could throw all the money in the Bow River for all she was concerned. Even though she enjoyed the lifestyle afforded to her by a business unique anywhere on the globe, she'd happily live as a tramp to unlock the questions that lay scattered and broken amongst the expensive spectroscopy equipment neatly adorning the walls of her laboratory.

"That's not enough for me. I need to know. Our equipment just isn't advanced enough to break down the constituent parts. We need something bigger."

"What do you mean, bigger? You've spent millions on the most advanced equipment available."

"Millions isn't enough. The equipment I'm thinking of has a lot more noughts on the end."

"You've clearly lost your mind. We can't afford that amount."

"I wasn't thinking about buying one. The equipment I need is a little big for our lab anyway," said Emma with a smile.

"Well, how big is it?"

"Twenty-seven kilometres."

"Have you been sniffing something in that lab of yours?"

"No, I'm talking about the Large Hadron Collider in Switzerland. I've been talking to some of the experts there about our compound. They're eager to fire it around their machine to analyse its structure. I'll be away for a few months."

"Thank God for that. I thought you were about to bankrupt me. When are you going?"

"As soon as I've prepared the samples and gained approval for moving it to Europe."

The telephone sitting on a small table to Victor's left started to flash, an indication that work was calling.

"Yes," he said, answering it almost immediately.

"Sorry to bother you," said the receptionist. "We have a walk in. Are you free to see him?"

The Serpo Clinic sat at the top of a valley on roads you'd only attempt if you were a rally driver or certifiably insane, and that was in the summer. In early autumn, as it was now, you were lucky if you found any evidence of a road at all. Most patients were rich enough to arrive by helicopter. Although they advertised the clinic, it was through carefully selected channels, designed to thoroughly research candidates that passed the tests of affluence and suitability. They were not accustomed to 'walk-ins'.

"Really, are you sure?" replied Victor.

"Quite sure, he's standing in front of me now," she replied.

"Well, I won't see him until he's paid his deposit. That'll put him off," he mouthed to Emma who was packing her things back into her handbag.

A dull thud came out of the telephone. "I think he's got enough, sir, but I might need to count it."

"He's paid one hundred thousand dollars in cash!" gasped Victor.

"I suspect you'll want to see him, then," said Emma, leaning in for another kiss before leaving. "I'll let you know when I have more details on the trip."

"Ok," replied Victor. "Send him in please."

The doors flew open and a man strode confidently into the room as if he was expecting a standing ovation. Unlike his last candidate, this man showed no signs of anxiety or stress. The sun from the skylights skipped off his claret suit, taking focus away from a face that no one else on Planet Earth could claim to be theirs. As he closed the door behind him, the back of his bald head showed an intricate tattoo that stretched from ear to ear. The only hair on his head was a white goatee beard that encircled a broad, toothy smile. Despite being in his late-fifties it was clear this gentleman worked on his slender build.

"Welcome, how can I help you?" said Victor.

The man didn't reply but his piercing blue irises, fixed on Victor, gave no doubt that his ears had heard the welcome. He walked purposely to the sofa and lay down, kicking his polished shoes off in one smooth motion.

"Well, Mr…" Victor waited unsuccessfully for a reply. None came. "We're not accustomed to having walk-ins at this clinic. It's normally by appointment only. But as you have paid your deposit and I have the time, let's begin. In order to decide on your suitability I have to ask you some questions. Is that ok?"

The man nodded, giving no reassurance that any of his answers might come out of his mouth.

"Your name?"

"Let me introduce myself. I'm a man of wealth and taste," came a gravelly response.

"You are allowed your anonymity, if you pay enough for it, but there are some questions that I do need accurate answers to. Age?"

"Oh, I've been around for a long, long year."

"What is this? Who are you?" demanded Victor.

"Pleased to meet you, I hope you guessed my name!"

"Well, I haven't," said Victor angrily.

"Amongst others they used to call me Byron T. Casey."

*****

All the encouragement in the world wouldn't motivate the Clerk to leave Limbo. Whatever the Clerk was, or had been, his place was most certainly here. He argued that his job had not changed. It was still his role to accompany souls into the vast chamber of Celestium, and chaperone safe passage to their final destination. David didn't hate the Clerk for it. There was no hate left in him to use. Once the logic of the man's actions had been computed and rejected there was nothing more that David could do.

In the darkness of the Alpine panorama he sat for a while contemplating his next move. The less notorious southern side of the Eiger framed the starlight setting in the distance. There was no point leaving. The only safe return was to take the train via the visitor centre in the morning. He'd prepared well. Ropes and climbing shoes had been packed to allow escape from the grand fissure that housed the sphere. And his own abilities to find sanctuary in the wilderness were as natural as his inability to lie. The night's weather conditions didn't warrant it.

Growing up on the mountain slopes of Patagonia, in the shadows of Osorno the volcano meant his anatomy was quite suited to camping out. At four thousand metres the Eiger was only just higher than the hut he was born in. As the kettle boiled on his small, portable stove he lay down on his sleeping bag under a small outcrop of rock that hung from the side of the slope.

What next? Laslow's name had been removed from the list and replaced by Byron's. He drew his finger down the page. There was no clear way of taking revenge on the whole of Hell, not unless the rest of his soul took the opportunity. The next feasible name on the list was Dr. King.

At first there had been no overriding desire to wreak revenge on the old preacher. He'd only made it onto the list because of the circumstances surrounding John's exorcism. Things had changed since then, though. The inscription on John's grave had included the same name: King. Whether there was a connection or not didn't matter. If you were on the list you were going to get a visit.

David had an alternative reason for wanting to track Donovan down. Dr. King was not only a doctor of theology but also a doctor of psychology. When you were fairly certain that you had no physical capacity for any emotions, psychology was going to draw a blank. But how about his dreams? What could King tell him about those? Why did he have such vivid, unconscious experiences that never materialised after waking? The stars twinkled and David raised his mug of tea to salute the other parts of him many light years away.

CHAPTER SEVEN

THE TAMING OF THE SHREW

As the final wisps of Paul's recycled soul passed out of existence, the onlookers started to filter away. They'd got the thrill they were waiting for and the collective disappointment, that comes from anything hyped up so much, was infecting their mood.

"Not as good as last time," Jeff the lizard was heard saying as he scurried off in the direction of the desert biome.

The timing hadn't been good for Sandy's plan. This was the only time these creatures gathered in the same place in such numbers. Who knew when that would happen again? Before long his captive audience would be spread over an area the size of Belgium. How would he identify the right candidates to help him take on the demons? What had seemed ambitious but achievable no more than half an hour ago now seemed impossible. It was also the second most interesting topic in Sandy's head.

"How are you feeling, Ian?" asked Sandy, collecting the white plastic bird off the floor like a trainer supports a defeated bantamweight boxer.

"Dizzy. I'm not quite sure what just happened?"

"You got your arse kicked by a tiny shrew with behavioural problems."

"No, I didn't. You must have missed the start. I got a couple of decent jabs in. He was scared, you could see it in his eyes!" said Ian, demonstrating more bravery now that he was further from the scene.

"Of course he was," replied Sandy.

"What's his problem anyway?" added Ian.

"I think he has many. One of which might well be that he's John Hewson," replied Sandy. "Although it appears he's developed some rather disturbing characteristics. We need to get to him before he disappears."

Finding the shrew was easy. The great kingdom of species were all filtering away down a narrow gully that led up from the beach between the dunes. Every three seconds or so one of them got an electric shock and leapt out of the way. As Sandy and Ian watched the exodus from the air they could pinpoint from the affected animals just where John was. They waited patiently for him to exit the gully and head off in the direction of the forest biome. The pigeons weren't the only ones watching him from the air.

As close as physically possible to what was both the roof of level zero and the floor of level one, a magnificent golden eagle was hovering effortlessly above them. The direction of flight suddenly changed and with the accuracy of an Exocet missile the eagle went in for the kill. With air resistance having been given the day off, the eagle was at John's position in seconds, its talons raised, sharp and inviting. The eagle's prey responded with the type of shock that might be delivered by an electricity substation. By the time Ian and Sandy reached the spot, Malcolm was spread eagle on the ground.

"Ha! That'll teach you…bitch…*cough*…what have I done, that's awful…arse biscuits," replied the overly confused rodent.

"John, stop!" shouted Sandy. "We need to talk."

"Oh, it's Sandy the traitor…*cough*…it's all your fault…flange…it's all my fault…bumholes…I cursed you to your fate, how can you forgive me…gusset."

"What's happened to John, Sandy? He was always so well...balanced?" asked Ian, trying to choose his words carefully.

"I'm not certain but something has. John, how did you get like this?" asked Sandy.

"I escaped...bastards...I split up my soul...going to take revenge," he replied, constantly flinching from the little sparks discharging from his body and forcing him to blink rapidly and clear his throat valve. "I have things to do...must put things right...*ahem*...kill... they must pay for what they have done...knickers."

Behind the one rodent argument, Malcolm came around from his bout of unconsciousness with a groan. "Ow, what happened?"

"I think you forgot about the notion of 'not' acting like an animal," replied Sandy.

"But I am an animal. It's not like I can be an accountant again, is it? Who's going to need their tax returns done here? There's just nothing else to do other than act like an animal."

"We all have to adapt," said Sandy. "I don't think we've met yet. I'm Sandy. What's your name?"

"Malcolm's an arsehole," replied John, giggling with laughter and hopping on the spot like a child desperate for the toilet.

"How did he know that?" replied the eagle.

"It's not important," countered Sandy before John could offer any further abuse. "I have a plan. I want you to send a message to as many animals that you can get to safely. Go to every biome and tell them I need to find a team of animals willing to break out of here. I want only the most cunning, wise, strong and nimble to apply. Tell them to congregate by the willow tree in the forest biome for try-outs."

"You're mental, you are. Why would I do that? I've got a good life here, no one bothers me," replied Malcolm.

"If you don't...crevice...then I'm going to hunt you down...jockstrap...I know where you live...fucker...

I'll rip all your feathers out," replied John, getting more and more irate as he attempted to bite an animal considerably bigger than himself. Sandy held him back, although it cost him a couple of nasty burns.

"Ok, I'll do it, but I'm not sure how many creatures are as bonkers as your friend here."

Shaken but still capable of flight, Malcolm soared into the air to complete his newly acquired mission. The pigeons and the shrew watched as he headed for the Arctic biome over in the distance. It was incorrect to say that Sandy had a plan. It was more of an objective, really. He knew what he wanted to achieve and hoped that in the fullness of time some strands of genius would form themselves into something resembling a plan. If not, they'd just use their wits and propensity for causing havoc.

"John, we need to find you a hiding place. It'll only be a matter of time before Primordial finds out that you're in his domain without his knowledge."

"I could take him…butt crack…scares the shit out of me…let's go," replied John, apparently at odds with himself over the outcome of any rendezvous.

When the only demon that surveyed the inhabitants of this particular level of Hell had the ability to sink into the ground and appear at leisure, hiding was a challenge. Nowhere at ground level, or sea for that matter, was safe. Being one of its newest residents, Sandy wasn't an expert on demons yet. But he was a canny type, gifted at problem-solving and bouts of brilliance.

If Primordial was essentially a soup of elements and bacteria born alongside the first organisms of life, he probably couldn't fly. Slide up things, yes. Squeeze through tiny gaps, yes. Fly into the air, no. It was time to test that theory out. What was the worst that could happen?

"John, Ian and I are going to take you somewhere safe so that we can talk. It needs to be high up, I'm afraid, and it would be useful if you didn't shock us en route."

"Can't control it…shit…I love you guys, you're so kind to me…feathery arseholes…"

"Ian, we need to work as a team on this one," said Sandy. "I'm not convinced our friend here is going to be able to control himself."

"Whatever you say, Sandy."

The relay started with Sandy, but switched between them every three or four seconds. Once Sandy had been given a shock and spontaneously dropped the rodent, Ian had to catch him before he hit the ground. This process continued with both pigeons engaged in a foolish prank of who could put their hands on an electric fence the longest yet still stay conscious. When they finally landed at the very top of a thin, eroded rock tower in the canyon biome, their plastic feathers were sticking out like an avian Afro.

This wasn't truly in the sky as Sandy had planned, but how could they keep flying with John in this mood? The tower was the next best thing. The column stretched a hundred feet from the ground, smooth from the repeated friction of the wind that blew through the valley. The head of the tower was slightly wider than the thin body, allowing them even more protection from the overhang. At the very least they'd hope to see Primordial coming.

"What's happened to John?" asked Ian.

"Who knows? It seems to me that he's developed a form of Tourette's. He can't control his emotions."

"Revenge…dirty girl…I'm going to burn them…… when I save Faith…it's all my fault…no, it's not, it's yours…baps," John garbled.

"So what good is he to do us?" said Ian. "He's more of a liability than I am."

"Let's not exaggerate," replied Sandy. "Given the choice, I'd still be taking potty mouth over you."

"But he can't even walk straight without discharging everywhere," replied Ian.

"Well, not at the moment, but if I remember rightly, you can teach someone to manage their Tourette's. John didn't used to have it so maybe we can help him…"

"Two souls…yes, I have, I have two…fucker…two souls in me…QUIET…don't tell them…bite them… they don't like each other very much…go do one," said John, dancing all over the top of the tower, precariously close to the edge a number of times.

"Two souls? Are you saying you're possessed, John? Who else is in there with you?"

"Both Johns…don't tell them, you idiot…the good part…stop it…ignore him, he's disjointed…tosser… and the bad bit…well done…loser…"

"This is going to take longer than I thought," said Sandy.

"I don't think so," replied Ian. "Remember when you and I were learning to fly?"

"Obviously. What's your point?"

"Well, we solved the problem by understanding how our bodies worked, didn't we? All we need to do is help John work out his."

"I see your point in principle, Ian, but we have no idea how to do that," said Sandy. "What did you mean by both Johns, John?"

"Negative soul…fuck pigeons…smelly dirty… scumbag…and a positive soul…I'm so embarrassed, he's so rude…flying rats…rest of me sent back."

"What rest of you? I'd have thought there was enough of you in there already," asked Sandy.

"The boring bit…girlies…sent that bit back…bite me…REVENGE!" screamed John at the top of his octave range, which fortunately was not that high.

Sandy had a quick look over the edge of the column to see whether there was a pile of soil trying to scale it. There wasn't and he sighed his relief.

"Ok," said Sandy. "I think I'm getting it. It appears that John has splintered into different parts of his soul and is struggling to manage the competing factions."

"Interesting theory," replied Ian. "I was going with sex pest."

"That's the Tourette's, you idiot. They have physical and verbal tics that come on when they're unable to control their emotions. If I'm right, and normally I am, he only has emotions in there. No superego to restrain the wild horses of his id."

"Well, if he has tics that's pretty easy to deal with. My mum's cat used to get them all the time. She had this little device with a hook on the end of it. The trick is to turn the device so you get the whole head out," said Ian, attempting to indicate the movement with only the use of his wings.

"You're thinking of ticks, you fool," replied Sandy, clipping Ian around the back of the head. "He's not got lots of insects sucking his blood, has he? How's that going to work? None of us has any blood inside, just plastic and electricity. A tic is an involuntary movement or verbal response."

"My mum's cat used to scratch a lot, though, just like he's…"

"If you mention your mum's cat once more I'm going to be forced to throw you off this rock. The only way of dealing with these types of tics is through John's own willpower," replied Sandy scornfully.

"Willpower…my arse…go screw yourself…"

"Which is clearly not going to be easy," added Sandy. "I seem to remember that you have to get involved in something called habit reversal. Maybe I could try it on both of you."

"Habit reversal: how do you do that, then?" asked Ian.

"Well, there are lots of ways. Relaxation works for some people."

"Couldn't we just use psychological torment, refuse to feed him and damage his self-esteem?" stated Ian.

"No, let's go with relaxation."

"But how do you relax a shrew?" asked Ian.

"Beats me. But if there are several Johns inside him, one of them must have some happy thoughts. If we can coax him to find those, maybe he can control himself?"

"Bollocks to that…sex biscuits…worth a try," came schizo John's response.

"Right. John, I'm going to ask you a series of questions. Before you answer I want you to take a deep breath and really focus on your happy place. Ok?"

"Go swing…it's difficult," replied John.

"For all of us, John, believe me. So what do you want most right now?"

"Arse biscuits."

"That's not even a thing. Try again, remember breath slowly and think clearly."

The shrew closed its eyes and drew squeaky breaths through the thin, plastic valve that occupied the space where the mouth was for all creatures in this realm. The electricity that had been coursing through his body diminished momentarily and his body movements returned to stationary. Slowly he wrestled his negative emotions into submission.

"I must return Faith's shadow…*ahem*…nothing else matters…*cough*…will you help me…?"

"Of course," said Sandy.

"You suck," added John.

"That was good progress, John, at least until the end part. We will help you. I have plans of my own. We can kill two birds with one stone, if you forgive the pun."

"I think," said Ian, acting as current lookout, "you might want to take that back. Look!"

It wasn't a stone that might be responsible for killing two birds on this occasion. Stones didn't take human form, unless they were Brimstone, and he wasn't a good climber. Not as good as the humanoid pile of mud and ooze that was currently halfway up the column of rock.

CHAPTER EIGHT

BETTER THE DEVIL YOU KNOW

"How have you been, Victor? I see you've landed on your feet with this place."

Victor remained motionless, jaw left open so that it rested on his Adam's apple. This couldn't be Byron. Byron was a big, fat guy who wore glasses and teetered on the edge of a heart attack, bolstered by the constant cigarettes that were lit faster than oxygen would burn them. Plus, and this was a big plus, he hadn't been seen for over a decade, even though many, including Victor, had set a network in place to find him. Seemingly reading his mind, the man stood up and did a catwalk-style turn.

"What do you think of my renovations? It took a long time to get this tub of lard back into shape."

"Who are you?" said Victor for the first time out loud.

"I told you," repeated the man, starting to show an angrier side to his character. "I was Byron T. Casey."

"And now."

"Ah well, that is the question, isn't it? If these are the remnants of Byron, updated and improved, who is he really? Go on, have a guess."

Victor despised being played for a mug. That was his job. Those that lose power are the worst in the face of it. Like a playground bully who moves schools only to find there's a meaner, bigger kid in the next playground. Well, this was his playground and he was damned if he was going to move aside for some imposter with a scary tattoo and a sharp suit.

"How dare you come here and play me. Don't you know who I am?" replied Victor defiantly.

"Don't you know? You're the legendary Victor Serpo, aka Agent 15. The man who brought down a government without even trying. The man who destroyed a great man like Byron and drove him into my parlour, a fly to my spider. The man who tried to vanish into the night like a shadow into dusk. Spiders spin webs further than their meagre bodies look capable of. I am that spider and my webs reach everywhere."

"I think you may have misunderstood some of the facts of the matter. John Hewson was more influential than me in that chain of events. Maybe you need to set a web for him."

"You always were so quick. God, I missed that. Such a useful commodity in an ally. That's partly why I am here."

The man sat down again and reached into his pocket. An apple was revealed in the palm of his hand as crisp and shiny as the fabric of his suit. He massaged it in his palm for a while, feeling skin slide against skin. Eyes shut, he lifted it up to his nose and sucked the air into his nostrils, before running his tongue from stalk to stamen.

"Apples have always been my favourite," he said with a grin. "So much history in this simple piece of fruit. Instrumental in drawing back the curtains of gravity, maker of discord in the hands of the goddess of strife, and inspiration behind much of your modern-day tech. Forbidden in the annals of religious history as a symbol of man's corruptibility. Do you have a knife, Victor?"

"That depends for what purpose."

"If I wanted to kill you I wouldn't have left a bag with one hundred thousand dollars on your receptionist's desk."

Even though he'd stopped being an agent sometime ago, Victor was always armed, but never with a blade. That was far too Middle Ages. Why would he give up his gun? It might come in useful, particularly when psycho patients licked apples and suggested they used to be an overweight former boss. Victor walked tentatively over to the cabinet, sitting against the wall at the far side of the room, conscious to keep one eye on his mysterious guest. He returned with a small penknife.

"Thank you. Victor, imagine that this apple represents one human. Each human develops a smooth, shiny exterior that hides the juicy flesh beneath. Desperately they heap effort into keeping their skins from developing blemishes, to avoid any visible proof of the rotting flesh that festers under the surface. They're all born with a natural instinct to avoid the discovery that sits at their core, and it's a complete waste of time." The man cut a third of the apple away and threw it over to his host. "What do you see?"

"I see a piece of apple, slightly rotting and bruised around the pips," replied Victor, still doing his best to reinforce his guest's compliment to his speed of thought.

"That's my piece of the human soul. I don't need to cut it, I can see straight through the skin of every human roaming this planet."

Victor in anticipation caught the second piece of apple as it looped across the room in his direction. "Whose is this piece?"

"That is God's piece, an equal third with the same ability to see deep beneath the surface. But God has eaten too many apples. He no longer enjoys the taste of flesh and pulp," said the man.

"So who does the last piece belong to?" asked Victor.

"That's the thing, no one owns this piece. This is the neutral element to a human's soul. It lacks feeling or a need to enhance its appearance, being more interested in the simple reality of its existence. Until someone claims this piece, John is lost to the rest of us. I can no longer influence his movements or thoughts because he has cut away the two pieces of the soul that now sit in your hands. Yet I must find him before someone claims the last piece as their own."

"That story would be much more effective if you used an orange," replied Victor.

"What?"

"Well, you wouldn't need a knife for an orange. You could just peel back the skin and take out the right number of segments."

"Oranges! When have oranges ever been used in a good metaphor? There's nothing notable about an orange. Give me one example of a famous orange."

After a quick brain scan, Victor had to accept the orange was indeed the lesser cousin when it came to notorious bits of fruit.

"Well, come to think of it, I can't think of any."

"Exactly. Apples are where it's at, trust me. I think you're missing the point anyway."

"No, I think I get the point. Your story suggests that you are the Devil and John's soul has been broken."

"Exactly."

"An excellent party piece, but I don't believe a word of it. Preposterous. Somehow you've put this elaborate story together to extract money or advantage from me. Well, it won't…" His speech was cut off by a deep pain that started in his left arm before shooting up towards his heart. The man took a bite out of the last remaining piece of apple and grinned.

"This is not a game," said the man's voice in Victor's head, even though his mouth was brimming

with apple. *"I can speak to you as easily as I can any person on Earth. All except one, that is."*

"Ok, this isn't a game. Stop it now."

"Very well," replied Satan, casting the remaining apple segment to the floor.

"But how did Satan become Byron?"

"With the help of our mutual friend, of course. John's mission, unknown to him, was always to bring me a fresh body at the point of the solstice. It was never about pigeons or the end of the Universe. Over the centuries I've been forced to squat in a body with other mortals. There were always plenty of volunteers. The weakness of man is always corruptible, if you can find the right pressure points. With Laslow it was to save his precious wife. In the fifteen hundreds I was Ivan, only known as 'terrible' after I took up residence, I might add. There is a war coming, Victor. In fact it's already started and a warrior can't fight in tandem."

"And John brought you the perfect suit of armour."

"When Laslow shot John in Limbo he forced both John and Byron's souls from the body. It wasn't a perfect specimen, but I have managed to prepare it for battle over the last few years."

"But that would kill Byron's body, wouldn't it?"

"In normal circumstances. But they were not normal. It was the solstice. The pagans were right in their belief that certain flowers had an incredible healing property when administered at the correct moment. I left Laslow's pitiful body and entered Byron's, using the yarrow flowers to heal his flesh and fill it with courage."

"Well good for you. Well done. I'm not sure what this has to do with me?"

"That part doesn't. You may come in helpful one day in helping me locate the remaining part of John before he creates any more havoc, but that is not my main purpose for being here."

"So all the apple carry-on was pointless, then?"

"No, not at all. It was still an important visualisation of why I came here to see you. Do you know how the mechanics of Emorfed works?"

"Not really, I'm more interested in the huge amount of cash it generates."

"And fair play to you. I wouldn't be a good role model of evil if I didn't congratulate you heartily," he said, clapping his hands a single time. "Yet it must stop immediately."

"Close the Serpo Clinic? Why?"

"Because it is damaging my home. In comparison to my earlier analogy, Emorfed is the knife that I hold in my hand. It can cut away the two pieces of the soul that you hold, leaving the neutral third. Like a surgeon's knife cutting away a cancerous growth, Emorfed cuts away someone's pain, suffering, and also any joy. Emorfed is freedom."

"Well, I know all that, but why is it affecting Hell?"

"Those positive and negative pieces of the soul become a shadow. They come to us, yet they cannot be cleansed. They have a life of their own and can only be housed in glass."

"Why glass?"

"It doesn't conduct electricity, in fact it's one of the best insulators around. The problem is there aren't many sources of real sand in Hell. I'm told he's already shrunk considerably since all of your patients have been arriving."

"I can close the clinic, but I can't do anything about the more than six hundred patients that we've already treated."

"On the contrary. A man with your résumé would be well placed to do just that."

"What do you mean?"

"We must kill all your patients."

"Why?"

"It's the only way to reconstitute their souls and stop the shadows destroying Hell."

In a location designed and purposely built to be a place of calm, a message of death was being extolled. Victor was used to killing people on the behest of a powerful employer. Who was more powerful than Lucifer himself? But over six hundred, not even he had killed that many before. His clients were spread all over the world. Their wealth and power meant they were well protected. It would take an age.

"But there are six hundred and sixty-four."

"No, there are six hundred and sixty-six. You're forgetting about two victims that took Emorfed before you opened the clinic."

"Who?"

"Byron's daughter and a man called Herb Campbell, former Manager of Nash Stevens. These two may also hold the key to finding John. John is bent on revenge, which means he may be looking to protect or save them in some way."

"What's in it for me?" asked Victor.

"You'll be paid, of course: the first down payment is sitting out there in your reception as we speak."

"But Satan, it's a massive job."

"I think we'll keep to Byron if it's ok with you. It raises eyebrows if you refer to me as the epitome of evil."

"Of course."

"I thought you'd be more positive about it. You were already running low on Emorfed: your business is a year from bankruptcy. This diversification will keep the business solvent."

"That's true. Ok, I'll do it."

"Excellent. There's one other thing. You need to make the deaths look natural."

"Why's that?"

"Because someone else will be watching us."

"Who? John?"

"No, I doubt that, although it would be excellent if he showed himself to us."

"Who, then?"

"Baltazaar."

"I'm not familiar with him."

"Oh, but you should be. You're holding his piece of apple in your hand."

CHAPTER NINE

GOD PROTECTS THE KING

There's something deeply satisfying about working the land for income or survival. Of all the professions that rise and fall in demand and popularity, it's unlikely the bottom's going to fall out of farming.

"Jimmy, what do you want to be when you grow up?" said the teacher.

"I'd like to be a farmer, sir."

"Hmm, stupid boy. There's no future in farming, son. You should think about being a software developer or social media guru. That's the future. The world doesn't need a load of farmers."

"But sir, farming has been an essential part of humanity and community for thousands of years and people will always need to eat, won't they?!"

"Stop dreaming, boy. Give it up, you'll never make it. Annie, what do you want to be when you're older?"

"I'd like to be a reality TV star."

"Good move, excellent choice. See, Jimmy, I'm glad some of your classmates show some real ambition. Farming, I ask you. Whatever next?"

It may not be fashionable in the eyes of many a young school pupil, but to some, still nostalgic for how the world was, it's a noble career path. To curate the soil in ancient arts passed down from father to son, planted in the brain like a seed might be sowed into the ground in March, with skills more complex than the highly paid stockbrokers that cultivate their own profits. What could be more humble or rewarding than that? The terroir, as French vignerons call it, is a religion in all but name. Prayers will be offered for a rich harvest at the same rate that excuses are apportioned to its failure. Not everyone, though, was convinced by the divinity of soil.

The summer this year had scorched much of the ground in Cornwall to the detriment of the produce who struggled to grow and the people that struggled to manage it. On this small island's only farm that responsibility rested on the shoulders of two women.

A battered jeep trundled over the brow of the hill on its daily delivery run from the quay near All Saints Chapel to the hotel. Its arrival, as precise as any alarm call, signalled the onset of lunchtime and the two women laid down their hoes and stretched out their backs to more evenly spread the blood around their bodies.

"Any better on your patch, Fiona?" said the elder of the two women, whose appearance looked well suited to manual labour.

"Awful," replied Fiona. "If we don't get some rain soon we'll struggle to harvest enough to live on, let alone sell."

"Chin up," said Violet picking up a rucksack from the ground. "There's not a lot we can do about it and I'll be damned if I'm going to start praying to the soil for luck."

The farm was made up of a series of small fields scattered across Bryher, the smallest inhabited island in the Isles of Scilly and the most westerly point of England, far out to sea off the tip of Cornwall. The field they'd spent the morning working was in a shallow valley in the centre of the island sheltered from the sea elements by Samson Hill and banks of withering brown ferns.

The only access to Bryher was from the larger islands of St Mary's or Tresco via public ferry or private boat and most residents were more likely to own the latter than they were a car. The only sensible mode of transport on an island not much more than a mile long was quad bike or bicycle. Fiona and Violet used neither. The many pockets of their farm, separated by mossy drystone walls or banks of prickly gorse bushes, was never more than a five-minute stroll to their small, white cottage that sat on the edge of the western shoreline.

"I'm not sure we'll need many pickers at harvest time this year," announced Fiona as they ambled down a sand track that descended between attractive, grey stone cottages on both sides.

"How many did we have here last year? Five or six?" said Violet.

"Six."

"I think the most we'll need is one extra pair of hands at this rate. The locals looking to earn an extra quid or two aren't going to be very happy."

"I'm sure we'll be ok and the locals will understand it's out of our hands," said Fiona encouragingly as she stretched over to hold the other woman's hand.

The island's robins and sparrows, less anxious and fragile than their comrades on the mainland, bustled around blackberry bushes and provided a distinct soundtrack of the island. The sound of the ocean lapped against the rocks as the women made a turn onto a dusty driveway that led up to three attached cottages clung to the beachside on the edge of a semicircular bay.

Every day the two women thanked their luck and persistence for this paradise setting where they'd made their home. Without a certain Byron T. Casey they would never have come to live here or afforded the privilege. Both women had been held against their will in the underground passages of Whitehall, although no evidence for their imprisonment was ever presented to them. After the scandal of Emorfed the new government were more than happy to buy their silence. Financial compensation that more than paid for the farm and the cottage.

Still holding hands, they approached the larger of the two end cottages. A small boy sat on a wooden fence waiting patiently for their return. A grubby-looking child whose skin showed he took every opportunity to explore an island where little was out of bounds and everything was worthy of adventure. This was his island. When only eighty or so people lived permanently here, no one else of his age could lay claim to it. Today he'd been down to the beach for a few hours playing amongst the rock pools. His brown, curly hair had captured more seaweed than his hands had caught fish.

"Hello, Mums," he called when they were within earshot. He jumped down to greet them.

"Here's our little guard dog," said Violet. "So, have you been vigilant?"

"Absolutely. I haven't moved from this spot all morning."

"Other than to go to the rock pools, I see," added Fiona with a chuckle, picking a piece of seaweed from his hair.

"It was all part of my secret operation. You don't know what might be hiding in them," he offered in defence.

"Crabs, I'd think," replied Violet.

"Or pirates," replied the boy.

"Pirates are a bit big for rock pools, I think. Where is Faith?"

"Aunty is at the back of the house soaking up as much sunshine as she can. Even though she's in the sun every day she still shivers when she's in it. I don't get it?"

"When you're older I'll explain it to you, Scrumpy. She's perfectly fine: the brightness makes life more pleasant for her."

The boy lost interest in the answer halfway through and started searching the ground for good, flat stones for skimming on the lake this afternoon.

"Well, it's time we got everyone some lunch. There aren't many pickings from the farm so thank God they invented supermarkets," said Violet.

On the lawn to the right of the house a young girl sat with her legs crossed and a book open across her lap. Her long, white unicorn hair flapped around in the breeze but her focus on the book was never lost. The pale, white skin across her body was impervious to the scorching temperatures around her. Where it was hard to distinguished between the boy's tan and the dirt that he'd acquired, the same was not true of the girl. Clean and pure, her skin sat contrasted against the brown grass of the lawn. A couple of years older than the boy, she ignored all three as they walked up the path.

"Hold on, Mummy," shouted the boy, as the two women drew closer to the house.

He made his way into the immaculately pruned walled garden full of bright colours and strange flowers. The girl didn't move, captivated by the puzzle in her book that sent somersaults around her brain. The boy skipped over to the girl in the pose of an aeroplane, making noises to fit the reconstruction.

"Sis, it's time for lunch."

Unable to move from the spot, her plain voice gave a short response. "I'm working out the puzzle."

"Even you must get hungry. Come on, Grace, I'll race you."

She lifted a single skinny, white finger to her lips as if to hush the world, and after the briefest of pauses she stood up. "Solved it."

*****

Cities were full of people: that's why they were called cities. A mass of citizens living in a collective group or society. David couldn't understand what advantage there was in squeezing so many people into so little space. It was obvious that people loved cities, otherwise why were they there? In their billions they followed, one lemming after the next. Yes, there were more jobs in cities, and of course with jobs came entertainment, theatres, restaurants and more people. Lots more people. The more people that congregated in a place, the more other people wanted to join in, desperate not to miss out. Most cities lacked space for this very reason. What was fun about that?

People were forced to live in smaller and ever more expensive accommodation. It wasn't unusual for a single person to live in something no bigger than a one-room shoebox for the price per month of a small family car. They still paid it. Drawn in by an undiagnosed addiction to opportunity and excitement, naively the mass of human traffic is tricked by the city's need to feed on those that lose their bottle or fall to the many traps that it secretly builds behind the illusion. Crime, vice and violence were all generated by the collective selfishness of a city desperate to corrupt all of its inhabitants in one way or another.

There were no such temptations to worry about in the countryside. Nothing to squabble over but the peace and quiet. Outside of the bustling metropolis of concrete orchards was a world where birds could be heard singing. The last time David heard a bird singing it had come from a budgie in a cage. The countryside might have lacked a really good pizza parlour or a nail salon, but as a child in Patagonia he never missed them, so he probably wouldn't miss them now.

David struggled to get a glimpse of the outside world through the jumbled contents obscuring his only window. The fridge-freezer blocked at least fifty percent of the three-foot-high window. But if you stood on a stool, held onto the ceiling light and craned your neck at a ninety-degree angle you could just about make out the round dome of the Radcliffe

Camera. Only if it wasn't pissing it down and grey in Oxford on the particular time you tried to look. Which realistically meant about four days of the year.

Fortunately for David, this city home wasn't permanent. Once he'd had the opportunity to meet with Dr. King and figure out whether, and how, he should be punished for his part in John's demise, he could move on. Hopefully back to a place where everything was not governed by road signs and traffic lights. Dr. King taught psychology in Oxford, not far from the view that was hampered by clouds and David's fridge.

Everyone in Oxford seemed to own a bike. Their conscientious motives to save the planet appeared not to stretch to the potential damage inflicted on those 'not' riding a bike. Unless you had two wheels and a lump of metal wedged up your backside you were apparently fair game. David tiptoed his way through the city, navigating the narrowest and least bike-friendly passageways he could find. A number of these two-wheeled death squads still did their best to hunt him down.

Dr. King was deep into his ninth decade, but still gave daily lectures and seminars at the Experimental Psychology Department, a walkable distance from the centre of Oxford. His great age didn't seem to worry the Deans who offered him the position some years ago with the proviso that he did not take up a full-time clerical position. The occasional sermon was fine. Their interest was in his work with the mind, not the spirits that he was also famed for. When David reached his office door he tapped on it firmly.

"Enter," came the deep Irish welcome.

The office was low frills. There wasn't a couch for patients because in truth they weren't welcome here. The replacement for a couch was a desk and a couple of chairs positioned in front of it. This room was equipped for talking to students about psychology, not for the afflicted who needed help to understand their own. This room was focused on theoretical debate of the mind, rather than any deep, forensic search of one.

"You must be David."

"Yes," he replied.

"It's most irregular for you to ask to see me. There are many psychiatrists, psychotherapists, counsellors and even less qualified people, if that's possible, who would be more than happy to see you in Oxford."

"None of them can help me," replied David.

"Well, that's no surprise, I'm afraid. Take a seat."

"Thank you," said David as he sat tentatively in front of Donovan's desk, "You come highly recommended."

Donovan rubbed his wrinkled face and leant backwards a little so that his thick glasses could focus on the young man. He spoke with the eloquence and clarity of a much younger man and, although his features could not be mistaken for youthfulness, he appeared nowhere near the age that had been indicated. There was one other important difference from how David's mind remembered him. There appeared to be no stutter. In every other way, though, he was definitely the man who had chanted the soul out of John's body in a house in Kensington all those years before.

"I'm grateful that there are people in the world that still remember who I am, let alone recommend me. You'll appreciate I have limited time, as this is not part of my normal routine. What seems to be the problem?"

David tried to explain. The issues in his head only occurred during asleep and away from his own unique ability to rationalise what he saw. Was it even happening? Or was it some strange flashback of things that were and things that might yet be? These weren't normal dreams, after all. Most were effectively reruns, déjà vu moments trapped in the fabric of a brain that his soul was unable to fully occupy.

"I have dreams," replied David unable to offer any bias as to what he felt about them.

"What sort of dreams?"

"Of things that I think happened before I was born and stories I was told as a young boy, now repeated at night in perfect clarity."

"Quite often patients with recurring dreams demonstrate some unresolved conflict or stress point," offered Donovan.

"But they are different dreams that recur frequently, sometimes all of them in the same sleep."

"Then you must be experiencing many different unresolved conflicts. Give me an example of one of these dreams."

Dr. King removed a pad in preparation to jot down anything of interest or note, at all times keeping eye contact firmly on David. David chose carefully which dreams to reveal. He had dreams that would be familiar to Dr. King and at this point he didn't want to make any connections he might remember.

"There is one dream that I have that resembles no emotion or memory stored or seen. In the dream I wake in a meadow of ivory white grass. A gentle breeze washes over me as I open my eyes to a sky tinged with red. Between myself and a red sun, burning in the sky, a translucent barrier holds in the atmosphere. On the other side a cloud of blue material attempts to enter but the translucent barrier cannot be breached. I appear to be the only one alive in a world of regimented beauty. My whole existence brims with…what do you call it?"

"Happiness," offered Dr. King sympathetically.

"Yes. But when I wake there is no happiness in me and I have no desire to rediscover it."

"You know, of course, that the place you describe only exists in your mind?" said Donovan.

"But it's so vivid. The touch of the grass upon my hands, the breeze against my face, is just a fraction of the reality that presses down upon me."

"The brain is a magnificent organ, David. This world, however real it may feel, is a figment of your subconscious. Why the brain has created such a location for you is what we must discover. Dreams, you see, are based on our feelings and perceptions towards experiences in our lives."

"That's just the point, though. I don't have feelings. I'm not capable of it."

"What you tell the girls of this city is none of my business."

"No, I mean it, it's not a girl thing. I really don't. I have never cried either in sadness or humour. I have never screamed in pain or anger. I have never shown pity or felt disappointment. Never once in all my years."

"Not that I believe you for a second, but maybe your perception of having no feelings has created a world full of them. A place where you can connect to the things that you feel are missing in life. Do all these dreams have a similar pattern?"

"No. I can't find any pattern between them."

"And you have no particular life concerns. Money, girls, gambling, drinking, estranged family members, job anxiety, university stress?"

"No. I told you I'm not susceptible to the worries that normal people suffer from."

"So why have you come here?"

"The dreams. They're not normal surely?"

"Well, they are what they are," replied Donovan, feeling his time was being wasted but wanting to humour this strange teenager. "Tell me another dream. Let me see if I can identify any patterns."

"There is a dream that has surfaced in recent months. It feels the most real at the time, as if I am playing a part in it as it unfolds, rather than watching from the sidelines."

"What happens in that dream?" asked King calmly.

"I'm standing over a middle-aged man lying lifelessly on the floor of a hallway. The body has a gunshot wound to the heart and a pool of blood is gently flowing over the floor. I turn and walk out into the corridor. There are no signs of a forced entry at the front door, but there's a man with a gun. He talks directly to me. There is no haste in his actions. He's just murdered a man and yet he wants a conversation. In a calm voice he says, 'How many times have I killed you? See you next time.' And then he slowly walks away."

"The man is referring to the gentleman on the floor in this scene, is he not?"

"That's just the thing. He says it to me, as if the body and I are one and the same. The dream then shifts to a cemetery. I'm standing over a black marble gravestone and there are markings carved carefully into the back."

"The markings must identify who is buried there," replied Donovan rather too directly.

"These marking are not on the front of the gravestone but on the rear."

"What do the markings read?" asked King, suddenly more fascinated with this dream sequence than the one before.

"God protects the King."

"Interesting. In the dream whose grave was it carved on?"

"I don't know. I never see his face or the front of the grave in the dream," replied David accurately.

This was exactly how he saw it in the dream, even if he had seen it differently in real life. A lie could be hidden if the question asked was wrong.

"Do you know what it means?" asked David.

"Yes, I do. It doesn't come from any of my psychology teachings, though. I know this phrase from my study of theology. The phrase is based on a Phoenician description."

"Who are the Phoenicians?" asked David.

"Phoenicia was an ancient civilisation based in the Eastern Mediterranean close to what we now refer to as the lands of Israel and Lebanon. They first appeared around 1500 BC and are recognised as being the first race to use a formalised alphabet. They were also the first civilisation to organise their society into city states."

"At least I know who to blame for my cramped apartment," said David. "What do the words mean?"

"Well, in the Phoenician culture and alphabet the word God is 'Bal' and the word for King is still in use today in European languages, although its spelling has changed. Tsar Nicholas, of course, was one of the last to hold the title. Your inscription is a name, Baltazaar."

David desperately tried to process the information with little success. None of the timing or detail made sense. Weeks before he arrived in the country and visited the grave etched on his own history for so long, someone had spent hours chiselling the Phoenician name of one of the people on his list into the back of it. But why? This wasn't divine intervention. He knew that John had received unexplained help during his attempt to bring Sandy and Ian back to Hell. When he'd really needed help it had come to him. But that had never happened to David. There were no voices, no signals and no directions. He had always been on his own in his search for revenge on those who had hindered him.

"What do you know about this Baltazaar character from your theological teachings?" asked David.

"Very little. You're talking about a culture that predates Christianity by more than a thousand years, and the ability to write it down on paper by even longer. Only mystery surrounds this character. Anyway, it's interesting that you should think that up in a dream. Do you have any religious beliefs?"

"Let's say I'm aware of the possibility, but it's not really for me," replied David.

"Agnostic, are you?"

"Something like that."

The clock on Dr. King's wall clicked through the hour mark and acted as a prompt for his next appointment.

"Well, I do need to go, I'm afraid, otherwise I'll be late for my next engagement."

"Of course. I appreciate you seeing me in these circumstances. There was one question that I wanted to ask you of a personal nature if you don't mind?" asked David.

"Well, if I can I will," replied Dr. King.

"The person who recommended you said I needed to be patient as you had a rather pronounced stutter. Yet in all the time we have been speaking you've not stuttered once."

"Well, your friend must have known me from a very long time ago. My stutter hasn't affected me now for some twelve years."

"How did you treat it?" asked David curiously.

"I didn't seek treatment for it. It happened whilst I was performing an exorcism on a famous popstar. Strangely my exorcisms never worked that well, but on this day it was quite effective. Ever since then, I have lost any trace of my voice impediment. Now I really must insist you leave, or I won't get to my funeral in time."

"I thought you weren't involved as much in the Church anymore?" replied David who had done more than enough homework on his roles and responsibilities.

"It's for a family friend so I'm allowed by the college to lead more personal duties of God."

"I'm very sorry for your loss. Who was it that passed away?"

"My good friend Herb Campbell sadly passed away last week. Took his own life, poor soul."

"How is that possible?" asked David.

CHAPTER TEN

BUILT ON SAND

When the hooter sounded it ushered in a shift change at the front gate of Hell. It was impossible to say how long shifts lasted or indeed who was responsible for sounding the hooter. When time was effectively non-existent you could make it up as you went along. It was incorrect to say that there wasn't any time because stuff happened all the time. Stuff needed time. Whether seconds, minutes or hours had passed was irrelevant. Just because barely a second of Earth time had passed since the last shift change had no bearing on the amount of work the demons had put in.

The outgoing Shift Manager set the Soul Catcher to pause and the five demons stretched out their bodies, each one built from a unique element of the periodic table. Off into the distance they trudged to do what demons do when they're on a break. Not all of them had that luxury. The senior demons, like Brimstone, only really got time off for good behaviour when something brown and smelly hit a spinning object used for cooling people down. Fans weren't popular in Hell. Shit was far more prevalent.

Brimstone stood at the entrance waiting for the next team to drag their sorry arses into work. They were never late. After all, none of them were French, the only race capable of being late in a place where time doesn't exist. The new team assumed their positions at the various points amongst the complex machinery. Two stood at the conveyor belt waiting to direct the vessols to the correct levels. One sat at the controls overseeing the lists that illustrated in- and outpatients. The other two were responsible for loading vessols to the bulbous end of the contraption where a valve protruded from the base.

None of them relished their work. Where was the job satisfaction? Routine was the name of the game here. Demons didn't need recognition and they had no great ambitions for a higher office. The mind of a demon didn't have that capacity. But they did get physically tired. When your shift appeared infinite and your body ached from the dual challenges of manual labour and too few of you to pull the weight, there was no shortage of disappointment.

"Right, team!" shouted Brimstone as they all reached their normal positions. "Ready to go?"

The five demons crossed their arms and shot Brimstone messages of discontent. It was clear who they blamed for this monotony.

"Mr. Shiny, can you remind us of the team motto, please?"

Mr. Shiny, a lanky demon with skin that reflected the scenery onto himself, was one of the demons standing by the conveyor. He looked at the others for encouragement, hoping they might nudge his memory into action. Finally it came to him. "Where there's a soul there's a way."

"Very good. Let's remember that, shall we? There are plenty of souls ready to greet us and there are many ways we can punish them. Let's begin."

Brimstone signalled for the machine to be fired up, and with a pulse of energy it rattled into life. The vessols started to fill up and join the conveyors. Brimstone stood as he always did in the centre of the cavern purveying the activities. This was only one of two jobs he had to oversee today. The second had become increasingly frustrating. Even though they'd scanned every one of the levels from one to twelve they still had not located John's remains.

Brimstone was starting to believe he wasn't here at all. It was possible that he had been. But it was also possible that he'd come to some sticky end while exploring. After all, there were plenty of opportunities for accidents in a place like this. Until there was evidence of that, Asmodeus would not let it go. He wanted to make an example of him. Plus, John was just too important to be on the loose.

"WE'VE GOT ANOTHER ONE," came a shout from the control seat.

Up in space a dark blue mass with the ferocity of a comet was directing its force towards the translucent barrier. It ripped a gully in the subservient atmosphere of electric blue energy that collected at the mouth of the Soul Catcher that poked through into another dimension. They knew what it was and they knew what it meant.

"Navy Blue Warning," shouted Brimstone. "Get ready."

The rogue soul hit the tip of the Soul Catcher with the force of an earthquake. The demons had acted quickly. After all, this was not an isolated event. Many shadow souls had come this way since John's disappearance. The other souls inside the bulb had mostly been siphoned out and the ones out in space had been barred from entry. All except for this one, of course. This type of soul did whatever the fuck it wanted. You couldn't close the door on a thug. The shadow soul expanded out against the inner walls of the Soul Catcher searching for any signs of weakness.

"Call Mr. Silica. Tell him we are in need of his services," said Brimstone to Mr. Shiny.

It didn't take long for him to arrive. He'd been put on standby and relieved of his normal duties due to his unique role in managing this ever-increasing plague of shadows. The process had taken its toll. Brimstone rarely looked down on his peers, but now he had to kneel to get to Silica's eye level.

"Silica, how are you doing?" said Brimstone sympathetically as the stream of sand rebuilt itself into a dwarf-sized humanoid figure.

"I'm a little tired," replied Silica. His voice had become higher and softer as if someone had recently and regularly been kicking him in an area that boys should never be kicked in.

"We have another one, I'm afraid. Can you spare us another vase?"

"There's not much of me left."

"What about that bit there?" offered Brimstone, pointing to a region somewhere around his midriff.

"That's a kidney," he squeaked.

"Well, you don't need that, do you? Think about the good that it'll do. I'm sure in a while you will think back with a sense of pride and satisfaction."

"Easy for you to say. I don't see you giving up any of your organs."

"But mine are worthless. They'd be rejected by the host. But you. You're a match every time."

Mr. Silica had always been a decent size, back in the day. Not the biggest demon in Hell, but certainly noticeable in a crowd. Not any longer. So many shadows had broken into the Soul Catcher he was starting to lose count of the number of donations that he had made. It couldn't go on forever. There would come a time when he was called to the front gate and a single grain of sand would jump about trying to get noticed.

"Ok, take the kidney," he said reluctantly.

Even though Brimstone was incapable of offering any donations himself, he was still an important part of the process. He was the surgeon to Silica's patient. To make glass you needed sand and incredible heat, and Brimstone was full of it. Brimstone's face was a constant stream of molten material. He scooped off a bead of lava and flicked it into Silica's chest, instantly turning that region from a solid to a liquid. Brimstone removed it with care and started to blow it into a bubble.

"Mr. Shiny. Get Mr. Aqua down here, would you?" he said, as he manipulated the glass with an artistry not normally associated with a walking lump of rock. This was Brimstone in his element, making an object of beauty and precision, rather than running a machine whose only purpose was a portal of misery to what lay ahead. Just as Silica had done moments earlier, a stream of water flowed into the cavern. It rose up into a column, spinning furiously to stop it collapsing to the floor again.

"Thank you for getting here so quickly, Mr. Aqua. As usual, this will sting a bit," said Brimstone, placing a molten glass vase and separate stopper into the water to cool it down.

Mr. Aqua made a fizzing noise not dissimilar to an electric bulb blowing.

"That should do it," announced Brimstone.

Once it had cooled sufficiently he marched the vase to the end of the Soul Catcher where the shadow was still beating the panels, desperate to escape. When the vase was in place around the white tip of the exit valve, he waved up to the control panel. The Soul Catcher shuddered into action as the shadow burst out and into the glass receptacle. Brimstone secured the stopper and quickly placed the vase on the floor where it rattled and groaned.

"Mr. Shiny, if you'd be so kind as to take that up to level twelve and place it with the others. Back to the infirmary for you, Mr. Silica. Go get some rest. Who knows when we might need you again?"

"Brimstone," replied Shiny, moving gingerly towards the vase, "I don't think we got all the normal souls out before the shadow arrived."

Inside the Soul Catcher a solitary blue cloud was limping its way around the circumference like an amateur marathon runner had just hit the proverbial wall. The demons knew the consequences that accompanied a normal soul being housed with a shadow. A shadow had no control over itself. It did whatever its emotions told it to. If its emotion said hunger, it ate. If its emotions said to fight, it fought. If its emotion said love, it shagged. Brimstone looked into the bulb and contemplated whether the poor thing had been eaten, beaten or buggered.

"There's only one way to deal with this," said Brimstone to the others. "Let's see what we have in the storeroom."

Any soul that wasn't expected or balanced would not accept a normal vessol. Brimstone knew that all too well from his experience of dealing with reincarnates and a certain John Hewson. It wasn't an exact science as to what would work, so they kept an array of alternatives in a storeroom just off the main cavern. There were all sorts in there. People, creatures and objects. It was all about trial and error. As Brimstone rummaged through the various options that were organised in alphabetical order on shelves that ran in a circle no more than three feet high, he noticed an anomaly.

On the rack listed as 'S' there was a sea lion, a squirrel, a Scouser, and a space. The space wasn't supposed to be there. Brimstone knew only too well what should. A shrew.

"John's on level zero," shouted Brimstone at the top of his voice. "Call Primordial."

*****

Hide-and-seek was a stupid game for people who lacked imagination. It had only been played for centuries because no one had the good sense to invent game consoles yet. The odds were always stacked in favour of the seeker. The hider never had sufficient time to make the decisions fast enough, causing them to panic and hide in the most obvious places like under the bed or in a wardrobe. The seeker would regularly cheat by either counting more quickly than agreed, opening their eyes a fraction or, in the most cunning of cases, walking, looking and counting at the same time. The hider never won because they were either found or gave up through boredom.

Whether Primordial was still counting remained to be seen, but two pigeons and a schizophrenic shrew were most certainly hiding. Had Primordial seen the two pigeons flying from the rock column? Did he know that they were carrying their difficult passenger? The assumption must be yes, which meant they had to move quickly if they were going to keep John secret. That meant they kept moving until they were certain of their strategy.

Their current hiding place was in the shade of a willow tree, the deciduous equivalent of lurking behind an armchair. Secrecy was not their primary reason for being there. It was in this location that any creatures wishing to join Sandy's army would come, but when? There was no such thing as night and day in Hell, only now. This made it a bit difficult to make any concrete plans. All that had been asked of Malcolm was to gather candidates and direct them here. The time was now and some at least had come.

It was hard to say what might have motivated them to gather. Intrigue, boredom, insanity or a general desire to escape might be amongst them. Based on the strange selection of candidates currently loitering in the clearing, it was hard to identify anything other than 'insanity'.

"Malcolm, I think I said, 'Bring me the most cunning, wise, strong and nimble,' that you could find," said Sandy.

"That's right," replied Malcolm, "and I said you'd only get those that were one horseman short of an apocalypse."

"Well, you didn't disappoint on that front," replied Sandy.

Scattered around the clearing were a collection of life's cast-offs, waiting in sporadic formation for their chance to prove themselves worthy. In all there were five. A black cat sauntered about ignorant of any of the others. A sloth was showing off by attempting the world's slowest press-ups. An ox was on its front knees in quiet prayer whilst a gibbon attempted vainly to tickle its nostrils with a long piece of bullrush. He scurried away every time the ox opened its eyes. Finally, although it was hard to make it out at first, a tarantula sat alone on the furthest side of the clearing shooting webs from its spinnerets.

"It's a start. Ok, everyone, listen up," said Sandy.

A few of them paid attention to the announcement. The cat pointedly looked in the other direction.

"As you might be aware I am planning to break out of this place and I need some help. There is an artefact on level twelve that must be recovered and returned to Earth. Our mission will be difficult and it's possible some of you won't make it. If my theories are correct and we achieve our goal, we may also have the opportunity to suppress the demons."

"I'm not sure they're all listening," added Ian unhelpfully.

"I'll call you forward one at a time for an interview. Sloth, you can go last, but feel free to start moving now and you might get here when we need you. Ox, you can go first."

The ox made the sign of the cross with one of its hooves before approaching the willow tree. Sandy hopped onto a broken branch to elevate his importance.

"Welcome. What's your name?" asked Sandy.

"Abraham, but you can call me Abe," replied the Ox, bowing his head slightly in reverence.

"And why did you decide to come?"

"Because I have never lost faith. My heart is full of love for our Lord. In his warm embrace, with his guidance and love, we will overcome all hardships and spread his message to others," said Abe, dropping to his knees once again.

"You are aware that you're in Hell, aren't you?"

"Of course. That doesn't mean anything."

"It sort of does. It means God wasn't keen."

"I think it must have been an admin error," said Abe. "Happens all the time."

"I thought God was supposed to be all-seeing. Surely he doesn't make admin errors."

"He's just testing my resolve."

"In that case you're doing remarkably well. I still think you might need to adjust your belief systems a little," said Sandy calmly, eager not to offend him.

"Never. Faith can move mountains, Matthew 17:20."

"Well, let's hope so, it might come in useful. Part of these interviews is to establish your skill sets and usefulness to the team. What did you do when you were a human?"

"I praised the Lord and basked in…"

"As a job," said Sandy interrupting before a new biblical verse could be recited.

"Evangelical window cleaner."

"Do you mean you were really just a window cleaner but tried to convert anyone you met?"

"Well, the evangelical bit was important in the scheme of things," replied Abe.

"Are you trying to say that people looked out of their windows and thought, 'These are a bit dirty, we ought to get a window cleaner in? But let's not just get one of the many competent window cleaners who work this area. What we really need is a part window cleaner, part restorer of faith'?"

"All part of the service."

"No, you go to a church for that kind of service. Do you have any special talents that might help us on this mission?"

"Encouragement, an unwavering belief in the Almighty, I'm very popular with the Chinese, and I'm excellent at ploughing."

"All essential in the circumstances," scoffed Sandy. "And what would you do if you faced a demon, other than praying?"

"Oh, I suppose I'd kick it in the head on the instructions of God!"

"That's good enough for me, you're in. Next."

The remaining animals waited patiently for their breed to be called. Abe returned to the clearing and lay down in the grass quietly meditating.

"Cat, your turn!" shouted Sandy from under the willow's branches as Ian continued to work in the background on John's therapy with indifferent results. The cat didn't move. He'd come when he was ready. It might be now, or later, or never. When the mood took him, really. The gibbon attempted to jump the queue in the cat's absence, which seemed motivation enough for the cat to move.

"Hello, here at last. It's ok, we're not waiting for a certain demon to arrive, no hurry."

The cat looked at him impassively.

"What's your name?" asked Sandy.

"Sir Roger Montague, the third Earl of Norfolk," said the cat with a smile.

"Bollocks it is," replied Sandy.

"You don't know, do you? If I say that I'm the third Earl of Norfolk you'll have to prove otherwise, won't you?"

"Fine. Well, Roger, why did you come here?"

"Sir Roger," added the cat.

"Sorry, Sir Roger. Why did you come here?" A pigeon's anatomy lacked lips, which was a shame because he was desperate to bite his.

"I wasn't actually invited. I was just passing, thought I'd stop to see what was going on. You can't do it without me, you know. It's impossible in fact. I should be interviewing you, rather than the other way around."

"You're a little arrogant…"

"No, it's just fact. I've already escaped from this level nine times before, you know. It's no biggie. Sometimes I escape without even meaning to. I even got up to level twelve once before," replied Roger as he nonchalantly licked his paws and focused his eyes on anything other than Sandy.

"Impressive. How did you do it?"

"Plans. Strategies. Really good strategies. Some of the best strategies you've ever seen. Period."

"But no details apparently," added Sandy. "What did you do as a human?"

"I was the first astronaut to walk on the moon," replied Roger without the slightest pause for thought.

"I'm pretty sure that was Neil Armstrong, not Sir Roger Montague the third Earl of Norfolk, who for the record died some considerable time before the nineteen sixties."

"Roger was my original form, but when I was reincarnated I came back as Neil's cat. He snuck me aboard the *Eagle* and I nipped out just before he did."

"Do you always lie…?"

"I never lie."

"…Or are you broken?" replied Sandy.

"I don't care what you think. I'm a cat, we don't give a shit what anyone thinks. Believe me, don't believe me, it's up to you," replied the cat getting up and strolling back into the clearing.

"I'm not done with the questions yet," shouted Sandy.

Roger ignored him and scurried up a nearby oak tree for a snooze. Sandy wasn't feeling overly impressed with what he had to work with. A sociopathic cat was a step up from an evangelical ox, though. The cat was in, if he could be arsed to turn up, of course. The sloth was still some distance away so Sandy called one of the two remaining candidates.

"Tarantula, you're up next."

The spider had been avoiding any contact with the others as if in some way there was only one spot on the team and fraternising with the others might put him at a disadvantage. He scurried over to the spot at a blistering speed.

"Wow. I can say without fear of contradiction that you are already my favourite candidate and I haven't asked you anything," said Sandy, impressed at least by the creature's velocity. "What do they call you?"

"Vicky."

"Well, Vicky, I can assure you that this is an equal opportunities mission and all candidates will be treated with the same level of fairness. Why are you here?"

"I hate demons."

"That's a good start."

"And cats."

"Me, too," agreed Sandy.

"In fact, I'm not fond of anything with less than eight legs. Ox can fuck off, too, always trampling through all our webs. They shouldn't be allowed in here."

"I think this part of Hell is open to anything that's been reincarnated," prompted Sandy.

"Now, yes. But back in the early days it was just insects and rodents. They'll let anyone in these days. Mammals are the worst. They take up all the space and kick all the indigenous breeds out."

"Right. That sounds a bit racist to me, if you don't mind me saying so."

"I'm not a racist. They always say that when someone tries to protect what was once theirs."

"I don't think it was yours in the first place. You can't claim a place just because you were there first and stuck a flag in the ground."

"Pigeons can fuck off, too. All the cooing and shitting everywhere they want. Have some respect for others."

"Ok. So I'm retracting my earlier statement and contradicting myself fully. What did you do when you were on Earth?"

"I worked in the immigration department at an airport."

"Why am I not surprised? Apart from racial discrimination, do you have any specialist skills?"

"You may have noticed that I'm a bloody big spider. I can do webs, really thick ones, too, and I'm a dab hand at scaring people."

"What about demons?"

"Hate them."

"Yes, I think we established that. I mean, how would you deal with one, if you were needed to in a crisis?"

"Probably shoot webs at them."

"Not all demons are likely to be too concerned. What if you were up against one made of electricity or wind?"

"Oh in that case...probably run away."

"Excellent," replied Sandy sarcastically. "Send the gibbon over, would you?"

Before the gibbon was called, Sandy aimed his collective thoughts back up to Malcolm.

"Is this really the best you could do? I don't want to sound ungrateful but, so far, three of the five candidates I've interviewed are total nut jobs."

"Six, you mean? There are still three left to see," replied Malcolm.

"I can only see a sloth who's barely travelled metres since I started interviewing, and a gibbon playing tricks on an ox. Where's the third one?"

"Over there," replied the eagle, pointing a wing through the clearing to a point on the horizon.

Where the water's edge broke on the shoreline of the forest biome a huge creature wallowed in the shallows. It offered a welcome with a squirt from its blowhole.

"Blimey, that must have been a difficult one for the Soul Catcher. Well, given my luck with candidates so far, I suspect he'll probably have anger management issues or a pathological fear of feet."

CHAPTER ELEVEN

WAKE

The news of Herb's death had come as a shock. The fact that he was dead wasn't the big news. Any man who consumed the volume and strength of liquor that Herb had over a fifty-year spell was always likely to be teetering on the edge of some terminal mishap. No amount of cardiac surgery could prevent the single-minded nature of someone willing to self-destruct. It might come as the result of some barmy subconscious and drunken belief that he could climb a fifty-foot building with only his bare hands, or the more likely outcome of his arteries clogging up with plague. Yet none of these situations had taken Herb's life from him.

No drink had touched Herb's lips for over a decade. David didn't need to check this fact: he knew it to be true. Most people who attempted to kick the bottle are susceptible to a relapse, but not Herb. Once you'd taken Emorfed you had no such weakness. Life was unable to offer any type of temptation to a mind deficient of the required motivations. Which raised another important question: if Emorfed took away your ability to feel, love, hate, or the circumstances that brought about depression, how would someone in that state kill themselves?

Donovan King had been quite clear about that fact, though. Surely there must be more to it? If he was going to understand the situation, David would have to dig a little deeper. Starting with the funeral.

This created some challenges. Number one, Donovan was going to be there and David was keen to keep his existential background secret from as many people as possible. Number two it was highly probable that Herb's best friend, Nash, would also be there. If anyone was likely to know who David really was, it was him. David had first-hand knowledge of the lead singer from the 'Wind-up Merchants' and he was fairly certain the experience was mutual.

Nash had demonstrated more than just the special connection common between twins. It was highly likely that some of John's soul had attached itself to Nash as a consequence of his first use of the Limpet Syndrome. How else could it explain how Nash had come to John's rescue when Victor held him prisoner on the plane? David's soul, as neutral as the black wire in a plug socket, had only the slightest echo from parts of his soul that were left behind. Nothing was certain because most of his memories and emotions existed, presumably, elsewhere.

Herb's funeral was being held in his home village of Applecross which sat on the shores of the Scottish Highlands, sandwiched between the mountains and the water that stretched from it to the Isle of Skye. Herb had always been a proud Scot and it was fitting that his final resting place would take him back to his roots. The small church of Clachan, a few miles inland from the scenic village, set the scene for one of the most sparsely attended funerals in history.

Herb hadn't been a great collector of friends. Acquaintances were plentiful, but few of those even knew his second name, let alone harboured the motivation to travel to the back of beyond to drink his health. Many of Herb's true friends had been dead for decades. Burnt-out candles that left their imagery alive, still youthful way beyond the years that ticked by for others. In the early days of the music industry anyone who wanted to be remembered worked tirelessly to ensure they fizzled out well before their full potential had been reached. Most did so successfully.

Of those that were left, only a handful of part-time rogues and retired hellraisers had been capable or upright enough to travel to this spot. This made it even more difficult for David to remain anonymous. He couldn't just sit in the small chapel surrounded by old gits and expect to blend in. Donovan would spot him in an instant. The plan was to wait a short distance away from the church and watch. After the sermon was conducted, the grieving would retreat to the graveyard and David could determine who was in attendance.

*****

Nash was one of only five mourners in the chapel. They'd spread themselves as far apart as geographically possible, as all humans appear to do in circumstances like this. The chapel held just over a hundred, but each human was sitting at least ten metres distance to the next. The only connection the five of them possessed was the person that they'd come to bury. Apart from Nash, there was an elderly lady in a wheelchair, a hippy wearing a black leather jacket, a bald-headed man attached to an oxygen tank, and Dr. Donovan King at the front, holding the altar.

Nash brought the average age of the congregation down to somewhere in the mid-sixties. He was also the most traditionally dressed for the occasion, whereas the others clearly didn't know what the normal dress sense was for a funeral, his neat black suit and tie did its best to hold up religious convention. The hippy was actually wearing shorts and an Iron Maiden T-shirt, one definitely not Church-approved. As Nash's hands reached forward to the pew in front, his head and short hair nestled between them in silent thought.

This wasn't a sad occasion for him. It was one of reflection. Nash had accepted twelve years ago that the Herb he knew and loved had left the building. The essential characteristics that made him unique and charismatic had been removed and replaced by a soulless shell. Above all else, Nash was responsible for that transformation, and the guilt had never left him. The impacts of that fateful event were as evident on Nash as they had been on the man lying in a wooden box at the front of the church.

When life kicks you, you have two choices: fight or run. Nash had been running ever since. What he was running from wasn't totally clear. Certainly some of his retreat was down to guilt. Some of it stemmed from a diminished desire to be in the public spotlight. The glare of the media attention reflected their fake recognition, and his own deficiencies, back at him like a mirror. The band was nothing to him anymore. His only desire was to give something back and help others. One person in particular.

Donovan coughed loudly and purposely to gain the attention of the mourners. Nash expected him to be here, although he was intent on avoiding any repeat of their last meeting.

"Family and friends. We are gathered here today to bid farewell to Herbert Campbell and commit him into the hands of God. How ironic that, despite a life of excess, he outlived all but a few of his friends and family. He's smiling about that now, I can assure you. He dedicated his life to the pursuit of musical excellence, the development of talent and personal enjoyment. I think we can all agree he achieved it."

Nash nodded in agreement.

"Herb's mother," said Donovan, holding a hand open in the direction of the woman in the wheelchair, "tells me Herb had always been an experimental child. He had a deep inquisitiveness that included his homeland, this magnificent countryside, the arts and the local entertainment. A Scot, deeply passionate about his culture, he never achieved his own music ambitions, but was instrumental in so many other people's'. One of those to benefit most is with us today."

Nash acknowledged the reference, quite displeased that he hadn't managed to go unnoticed.

"Sadly, Herb's sense of adventure and proclivity for mischief were restrained in recent years. He fell victim to the government's efforts to poison the nation, a living example of the torment that would have befallen so many others if it had not been stopped. It changed who Herb was, casting a shadow over him. Somewhere deep down a longing for the life that had been taken from him drove him to choose the manner and time of his own passing. Although, from what I have read about Emorfed, I find this hard to accept."

He wasn't the only one to think this. Nash was convinced that no such suicide had occurred. The autopsy stated clearly that Herb had died from an overdose of painkillers. That was not in question. What was in debate was whether Herb himself had willingly taken the overdose. No one with Herb's unique outlook on life had the will to do anything that might be harmful or self-destructive. That was the old Herb, not the new one.

Nash had cared for Herb for many years after the incident with the contaminated water. He had first-hand experience of how he behaved in the years that followed. An Emorfed victim was not incapable or inactive. They slept little, ate infrequently and spoke only when spoken to. But they could move, walk, clean themselves, read and write. Above all else, a puzzle or a crossword might just keep their attention. What remained impossible was feelings or emotions. Neither desperation nor pity were available to pull a trigger or tie a noose.

The service was short. A couple of rock songs replaced the normal hymns, and the hippy read the eulogy. Nash was pretty sure it was a recital of 'Death or Glory' by The Clash, certainly not content that most vicars would have approved of. It didn't seem right to celebrate someone's life with so few people and at such speed. Nash had developed a more traditional lifestyle than in his celebrity heyday, and religion had partly instigated his change in outlook.

As Donovan brought proceedings to an end he signalled to Nash that he wanted a word. A wooden cane supported Donovan's progress down the aisle.

"Hello, Nash. How are you?"

"I'm well," replied Nash.

"On your own?" asked Donovan.

"Most definitely. It's just me, no hitch-hikers whatsoever," replied Nash, concerned that Donovan was in some way scouting for future exorcism candidates.

"I didn't mean inside you. I meant you're not with your wife or children."

"I'm not married."

"Oh, still playing the field, are you? You always did have multiple women on the go from what Herb told me," replied Donovan with a wink.

"Not anymore. I only love one girl and she can never love me back. I found no pleasure in the company of the opposite sex after that. Why are you interested?"

"I'm not. I thought small talk was what people do when they meet after some time has passed."

"I appreciate the sentiment, I think. You've lost your stutter, I see."

"Yes. Your exorcism was responsible for that. A most unusual experience. Has John been in touch since?"

Other than watching him take off from the airfield all those years ago, he'd only had one further moment when he felt John's presence. A few days later, he was woken from his sleep by a convulsion in his body very similar to the one he experienced at his exorcism. Whatever had caused it was brief and, immediately afterwards, Nash felt a sense of peace he'd never experienced before. It was the start of the life he now led.

"No. John's gone. Why?"

"Just small talk. He's the only person other than Herb that connects you and me. Were you there when Herb died?" asked Donovan, changing his focus of interest.

"No. He lived in a care home towards the end. I visited regularly but having moved some distance away it wasn't always convenient."

"Do you think he killed himself, as highlighted in the autopsy?"

"No. It's not possible. Apparently the overdose was taken at night and he had no access to those drugs. How could he overdose in those circumstances?"

"He couldn't."

"So what's the answer?" asked Nash.

"Someone, or something forced him."

"But who and why?"

"That's just what I intend to find out," replied Donovan.

*****

There were too few able-bodied mourners to carry Herb's rather heavy coffin to the graveside. The funeral director had provided a team of six burly men to carry out the final journey. David watched as these hired heavies carried the wooden box from the chapel door to the newly dug plot, sunk between those that had made the trip at some point over the last three hundred years. As the coffin was lowered into the ground, David witnessed Dr. King perform his next duty.

Once every finality was completed, the dilapidated congregation were helped to leave the lightly drizzled scenery for the sanctuary of the wake in the pub in Applecross. Only one remained at the graveside. Nash was deep in thought, tears welling in his eyes only now the others had left him alone. Desperate to learn more of Herb's final days, David approached the solitary figure.

"I'm sorry for your loss," said David as he eased his skinny frame through the scattered gravestones.

Nash wiped his tears as he felt the presence of the unknown man approach.

"It's never easy saying goodbye, is it?" offered David in an attempt to demonstrate a certain level of sympathy.

"No. It isn't," replied Nash. It wasn't clear if this olive-skinned youth was being nosy or friendly. "Are you just visiting?"

"No. I have an interest in dead people," replied David rather too truthfully.

"Really. I find the living more talkative, although Herb never did much of it towards the end. Why are you so interested in dead people?"

"I like to work out their stories," replied David. "Work out what they were like in life and consider where they are now."

"Are you religious?" asked Nash.

"I accept there's a possibility that there may be higher beings in the Universe although I don't have faith."

"No, I don't have faith either," he said with a sigh. "But I have found God."

"Would you mind shedding some light on where he is?" said David matter-of-factly. Any information he had suggested, if he was there, that he was hiding or had been kidnapped.

"He's around, if you look for him," said Nash.

"How did he die?" asked David pointing to the newly dug grave below him.

"Who knows for sure?"

"What makes you say that?"

"It's complicated and frankly I've never met you before."

"I understand. It's just that as I was walking through the graves I thought I recognised you. You're Nash Stevens, aren't you?" asked David.

"How do you know that?"

"You were in a rock band! It's not that much of a secret. I'm a big fan. I know this isn't the best time but…"

"No, it isn't," said Nash sharply. He hated being reminded of his past in general, but not at a time of grief.

"He was your manager, wasn't he?"

"Yes…now, if you'll excuse me, I must be going, I have a long journey home."

"Back to Gloucester Road?"

"No, back to Cornwall… Hold on, how do you know where Herb lived?" asked Nash.

David had offered more information than he'd intended to in his pursuit of the truth. Herb was not famous: his address or details were not in the public domain as Nash's were. How could he explain how he knew this without the talent to lie? He couldn't. It was the equivalent of being caught with your hand in the cookie jar with a written confession in your hand and a sign that said 'it was me'.

"Someone told me."

"Who?" said Nash getting more agitated and advancing on the man.

"John did."

The colour faded from Nash's face faster than an adolescent on a roller coaster. Maybe this boy meant a different John? Even though he'd attempted to purge the name from his mind, along with all other elements of his past life, twice today it had been dragged out. Perhaps this was just a coincidence created by the anxieties held deep within him. John had left him unbothered for years now. Yet he only knew one John.

"John who?" demanded Nash.

CHAPTER TWELVE

ALL AT SEA

It wasn't a hard decision to let the whale join the team. Even without an interview he'd already shown more promise than every other applicant. It wasn't because he had any specific credentials for stealing something from one of the most dangerous places in the cosmos. In fact, his size and immovability were a distinct disadvantage. It also wasn't because he lacked the mental impairments that ran through the souls of every other member of the team. He was in for one simple reason: buoyancy.

It would be a lot more difficult for Primordial to find them if they were riding a whale than sitting defencelessly under a willow tree. Time, if there was any at least, would tell if Sandy was right. There was an added advantage. The ocean biome stretched up to the perimeter of the window that opened up onto the space in the adjoining universe. Sandy's universe. Only the reincarnated sea creatures and a few of the most agile flyers, with the stamina to stay there long enough, could get to the edge to assess the scene. If they did, it might just offer some answers to any alternative ways out of level zero.

Getting the whole team aboard the whale transporter took longer than expected. The anxiety of Primordial discovering them lurked ever closer on his thoughts as he attempted to encourage, cajole, bribe and lift this peculiar bunch onto their ride. Even though his anatomy hampered him physically, the ox had been the easiest. The cat was the most challenging. Despite his lies and an unwillingness to take orders from anyone, Sandy was fairly certain the poor wretch was petrified of water.

As the whale slowly swam out to sea, rocking the crew gently on its back, Sandy assessed what he had to work with. A racist spider, a sociopathic cat, a shrew with Tourette's, an evangelical ox, and a twat called Ian. It was hardly an elite unit. The discovery of the whale, and the opportunity for an innovative retreat, had curtailed the interview process. The gibbon and the sloth would have to demonstrate their commitment by first boarding the whale, and then facing an interview at sea. The sloth hadn't been happy, having almost reached the willow tree when Sandy had called a halt to proceedings.

The waterborne interviews hadn't been any better than those on land. It transpired that the sloth, whose name was Gary, had spent his human life as the world's least successful motor sports driver. Not that he accepted it. Delusion kept him hidden from a truth that was plain for everyone else to see. He was adamant he was still capable of going really fast as long as he had the correct equipment. Sadly the afterlife hadn't agreed. But on a positive front at least Gary wasn't a racist.

The last of the team was Elsie, a gibbon who had the annoying habit of deflecting all serious subjects and replacing them with humour. A natural prankster, she had a complete lack of perspective. When he'd asked her what she'd do if she met a demon, her answer had been to give it a wedgie. On the plus side her specialist skills included the ability to make an excellent paella. Above all other characteristics he liked her because she wasn't a racist.

Sandy was clear on how he wanted to use this band of misfits. They'd first help John retrieve Faith's soul, and in the process Sandy would use what he knew to disrupt the workings of Hell itself. After that, if it was possible, he would exert his own authority and reclaim some control of the situation. This strange posse may have lacked a certain level of sophistication but when it came to being annoying and disruptive he felt they'd be in their element.

"Where exactly are we going?" asked Abe the ox.

"God botherer…idiot…" blurted John.

"Remember your breathing, John," replied Sandy calmly. "Surveillance. How many ways out of level zero do you think there are?"

The cat answered almost immediately. "Nine."

"Three," countered Sandy.

"Whatever," replied Roger. "I know some of the best ways to get out of here. Secret ways. Once I disguised myself as a shower of gold and evaporated out of here."

"Roger, that was Zeus. You're not impressing anyone, you know. Feel free to answer if you're not a compulsive liar," said Sandy to the others.

"You know nothing," replied Roger, strolling off towards the whale's head in disgust.

"What."

There was a pause.

"Are," continued Gary the sloth.

"Yes," prompted Sandy.

"The."

"Spit it out…tit…" snapped John.

"Three."

"You're almost there…" said Sandy.

"Ways?" finished Gary, obviously knackered from the effort.

"The trapdoor, the cliffs and space," replied Sandy.

"What does it matter?" asked Vicky.

"We need a plan to get us from here to level twelve without being detected. On level twelve we'll find a glass vase. In that vase is the shadow soul of Faith Casey. But getting the soul is the easy part. We then need to take her soul to the Soul Catcher and send it back to Earth."

"Plus…*croak*…we need to get to the library…kill demons…knackers," added John.

"What's the library for?" asked Ian.

"Books…albino bird…you're a liability…breathe… it's where they keep all the records of human… *cough*…locations."

"Fine, so before we get to the Soul Catcher we have to get to the library," added Sandy.

"That's all well in theory," said Vicky, "but how are we going to do it?"

"By working as a team," answered Sandy.

In the history of teamwork no group had been less equipped for success. The pre-eminent expert on the subject, Meredith Belbin, would be turning in his grave, if he had one. All good teams needed leadership, generosity, compatible profiles and talented individuals. Sandy reflected on his statement.

"Scrub that. We just need a good plan. The first part of which is to decide the route we're going to take to get out."

"We can't take the trapdoor," replied Elsie. "That'll take us through the heart of Hell and into the path of the demons."

"I agree with the gibbon," replied Sandy. "Which only gives us two other options."

"Eight," shouted the cat in contradiction.

"Can we even go through the window?" asked Ian.

"Who knows?" said Sandy. "I suspect it can't be done whilst we're wearing these vessels. But what if we weren't wearing them?"

"We'd be sucked out into space with the other souls," replied Abe in horror.

"No one knows. Perhaps we'd go back into the Soul Catcher, perhaps we'd vaporise."

"I'm not keen on either option," said Abe.

"Which is why we're not going to try it," said Sandy. "In my view there is only one possible option. We must go via the wall."

Level zero was a basement that directly mirrored the levels above with a few exceptions. The levels from one to eleven were enclosed around cliffs that extended in a huge oval, each level set further back than the one below. Like a series of giant steps that ended at level ten where a roof capped the sequence. The library at level eleven was enclosed and level twelve sat on its roof, open to the elements of space. As the whale made its slow commute to the translucent barrier, the underside of these giant steps were visible above them.

"If you look above you'll see our route," said Sandy.

"Dear Lord who art in Heaven, hallow…"

"Abe, it's not the right time," said Sandy, as Abe went in for a quick pray.

"Why is God always painting?" asked Ian.

"What are you on about?" said Sandy.

"Art in heaven," added Ian. "What do you think he paints?"

"Shut up," snapped Sandy. "As I was saying, I think the cliff is our best option."

"We can't climb that," said Gary. "There's a massive overhang every hundred feet or so."

"Who said anything about climbing it?" replied Sandy with a grin. "It would be madness if we all blunder up there together. First we need to send up a surveillance team. Ian and I will fly up to see if there's any access. I want the rest of you to do some research on the window. Find out what it is and whether we can go through it."

"Are you sure you want me to go with you?" asked Ian.

"Not really," he replied, "but none of this lot can fly."

"I can fly," replied Roger. "Piece of piss."

Sandy and Ian lifted off the whale as it crept slowly and smoothly further out to sea. The underside of the levels were almost completely visible to the pigeons, allowing an almost exactly vertical flight plan. The distance wasn't a problem. It was probably no more than a thousand feet and they'd once flown from Bristol to London in a single day. As they passed each level, making a mental note of how many they'd passed, the distance between the cliff face and the window drew ever closer. At the top of level eleven the space between the two was just big enough for them to squeeze through.

The translucent barrier was a benign object. There was no movement in it or obvious danger. The thin veil lay over the whole of this domain, creating the effect of being trapped in a massive snow globe. Its only obvious characteristic was its ability to refract and distort the objects that could be seen on the other side. As the pigeons hovered in the gap they heard voices above them.

*****

It was getting a bit cluttered on level twelve. An area that had, until recently, only housed an oversized dining set and a few metal boxes floating in the air, now had a rather large sideboard. The vases had to go somewhere. They couldn't just be left on the floor like some unwanted relics that didn't have a natural home. These weren't the type of items that you ignored if you were a demon. At the behest of Asmodeus a stone cabinet had been erected so that each vase could be placed safely on the shelves. He'd wanted to put a glass front on it, but Silica was having none of it.

There were more than six hundred of these vases growling their displeasure through their own glass coffins. They rocked and rattled like bottles on a milk float travelling down a cobbled street. Not only were these unnatural objects unsightly, they were also dangerous. If Emorfed had the ability to remove the emotions from a soul, the shadows had the opposite effect. These entities had the potential to convert a fully fledged soul into a copy of itself. Stripping away the neutrality until all that was left was a malevolent ball of pure teenager: hormonal, illogical and desperate to ignore all sensible advice. What's more, the demons could do little about it.

The arrival of the shadows, though, hadn't been responsible for this second council of creatures. News had filtered down that made it essential to gather the senior team together. There were several points on the agenda, although very few of those attending had bothered to read them or check their pigeonholes.

"Are you sure about this?" demanded Asmodeus.

"Quite sure," replied Brimstone. "When John came to us the second time, he had the choice of a small girl or a shrew. He knew the shrew was there. When he returned what remained of his soul back to Earth, the discarded elements would need to find a home. It won't have been comfortable. The competing elements of good and evil forced into a plastic rodent will be hard to manage."

"Then he should be easy to spot. I'm surprised that Primordial hasn't already done so," said Asmodeus.

"Have you ever been down there?" asked Primordial, feeling his reputation ebb away. "It's an area of a thousand square miles. Level one, which is the equivalent size, has more than a thousand demons to patrol it. I have one."

"What are you saying?" asked Asmodeus.

"I'm saying if you want to find John quickly, then we'll need to increase the numbers. Who knows what he's planning? If the reference to Newton is accurate, you can be sure he wants to have some impact here," added Primordial.

"Any theories as to what?"

"Plenty. John is the last of the twelve. Before he used the Limpet Syndrome he was extremely useful to us. More than a third of the animals in my kingdom are there because of his expertise. But now that he's heard the truth, he will try to find the way?" said Primordial.

"You mean the third way," said Mr. Volts from an invisible position somewhere around the table.

"Quite."

"And what if he does?" said Asmodeus. "There won't be anyone there. He'll be alone in his own version of paradise."

"If he's the only one," said Primordial.

"Of course he is. There aren't any other purely neutral souls on Earth or we'd know about it. And if we can find the shrew we can bring that part back here. How many of us do you need to help find him?"

"I need everyone," said Primordial.

"I'm not sure I'll be much help," squeaked what remained of Mr. Silica, unsighted in his usual chair.

"You have a pass," said Asmodeus. "You can stay here."

"Is it wise for all of us to go, Asmodeus?" added Brimstone. "The worker demons have been acting a little militantly of late."

"I'm surprised at you, Brimstone. Getting nervous about the workforce. They don't have the bottle for action. They do as we tell them."

"Whatever you say," replied Brimstone, although his tone of voice suggested he wasn't as confident as his boss.

Asmodeus had spent too much of his existence separated from the real day-to-day running of Hell. Claustrophobically he'd sit amongst his metal boxes, dealing with matters of the state. The Devil would not have been so complacent. He'd have settled the nerves and reinvigorated their purpose. Asmodeus may have looked the part with his three-headed monster pose, but he had none of the diplomacy or gravitas of the real thing. An inferior at a time when only the genuine article would do.

"I was thinking I might go to the library," added Brimstone.

"Oh, don't fancy level zero either, then?" said Asmodeus.

"If you remember, I'm one of the few that have already been there."

"So why are you going to hide in the library?"

"Because the books are kept there. I wonder if John's might tell us anything new. The books are a record of people. It may just shed some light on what's going on."

"Fine. The rest of you gather all the senior demons. We move on level zero immediately."

*****

It was hard to escape boats when you lived on an island so small even Google Maps struggled to locate it. If you were eight years old and had spent a substantial part of your life on one, sailing was as natural as walking. Every cove had been explored and yet there was no boredom associated with going back. Today Scrumpy Foster-Stokes was a pirate. Yesterday he'd been an Elizabethan explorer, and tomorrow, who knows? There were no boundaries to his imagination.

He was already an expert helmsman for a boy so young. His parents hadn't encouraged him, it was just natural for a boy on the island to show an interest in the sea. Since the age of four he'd commuted every morning and afternoon back and forth to his school on the next island. That school boat was just the beginning of his infatuation. To truly explore the islands you needed your own dinghy. His was called *'Unicorn'* and it was just big enough for two. Rarely, though, was that the case. Other than the occasional holiday family, there were no boys of his age on Bryher and he was forced to enjoy his own company. Grace had a very different personality and didn't tend to join in.

The island was littered with possible destinations. There was the small, uninhabited island of Gweal just across the water from the house. Despite meaning 'place of trees', Gweal had a grand total of none.

Across the channel, on the western side of Tresco, was Cromwell's Castle. He spent hours in the seventeenth-century gun tower pretending to fight off the Roundheads or the French ships sneaking up the channel. None of these were his favourite. There was only one 'go-to' place when the tide was in and the sun was out, Hell Bay.

It was named so for a reason. On their approach to England this was the nearest point for ships travelling the Atlantic. Unprotected by other land masses, its seas were notoriously difficult to navigate. Sea currents amalgamated in union with the unpredictable weather patterns to contrive against the fragile, wooden galleons that sought the protection of the island. Many succumbed to the jagged rocks submerged like hungry crocodiles under the swirling surf. The legend of this place was more compelling than the actual evidence. Few wrecks had ever been found, but it didn't stop a young boy from looking. Today, unusually, the *Unicorn* had two explorers.

Outside of her own thoughts there were few places where Grace felt truly comfortable. Where Scrumpy revelled in the excitement a small island had to offer, Grace hid from it. She'd always been socially awkward, a characteristic she'd inherited from her mother. People didn't make sense to her. They moaned about things they had no control over or turned into hysterical wrecks at the merest sign of adversity. Her brain just didn't have any time or empathy for them. Scrumpy was the only person she opened up to.

Officially he wasn't really her brother. He'd been adopted by Fiona and Violet when he was two years old and Grace was just four. They'd grown up together, although one had managed it better than the other. All children on the nearby islands attended the same small primary school situated on Tresco. Mixed-age classes meant they spent more time together than most siblings of different ages. Although Grace showed little interest in the other children of her own age, there was something about him that intrigued her.

Adults made terrible subjects for assessment. They had too much anxiety and followed complex rules that no one understood. If she was going to expand her knowledge of how people worked, she needed a purer example. Scrumpy, was it? There was just pure joy in him. No agenda, no politics, just joy. If she was going to learn why she was different, she could think of no better teacher.

"Do you want to pull the mainsail, Grace?" said Scrumpy as they floated smoothly out into Hell Bay.

Grace was unmoved, as if the message was aimed at someone who shared her name. She sat erect and uncomfortable in the stern seat, arms by her side and white hair blowing into her face. Her pale complexion camouflaged her against the whitewashed paint of the six-foot dinghy. Other than white, the only colour that distinguished her features was the sky-blue irises in her eyes that gave the impression of great age and wisdom.

"Why do you enjoy this?" she asked.

"I don't know," he replied. "It's exciting."

"Is it?"

"Yes. Let's be pirates," begged Scrumpy.

"Why would I want to be a pirate?"

"So we can find some treasure."

"The chances of finding treasure are low."

"I found treasure before, though."

"You found bits of wood last time," she answered.

"Still treasure to me."

"How does that work?" she asked curiously.

"Everything is treasure. I found a bottle last week with a map in it. Reckon it leads to some proper treasure."

"Was that the one you threw into the sea yourself last week?"

"No," lied Scrumpy.

Grace's mind attempted to connect the pieces of information in order to predict the likelihood of what he'd said being true. The answer came back as less than half of one percent. She confused his sense of wonder with a delusional need for hope. Why would he do that? What was the point? Was his brain just not as developed as hers? Or was she missing something? She made some notes in her book and went back to a complicated-looking grid with numbers all over it.

"What's that?" he asked as the boat swung gently back into the cove with no obvious movement from the captain.

"Puzzle," she answered.

"Word search?"

"No. It's a cryptogram. It's exciting."

"Is it?"

"Yes. I like them."

"Why?"

"To see if I have the skill to solve it. You know where you are with a puzzle. Just apply the right solution and the answers are there. People don't work like puzzles. The solution is random and always changes."

"Your mum is a puzzle to me."

"She's not a puzzle because there is no solution for working her out. Not even Mr. Stevens can understand her and he's a professional."

The boat picked up speed as a gust surged into the small sails. They sailed out of the horseshoe-shaped cove of Hell Bay and into a complex and ruthless maze of rocks that jutted out of the ocean. Only someone with a deep, local knowledge could navigate them with the ease that they did. In the distance, bathed in sunshine, was the back of their distinct white cottage. A forlorn figure sat alone in a deckchair.

"I wish we could stay out here a little longer," said Scrumpy, having consulted his wristwatch.

"There's no rush," said Grace, placing a finger to her lips.

CHAPTER THIRTEEN

MONACO

Many cities of the world are defined by money. New York, with its iconic high-rise Manhattan real estate. Dubai, with its mock landmarks and fake, man-made islands. Not forgetting Las Vegas, fully advertising its cash appeal from every neon bulb. All have a good case to be counted as the world's money capital. None of them, though, quite compares to the small principality that hides like a tax evader in the cliffs of the Côte d'Azur.

It isn't enough to have money in Monaco. Money is the physical commodity most of us use in exchange for buying stuff, whereas the rich use it to fuel their wood-burning stoves in winter. The value of cash is an unknown and pointless concept to most of the residents affluent enough to be allowed to live there. It isn't enough to have money to be accepted here, it was all about wealth.

Everyone has money, in one form or another, but very few people have proper wealth. Wealth in Monaco wasn't measured in volume but in vulgarity. The more vulgar you were, the more wealth you had. If someone bought a big yacht you had to up the pressure and buy a bigger one. One aquatic Russian Doll trumped the next until all of them were too big to fit in the harbour. When they stopped competing with the size of their yachts, they moved on to people. If one billionaire booked The Rolling Stones for a private party their peers would pay vast sums in an attempt to resurrect the deceased former Beatles, just to prove a point.

The vulgarity machine becomes normal, churning out an endless line of clones each eager to outdo the last. No one raised an eyebrow if you wanted a solid gold jet ski, irrespective of its inability to float, or a working Rolex fabricated out of raspberry jam and marshmallows. Nothing was unattainable, including peace from your own demons. Wealth wasn't the only thing prevalent here. The Serpo Clinic had more than a few clients in the city.

Monaco hadn't been Victor's first stop. When you had six hundred customers dotted over the world you had to be organised. You couldn't just fly around willy-nilly just because you liked the idea of the location. There were many clients in the United States that he'd got to first before moving on to the European leg of the extermination tour.

None of his targets had caused him any problems. When you had secret service training and a general disregard for life you could get into almost any place in the world, if you had the right planning and connections. Once you'd achieved that, faking deaths was easy. There was no resistance. Victor had already taken it, and their money, sometime ago.

The last month had made him realise that he'd missed the thrill of it far more than he'd thought. Earning vast quantities of money was all well and good, but it lacked the thrill that came from more devious acts. It wasn't hard to sell Emorfed: the results were proof enough. There was way more pleasure in taking their lives than in taking their money. Plus, his new employer was paying him anyway. Clients gave him money for cranial peace at the front end of the supply chain, and Byron gave him the same amount for the rest of their soul at the other. All with the added bonus of air miles.

Byron was always close at hand, even if he wasn't always seen. It was a little baffling to Victor why the

Devil didn't do the work himself. The only reason for his involvement appeared to be the list that contained all the details of his clients. If Byron took it, he could easily have completed the task himself. Or maybe he couldn't? Was there something stopping him physically killing or was there an ulterior motive for involving Victor? This fact had troubled him for a while. It may not be exactly the same Byron he was travelling with, but the same flesh had betrayed him once before. Maybe it had something to do with John?

Byron had already explained his inability to speak to John directly. Apparently it was something to do with apples. This talent certainly worked well enough on Victor: he could personally attest to that. Byron was forever popping up in his head to give him last-minute pointers like an invisible back seat driver. Perhaps this gap in the Devil's weaponry would turn out to be the real reason for his involvement? Time would tell and for now he was just having too much fun to worry about it.

On top of revisiting his former life, he was also inventing innovative new ways for people to 'commit suicide'. They didn't all have to be suicides as long as they all looked accidental. So far he'd ticked off poisoning, falling down stairs, electrocution, jumping from a moving train, crushed by falling masonry, trampled to death by a herd of startled buffalo, accidentally wandering into a live Army firing range and being impaled by a wayward javelin. It was getting harder and harder to come up with something original. Aptly for the location, today's chosen method involved water.

"Are you ready?" asked Byron, attempting a whispered tone that for some reason he found extremely hard to perfect. It must have been a side effect from the mild case of tinnitus he'd developed as a result of overexposure to high-pitched screaming.

"Of course," replied Victor.

"According to your list there are six clients currently based in the city, although I think it would be prudent to deal with only one tonight. Might be a little suspicious if six billionaires all commit suicide at the same time," replied Byron, silhouetted by the moon's light seeping into their luxury apartment from the balcony.

The streets of Monaco housed more tower blocks than the laws of physics would normally grant permission for. Each had miraculously carved out a foundation for itself, immune to what might be obstructing it on all four sides. They weren't finished either. Even though Monaco didn't appear to get any bigger by area, more and more buildings were being erected. It even baffled Byron who was from a world where the laws of physics were routinely ignored.

"How do they do it, though?" said Byron.

"Do what?" replied Victor.

"Squeeze so many in," he replied, counting the buildings he saw in the immediate vicinity of their balcony with his finger. "They must be bending the fabric of space somehow. They're like a set of cosmic dominoes."

"I think it's got more to do with having the best engineers money can buy," said Victor. "Shall we get on with it?"

"Yes, of course. Let me review the list again," said Byron, picking up a piece of paper and drawing a circle around a double-barrelled name with a black biro. "Grant Parker-Moore is your target tonight."

"I remember this guy. He was one of the first clients we treated. I think he was a banker. Yes, that's it. He crippled his multinational investment bank by engaging in reckless trading which he wasn't able to cover up when the sub-prime shit hit the treble A-rated fan. He came to us because even here he couldn't escape from the trolls. Even the millionaires of Monaco hate him."

"I don't really care what he's done. He could be an award-winning humanitarian who donates all his money to orphanages for all I care," replied Byron. "If he's on the list, he has to die, simple as that. What have you got planned for this one?"

"I haven't done drowning yet. Seems a good place to do it."

"Excellent choice. Remember, no evidence. We don't want the authorities thinking there was any foul play involved."

"Why do you want them to look accidental?" asked Victor.

"I told you, I don't want Baltazaar to suspect that I am behind their deaths."

"Why not, exactly?"

"Because we are at war and Baltazaar has met Byron once before. This gives him a slight advantage over me."

"They've met!"

"Yes. I suspect you even asked Byron about it once upon a time?"

"Um, I don't think so," replied Victor more than a little puzzled.

"Did you not ask Byron how he'd come by Emorfed? You knew that it wasn't man-made. I suspect a man of your inquisitive nature wouldn't leave that fact without interrogation?"

"Oh, that. All he'd say was he was given it."

"Ta-da! And you have your answer."

"Baltazaar, but why?"

"All part of the war. He knew that Emorfed would create an army of shadows and they'd only be able to go to one place. They'd rip Hell apart and he would have his victory. All he needed to find was someone malicious enough to release it. Thanks to John, he failed, although you did pick up his mission reasonably well afterwards," said Byron with more than a hint of disappointment.

"Yes, I'm sorry about that."

"Well, you're making amends now, aren't you? What I didn't expect was that John would make contact with him."

"How did he do that?"

"When John used the Limpet Syndrome he opened up a channel to Baltazaar, and very possibly others also. The twelve have always been kept secret from him. If Baltazaar got to John first, he could use him as a weapon. A weapon that we have no way of defending against."

"What do you mean the twelve?" asked Victor, peeling back further layers of mystery.

"When humans first developed a conscience we started receiving neutral souls. They had nowhere to go. The system wasn't designed for logic. That's when the Limpet Syndrome first came into being. When the soul's purpose is not fulfilled it looks for ways to regenerate. Once that happened we built Limbo with the capacity to direct these neutrals as best we could. The system worked well. Twelve neutral souls were chosen as jurors to make unbiased decisions."

"So what went wrong?"

"Baltazaar went wrong. Though it's still not clear to me why. He and I don't get on. Even being in the same location has a catastrophic outcome. What we know is Heaven closed its doors and it left the afterlife with a problem. We no longer just had to deal with neutral souls. We had to deal with all souls. By this stage the jurors had no power to choose, all souls had to go to Hell. Which, by the way, suited us fine."

"And what happened to the twelve?"

"They served a different purpose. Somehow the human psyche worked out what was happening. The Limpet Syndrome started again. John and the rest of the twelve were the only ones capable of bringing them back. But there was a risk. The more we used them, the more we stretched them. Every time we needed to bring back a reincarnate we had to kill one of the twelve so they could return to Limbo.

Eventually one by one they, too, started to develop the same conditions. Once they started using the Limpet Syndrome themselves they became extremely dangerous."

"Why?"

"Because every time they did it they opened up a channel to Baltazaar, and if they continued to do it they might just open up an even more dangerous channel. A third way. That's why they had to be killed, captured or restrained in metallic boxes on level twelve."

"And yet John has found a way to escape it."

"Somehow?" said Byron sliding his crimson jacket on his shoulders. "Anyway, you must not keep Mr. Parker-Moore waiting."

Victor, dressed in a way that suggested he was auditioning for a part in the Milk Tray adverts, picked up his bag and made for the exit. Byron watched from the window with the reassurance that if he wanted to talk to Victor he didn't need the aid of a telephone. Victor closed the door and descended the fourteen floors via the lift and snuck through the foyer into the night.

Grant Parker-Moore's yacht was permanently manacled to its larger cousins in the main harbour of Monaco. Nothing was far from the sea in this city. Several minutes after exiting the apartment block, Victor could smell the distinctive odour combination of sea water and power, that accompanied the heart of this playboy's paradise.

Even at three o'clock in the morning the party was still in full swing in the bars and casinos that afflicted the city like a virulent rash. Victor made his way to the far end of the harbour walls where no boats were moored and the public only strayed in the day, or in the evening as the result of too much booze or not enough luck. There was no easy access to the yachts by land. All were guarded by man and machine. His route would avoid both.

Revealed from underneath, his outer layer he glided into the water in his black wetsuit and swam to the side of the boat with the agility and guile of a sea otter. The focus of his swim was no everyday pleasure cruiser. The vessel was a hundred and fifty feet long and constructed on four levels. He knew from his surveillance that Grant would be on the bottom floor in the bedroom at the bow, closest to the shore. Whether Emorfed patients slept at all was an open question. None of his previous victims had. They'd all died fully conscious and completely passive.

Two crew members were on deck, walking the perimeter on a casual, unplanned basis. Victor scaled the starboard side and slipped unnoticed into the shadows. As the first employee passed by he quickly and quietly ambushed him from behind with a powerful sedative applied around the nostrils. He dragged the man into a store area and waited for the next to arrive. Once both men were medically preoccupied, he entered the main part of the vessel, tranquilliser gun ready for any resistance that might come between him and his target. None did.

Grant was a widower with no desire to change the situation. As a result this was probably the least debauched yacht anywhere in the city. No parties, no vice, just peace. In Victor's opinion a little too much peace. He liked action and having the odds heavily stacked against him. It gave him a proper challenge and the opportunity to test himself. As long as he didn't have to deal with doors, that is. Thankfully the pills made that little problem a less regular occurrence. His apprehension stemmed from the lack of a deterrent, rather than the possibility of facing one. It didn't feel right to get this close to a mark unhindered.

He descended into the lower deck and still nothing impeded his progress. The door to Grant's bedroom was open and the lights, typical of all Emorfed patients, were beating fiercely down on the bed. A small porthole was the only external indicator that it was night-time beyond the bright opulence of the expensive interior of the cabin. The room occupied a large portion of the bottom floor and was filled with elegant furniture and expensive contemporary sculptures. At the far end Grant was sitting on the bed, wide-eyed and sweating. Victor couldn't hide his disappointment. It was like shooting big fish in a tiny barrel.

"Can't you at least move about a bit?" whispered Victor sarcastically, swapping his tranquilliser gun for a pistol. "Make it a bit of a challenge at least."

"Beware of the shadows," said Grant without fear in his voice.

"It's ok, Grant, I know all about the shadows. It's not my first time."

"He means me."

The voice came from a chair in a dimly lit alcove at the back of the room.

Victor instantly turned the gun on the source of the voice, his finger patiently sitting on the trigger as it waited on confirmation to fire. That's why it had been so easy. The deterrent was here in the room, guarding Grant all the time. The man sat calmly, unfazed by the sudden threat being aimed at him. A cane lay against the chair as the man slumped forward as if pushed down by some unknown force. A Panama hat was tipped forward over his features, and his hands were held together in a golf grip.

"I wondered when I'd catch up with you," he said.

"Clearly you're in the mood to be shot," replied Victor, not accustomed to conversing with a victim peering down the barrel.

"You're not going to shoot me, Victor," he replied.

"How do you know that name?"

"You'd be surprised who knows that name."

"I really would be. I can name only three and two are probably dead."

"Let's just say I'm aware of your work, particularly over recent weeks. I almost caught up with you when you were in Paris taking care of Madame Bonnaire. That was good work, by the way. Very clever to cause a fire in that way. You almost convinced me it was an accident for a while."

"I don't know what you're talking about," said Victor innocently.

Madame Bonaire's death had been a moment of genius in his mind. How often do you get to see someone spontaneously combust inside a locked room with all the keys on the inside?

"You can't play dumb with me. I know who you are. I can see every move you make before you even think it. You have your friend, Dr. Trent, to thank for that."

Victor's trigger finger flickered and he took a pace forward, "What have you done with her?"

"Nothing painful. My relationship with Dr. Trent has been purely platonic. You see, when I discovered that the patients from your clinic were all dying in apparently accidental ways, I was most aggrieved. I was particularly interested by the alleged suicide of one Herb Campbell. I did a lot of research in order to discover who or what might be responsible. You'll never guess what I came up with?"

"Tell me who you are or I will shoot you."

"You won't, trust me."

Victor wasn't used to being told that he couldn't shoot someone. If he had a gun and desire to use it, how on Earth were the chances of success less than absolute certainty? However perverse this self-confident notion appeared, the very statement of it made him doubt himself.

"Go on," Victor inquired.

"Well, I found out that a certain Dr. Trent had been one of the leading scientists responsible for the original trials of Emorfed and that she had mysteriously vanished with all stock of the remaining samples. It wasn't hard to track her from there to the Serpo Clinic. I was most in favour, by the way. The more patients you have, the better. It was a lot harder to track her down after that, but I knew she wouldn't rest until she worked out what Emorfed was."

"Where is she now?"

"On her way home to Canada, I expect. You see the good people at the Large Hadron Collider weren't as keen as she was to blast Emorfed around their little machine. It's amazing how religious some scientists can be. They like to play with things they understand or have a theory they can test. They had neither in this instance."

"And what happened then?"

"I told her the secrets myself."

"You know how to replicate Emorfed?"

"Oh yes. The simple answer is you can't. You don't make Emorfed, you farm it. But you need a Soul Catcher for that."

"A Soul Catcher?" said Victor, feeling intellectually way out of his depth in a contest that should have been all about physical dominance.

"A large device for catching souls," the man replied, simplifying it. "I have one, you see."

"What did you get for offering this information?" replied Victor, quite sure that this was not done from an angle of charity.

"I needed your client list. I can't let you continue killing them, it's just not the done thing. I like the shadows, they're far more compliant than the rest of humanity. Whatever Satan is paying you, I'll double it."

"Give me one reason why I shouldn't just shoot you and end this pointless conversation."

"I'll give you four words. God protects the King."

CHAPTER FOURTEEN

IMMOVABLE OBJECTS

Byron was experiencing something that had not occurred for many years. In humans it was called nerves. That strange feeling deep in your gut that no medical relief can dispel. The saliva evaporating from your mouth and your stomach turning like a butter churner. It's the sensation that appears in anticipation of some disturbing event, known or unknown. Right now, Byron's stomach was trying to pull itself through his throat, but it certainly wasn't nerves. Satan didn't suffer from them. His body only reacted like this when very specific conditions were in play.

Although Byron's body was still intact since the bullet pierced his chest, signs of which were still evident on both sides of his body, what lay within had no link to him whatsoever. The shivers on his skin were a psychosomatic reaction created by the mind that lay within the former prime minister. The mind and spirit were Satan's and those elements only reacted like this in the presence of one other.

This wasn't a regular occurrence. It couldn't afford to be. When an unstoppable force meets an immovable object, you don't forget it quickly. The result was usually painful. Byron was the unstoppable force, pure evil with a spirit as negative as it was malevolent. If his body's reaction was anything to go on, he would soon collide with the immovable object and produce fireworks the likes of which Monaco would never have seen before.

It was impossible to ignore the urge to move towards what he knew was out there. Victor had taken longer than normal, which just added to his need to act. He felt the sensations grow more acute as he left the apartment and moved ever closer to the boat belonging to Grant Parker-Moore. The hair on his arms stood to attention, as if static electricity was goading them to evacuate their host and break free for a new life. Protected from the ocean by a concrete shield that encircled it like a force field, the normally calm tide bubbled and crashed against the harbour edge ever more furiously.

In a localised area above the boat the clouds dashed forward to audition their dark disapproval of what was to come. The wind swept through the gaps in the high-rise buildings causing aerials to quiver and shake. Like two magnets being pushed closer together, Byron knew there was a safe distance that could not be breached. Any closer to the boat and a force would be created even more powerful than the tempest developing around him.

He shouted from the shoreline towards the yacht, "Baltazaar!"

As the water rose the boat rocked more and more violently, its fenders stopping the vessel from smashing into the harbour wall. At the back of the ship a door opened and closed slowly three times, and a man, barely visible against the darkness, crawled out.

"Victor," said Byron. "What's happening?"

"There has been a situation," replied Victor quietly.

"Is he in there?" asked Byron.

"They're both in there. Baltazaar and Grant," he replied.

"Baltazaar, show yourself," roared Byron, taking a few steps backwards to increase the distance between them.

Byron had always suspected that Baltazaar had found a way to return to Earth. The rumour had started with John's declaration that he'd spoken to Baltazaar during his exorcism. If what John had said was true, there was every possibility that Baltazaar would use that opportunity to return. This hunch didn't extend to what he looked like. He didn't need to know. The disruption in the atmosphere around him was enough to identify that he was there.

The dull thud of wood striking metal echoed up the stairwell. Every step coincided with a thud, each one following more slowly and loudly than the last. Finally the end of a walking stick came through the doorway. Supporting the weight from the rest of his body, a strong, elderly hand clutched the end, the other hand placed firmly on his Panama hat to mitigate against the forces of the burgeoning gale.

"Where did you get that old fossil from?" said Byron, making reference to Baltazaar's elderly frame.

"Don't be deceived. There's more to this old man than meets the eye."

"Is that an Irish accent?" asked Byron.

"Indeed. It gives me an aura of warmth and wisdom, don't you think?"

"Not really. It makes you sound like an old fool."

The forces of nature battled for the space between their long-distance face-off, as they eyeballed each other waiting to see who would make the first move.

"So then Lucifer, we seem to be at an impasse."

"I prefer 'Byron', if it's all the same to you."

"Very well. The disgraced former politician back from the dead, I see. You'll notice I have taken a more discreet, less well known body. As we are going on first names, you can call me Donovan."

"Where did you find him?"

"Donovan had the misfortunate of presiding over John Hewson's exorcism. When the channel was opened, I hopped on-board. His body is a little tired, I grant you. Though his standing in the community is second to none. That has been most useful."

"Why are you back?" asked Byron. "I thought you were done with it all?"

"I'm back because of you. If you hadn't been so obsessed at breaking out of your old form, then I wouldn't have been introduced to John. A twelfth and final piece of the jigsaw."

"It wasn't intentional," said Byron almost apologetically.

"You've stretched John too far. You've stretched him to breaking point."

"And you took your opportunity to turn him to your advantage. But it backfired, didn't it?"

"Not necessarily. You don't know where he is, do you? He could be causing havoc in your domain at this very moment, destroying what you have spent so long building."

"We'll find him. And when we do, I will kill him like so many of the others," said Byron.

"That's if you can. Remember neither of us can access him any longer. Who knows what he might do?"

"Why did you do it, Donovan? Why did you give Emorfed to Byron?"

"Because I knew it would piss you off," he said with a deep cackle of laughter that caused the clouds above their heads to burst forth with rain.

"But you have no interest in humans anymore. If you didn't want us to deal with all of the souls, why did you turn off Heaven's Soul Catcher?"

"We were full. We keep our souls, we don't recycle them for pleasure like you do," replied Donovan.

"Full, ha! You can't lie to me, Donovan, I'm the ruler of lies. Lies and me go way back. Why did you really turn it off?"

"Because people started losing faith. The souls sent to us by Limbo, judged over by John and his friends, weren't suitable to stay in Heaven. They kept questioning our authority and casting doubt on the rule of religion. They did not want to be in Heaven, they wanted their own domain."

"There's no such place for them."

"Not anymore. But inside festers a genetic mutation that knows some great deception has befallen them."

"It doesn't help the situation by closing one of the Soul Catchers, though, does it?"

"The human race is out of control," replied Donovan. "They don't even care about each other, let alone gods. That's why I was compelled to destroy all souls. Emorfed was the solution and you helped to deliver it."

"So that's what you've been using your Soul Catcher for. You've been drawing all the recycled energy from Hell."

"Yes. Once we'd collected enough I picked the person I thought most likely to use it. Someone, like me, who was driven by the same desire to rid the population of their weakness. Byron was the best candidate."

"But it didn't work. Most of Emorfed was destroyed."

"Until Victor here started the process all over again."

Quite out of custom for a man addicted to thrill-seeking action, Victor was currently hiding behind a piece of expensive outdoor furniture. Occasionally he'd tempt fate by glancing over the top of it to see who was winning the argument. Both had made him offers of employment and it might be wise not to take sides.

"On top of releasing the shadow souls you have potentially helped John find the third way. His neutral soul has been separated from the rest of him and he's currently on a revenge mission. I'd be surprised if you and I weren't on his list of targets."

"Good. Bring it on. I'll find John, but not before he has helped me destroy Hell."

"Over Byron's dead body. I won't rest until I have found every one of Victor's patients and retrieved their shadows."

"And I will stop you. Don't forget, I also have the list. I know where you will be going and I will be there before you. Just as I did for poor old Grant downstairs."

Unfamiliar with the concept of being threatened, Byron stood forward a stride. The waves surged up and over the deck of the boat. The clouds above them rumbled with thunder. The intensity of the storm increased exponentially with every step Byron took forward. The light fittings on the yacht started to rattle free of their fixings, and the wooden floorboards buckled and twisted under Victor's feet.

Realising Byron's intentions, Donovan raised a hand to the air. The cloud above him compliantly released a bolt of lightning into his palms, where Donovan carefully moulded it into a ball. He threw it towards Byron with the speed and accuracy of the world's most talented baseball pitcher. Byron easily ducked to one side and the projectile struck the boat moored next to Grant's, which immediately burst into flames.

Semi-clothed yacht owners and their party-goers rushed onto the decks of their boats, frightened by the raging external anomalies. The flames from one of their neighbour's superliners licked the quayside and threatened to pass from boat to boat. Millionaires shouted at half-sleeping employees to stop the natural passage of fire. Perhaps money couldn't buy anything after all.

In the distance a multiple set of sirens signalled that the authorities would soon be in attendance. Byron was undeterred. As he took another step forward the deck of Grant's boat ripped open down the middle. Victor, who'd been watching proceedings unfold, threw himself in the water before the boat did it for him. Donovan circled his hand around to manipulate the wind into a micro tornado. It spun around him before violently lifting him off the boat and down the boardwalk. As the pressure in the atmosphere sent needles of barometers off the scale, Grant's luxury yacht finally gave way, splitting in two and sinking under the waves. It carried with it the body of Grant Parker-Moore, who'd sat through the whole incident, unmoved and undeterred on the edge of his bed.

"Job done," muttered Byron, as the storm abated with the rapid retreat of Donovan into the distance.

"Don't move! Stay where you are!" shouted a policeman who was pointing a gun at him from within the car window that had just skidded into the foreground.

*****

David was stumped. His only leads seemed like dead ends. He was no closer to finding out why Herb had died. Dr. King had disappeared shortly after the funeral, and Nash had become so suspicious he'd left their conversation in a panic. The next three names on his list were either complete unknowns, like Baltazaar, or had yet to be located, like Victor. David was starting to feel that the odds of completing his tasks before his twelfth birthday were slim. And then what? What would he even do if he completed them all? What would life be like without a purpose?

There was only one notable highlight from his conversation with Nash. Just one thing he'd picked up that might be useful. One word. Cornwall. It was a long shot but what options did he have? He could go back to law school and forget the whole campaign until another day, or he could keep trying whilst his vacation continued. Cornwall was significant because he knew Byron had suggested it was a good place to hide Faith. Nash had been hell-bent on protecting Faith, even though John had persuaded him not to. Love doesn't tend to listen to logic.

Those two minuscule pieces of data had been the stimulant for David's current course of action. His car was proceeding down the M5 motorway, a short distance behind Nash's black hire car. He kept pace with the ex-rockstar as he weaved dangerously between lorries and trucks. Not bad for a pre-teen. If he was right, Nash would take him all the way to Cornwall and just possibly some new lines of inquiry. If he was wrong, then it was the longest wild goose chase in history.

CHAPTER FIFTEEN

FINDING FAITH

"What did you find out?" asked Elsie, as she pointlessly attempted to pick invisible bugs out of her plastic skin. The pigeons had returned from their excursion far faster than anyone had expected.

"They're coming down here," replied Sandy.

"Who are?" asked Abe.

"Burn you…shock you…melt you…poke you…I'm ever so sorry…ha ha ha…mugs," stuttered John.

"What John is trying to say, rather insensitively, is that all the demons are coming down here. Which means there won't be any up there. The time to strike is now," said Sandy.

It wouldn't be possible for all of them to travel to level twelve the way the pigeons had previously done. The last time he studied them, ox couldn't fly. Sandy had devised a plan for using his troops to maximum effect while personally maintaining a distance as far from the cat as feasibly possible. The elephants in the room, and thankfully Sandy didn't have one of those on his team, were the demons. What if they had to face one?

"Ok, gather around, everyone," said Sandy needlessly, given the number of places available to hide on the back of a whale. "We're going to split into three units. My unit, which will include John and Ian, will head to level twelve to recover Faith's shadow. Units two and three will attempt to distract the demons when they come here. At the appropriate time, unit three, Roger and Vicky, will move on to the front gate and the Soul Catcher to clear the way for our arrival. We will meet you there once we have been to the library."

"Bloody newcomers," said Vicky. "They all think they know about this place. Well, I've been here for longer than any of you…"

"Ahem, I think you'll find I was here the longest," said Roger.

"Fuck off, cat," said Vicky, shooting a sticky web in his face.

"I'm only going in unit three if I get to lead it," demanded Roger, his voice slightly muffled from the spider's web around his chops.

"No way. I don't deal with cats, let alone follow them," replied Vicky.

"I really don't have time for this!" shouted Sandy. "The demons are coming now! You'll just have to sort it out for yourself."

Vicky and Roger avoided each other's eyes.

"What I'd like to know, from our so-called leader, is how we're going to deal with any demons if we meet them," said Vicky.

"It's a fair point," replied Sandy. "We do need to be prepared for it. How many demons do we know about?"

"I saw one made from mushrooms once," said Elsie, giggling away to some personal in-joke.

"Well, that's a start. How do you kill a mushroom?" asked Sandy to the group.

There was a lot of head-scratching from the animals as they considered the scenario. Apart from Roger obviously. He knew but was disinclined to answer. It wasn't just about what might stop a mushroom demon, it was also whether they'd have the means to do it.

"Holy water would do it," said Abe.

"And do you have any?" asked Sandy.

"No."

"You could fry him in a bit of oil," said Elsie.

"No pan, no oil and come to think of it, no massive gas hob," replied Sandy. "It would help if you thought before answering."

"A demon with thrush…sicko…" shouted John.

"I," started Gary.

"Yes," said Sandy encouragingly.

"Would."

"Go on," said the group in mass expectation.

"Have."

"Loved to have answered more quickly?" prompted Sandy sarcastically.

"No," continued Gary.

"Idea…that's what you're trying to say, isn't it?" sighed Sandy.

"Yes."

Sandy shook his head in realisation that this was the worst brainstorming session since Coca-Cola executives got together and decided they needed a new recipe.

"Ok, so we're stumped on the mushroom guy. What about one made of gold? I think I saw one like that loading the vessols on the Soul Catcher once," said Sandy.

"Oh that one's easy," said Roger. "The gold ones are very susceptible to hypnotism."

"You've hypnotised a demon, have you?!" said Sandy.

"Easy. Cats do it naturally. I can't tell you how, it's just within us. He probably still thinks he's an avocado after the last time he crossed me."

"I think you've been hypnotised," replied Sandy. "Any other thoughts?"

"Holy water," said Abe confidently.

Sandy contemplated the idea that he'd acquired some sort of powerful freak beacon that drew useless cretins to him. It was the only explanation. Firstly Ian had stuck to him like a magnet, and now five other candidates were attempting to displace him as the most irritating individual since the discovery of the whoopee cushion. Ian could sense his moment to climb up the league table.

"We don't need to fight them," said Ian.

"What?" said Sandy, not expecting any pearls of wisdom anytime soon.

"Well, they're only looking for John, aren't they? They don't know about the rest of us. So as long as we keep him hidden we should be ok."

"Yes…but how do we do that?" said Sandy. "You'd struggle to keep John hidden at an epilepsy convention."

"Hear me out," said Ian.

Sandy immediately hated himself for nodding.

"As far as we know, all the demons are made out of an element of some sort."

"Go on…" prompted Sandy.

"Why don't we disguise ourselves as a demon?"

"And how are you going to hide an ox inside a demon costume? I haven't seen many demons wearing shoes in the shape of a giant ox."

"Well, maybe not all of us, but if you and John are going upstairs, maybe a few of us could build a costume down here."

"There are many issues with your plan, Ian, but I'll just pick one out at random. What are we going to make a demon costume out of?"

"Leaves?" said Ian hopefully.

"There's no leaf demon."

"Ian's a tit…loser," blurted John in between bouts of habit reversal. "What do…don't tell them…demons hate…love…hate most of all…?"

The animals looked around at each other surprised that John had managed an almost completely coherent sentence.

"Holy water," said Abe.

"Shadows…" said John with a cough and a twitch.

"What's your point, John?" asked Sandy.

"Release…arse weasel…the shadows…bad idea…"

"But what will happen if we release all the shadows?" asked Abe.

"All hell will break loose…god bothering donkey… that was mean I apologise…ox-y-moron…haha…"

"I like John's plan more than Ian's," said Sandy.

*****

As the water of the lake swirled around the banks, like a bucket of water being swung around in the air, there was a palpable sense of anxiety. Very few of the senior demons had ever visited level zero, and even less knew how it worked. A few dozen different elements rubbed shoulders as each demon, in their own inimitable way, descended through the hole that separate the two lowest levels of Hell.

When your normal vista consisted of rock, metal bars and tormented souls in plastic bodies, it wasn't surprising that the demons stood mesmerised by their current surroundings. Some, like Mr. Fungus, sat dewy-eyed as if he'd discovered a secret nirvana that had been purposely kept from him. Others cringed at the sight of the unabated life residing here unrestrained. It felt to them like a place of rebellion, a place that lacked order and discipline. Where was the punishment? What was the point if you didn't get to revel in a bit of sadistic fun?

The bottom of the ladder, that only some of the demons had needed to use, came to an end on a hillock in the forest biome. In the valley below, trees ascended into the air like prison bars, blocking a view of multi-landscapes that disappeared over the horizon. The demons squirmed as the foreign nature of grass and weeds weaved around their toes. Everyone that 'had' feet and toes, that was. Mr. Aqua just felt like an over-elaborate sprinkler system. Primordial was waiting for them at the bottom of the ladder like a schoolteacher orchestrating a bunch of unruly students on a geography trip.

"Right," he said in a gravelly voice designed to draw their attention away from a number of residents sitting nervously in the undergrowth, frightened by this mass influx of new guests. "There are some rules."

"Rules?" said Mr. Volts, who was currently scorching the piece of grass underneath him, hoping he wasn't already breaking one of them.

"Yes. This is my domain. Do I come into your offices and tell you what to do? Do I mess around with your patients?"

The demons all shook their heads, thankful that he didn't. Of all the demons, Primordial was misunderstood the most.

"Rule one, you can't punish the creatures that live here."

"Aww, why not?"

"Was that you, Mr. Virus?" asked Primordial.

"No, I think it was Mr. Noir," replied a second voice that no one could locate.

Only a few demons were invisible to their colleagues. One was Mr. Virus, who was essentially a mass of microscopic virions. None of them knew how big he was, where he was or indeed whether or not he was responsible whenever they felt under the weather. The second was Mr. Noir. He was even more of an enigma. Unlike Mr. Virus, who you could at least sense when he passed by you, Mr. Noir's very existence was based on a load of assumptions.

Stuff is an interesting concept. Stuff is everywhere. We sit on it. We eat it. We sometimes bump into it. But is stuff always obvious? What if some stuff wasn't really stuff at all? At least not as we understand it. What if we owned stuff, but we didn't know where it was? Not like misplacing the TV remote for a couple of weeks, that's just lost stuff. Just because you can't see some of your stuff doesn't mean it's not there. Even now you're surrounded by a load of dark stuff that sits somewhere between the other stuff.

Mr. Noir must exist because strange shit kept happening. Why did stuff in Hell became heavier than it was meant to be for no obvious reason? Why did the light from torches bend in an unusual way? All of these factors made the demons believe that someone was responsible. There was a fundamentally more obvious reason for this belief, though. Sometimes he spoke. Not often, though. Mr. Noir wasn't great at interacting with others. In fact he didn't really interact with himself. Mr. Noir was built from dark matter, or at least that's what he claimed anyway. Unlike all the other demons, who generally had the good grace to stay in one place at one time, he was everywhere. Anywhere without stuff in fact.

"Mr. Noir, nice to have you with us," replied Primordial.

"I'm always with you," replied a voice.

"If you say so," replied Mr. Gold, making a madman sign with his hand.

"As I was saying," continued Primordial. "Rule one. No one punishes the creatures other than me. If you find John, then you can restrain him only. Is that understood?"

Everyone nodded and a deep sigh pierced the space between stuff.

"Rule two. Don't damage anything. You might be tempted to speed up your search for John by setting fire to trees or blowing down habitats or flooding valleys. It took ages to get level zero like this and I'd appreciate not having a massive cleaning bill."

"What about a few thunderbolts?" said Mr. Volts.

"No. Rule three. We will go about this systematically. If everyone just runs amok in every direction, John will be able to evade capture."

"I can't really do that, Primordial, I'm sort of everywhere," replied Mr. Noir.

"You should have already found him, then, shouldn't you?" stated Primordial. "We start here in the forest biome. Once that's done we move on to the desert biome."

"I can't go there," replied Mr. Aqua. "I have a note."

"Rule four, there are no notes. You do what I tell you. If you do happen to interact with one of the reincarnates you are welcome to question them."

"I tend to use Chinese burns along with my questions," said Mr. Bitumen.

"Not here you don't. These creature are very tame. Most just want an easy life so they won't give you any trouble. If we get a move on it shouldn't take us long to find John."

"I think we get it, Primordial. We've already wasted time listening to your rules," said Asmodeus disparagingly. "Any more?"

"Rule five. Don't walk on the grass."

Once a place of greenery, the hill was a smorgasbord of scorch marks, small fires and patches of filth. Everyone looked guilty.

*****

For the second time the pigeons carried John between them. Up the cliff faces of Hell they juggled him until they reached the gap between level twelve and the barrier. They flew it with much less trepidation than they had done previously. They knew access was possible and no one would be there to greet them. They squeezed through the gap as close to the rock as possible to avoid the unknown consequences of coming into contact with the translucent barrier.

In the distance the large table and scattered thrones occupied the centre of the floor, just as John had remembered it. The experience of being here made him deeply uncomfortable. So much effort had been expended to remove himself from this part of Hell and now he was back. Of the two parts of his character, one was more animated about it than the other. In this place his world had fallen apart. Here the truth had been revealed. A truth that still hung in the air like an apparition waiting to haunt him. A searing anger boiled inside him until it had nowhere else to go.

"Bastards…cruel, vicious, soul thirsty…fuckers…I will destroy them…REVENGE…!" shouted John as he ran full pelt towards the table in the distance.

"John, come back!" shouted Sandy, flying behind, but unable to catch up.

When John reached Asmodeus's throne, positioned at the head of the table, his rage attempted and failed to push it over. Not deterred, he unsuccessfully tried to gnaw chunks out of its wooden legs.

"John, stop," pleaded Sandy.

"They…gulp…took everything…arseholes…from me…" replied John, weeping.

"Then let's take it back," replied Sandy.

"I'm not sure…gulp…I can…I feel sympathy on top…arse...of anger."

"Sympathy! You don't need to feel that, John. You've been wronged, we all have. Make them suffer, make them beg to get it back."

"I…feel…I'm being…*cough*…used."

"We all are. We always have been. What about Faith? She's been used, too. Don't you want to get her back?"

"Yes…nasty demons…must be punished…let's tear it down…"

"There's a good lad, you know it makes sense. Now let's find Faith."

The stone shelves that housed the lines of shadows hidden inside glass houses stretched out in front of them. Each six-inch-high bulbous flask housed the same deep blue electricity in its stomach. None had labels. Some were more boisterous than others, jerking in their position in a vain attempt to be noticed. Was there any order to how they were stacked? Were the lower ones the first to arrive? There was no way of knowing if there was any system to this disorder?

They approached the bottom row, the only one they could reasonably access. To distinguish what was happening inside, Sandy placed an ear to a vase. A familiar argument ensued inside the glass as two sides of a personality were attempting to gain advantage over the other. Sandy whispered a question into the glass and, as if taken by surprise, it jumped into the air a fraction. He listened to the garbled reply.

"This one isn't Faith," said Sandy.

"How do you know?" asked Ian.

"It told me," replied Sandy, "in between some pretty experimental swearing."

The three of them followed the line of shadows, stopping to ask each a simple question. Not all the responses were delivered in the same manner. It was clear that these shadows had varying degrees of animosity and charity. It made sense to Sandy. If these souls were dragged from their humans before their time, they might have a balance towards negative emotions or a balance towards positive emotions. They would all have elements of both, but not all would be as dangerous as others. As they continued to talk to the shadows, Sandy made a mental note of the really angry ones.

"Any luck?" he asked the other two.

"Tongue my fart box...no...purple disease carrier..."

"Ok, Ian and I will have to fly up to the higher levels. John, you stay here and keep a lookout."

The pigeons flew to the next row and started the process all over again, standing gingerly on each stone shelf. While John stood guard his attention was drawn to an area of level twelve that he had a personal experience of. The only metal box not suspended in the air above him was the one that had formerly been his. Its crumpled shell, beaten and broken, was sitting on the floor with its side open towards him.

As he approached it he saw the inscription burnt into the side. He visualised how the two remaining parts of his soul had combined to create it. How was the other part of him getting on? Was it busy? A wave of joy washed over him at the prospect that his neutral splinter was free from pain. The vengeful emotion took over. Was it fulfilling the tasks that he'd set for it in those dark moments trapped inside this metal tomb? Was it able to without the anger that sat here within him?

The rest of the metal boxes stood like pillars above him. He felt their pain like few people could. What had they done to deserve such a fate?

"I think I've found her," announced Ian from the end of row three.

"Let me check," said Sandy, flying up to join him. He whispered into the vase, "Who are you?"

"I am the shadow. Help me. I want my daddy," came the distorted female voice from within.

"What's your name?"

"Faith."

"That's her. Ian, help me get her down."

"I love you…sexy hips…grrrr…naughty thoughts… we're going to save you, Faith…" shouted John uncontrollably from a distance away.

John's uncontrolled bellowing disturbed the only demon currently occupying level twelve. It wasn't a surprise that the animals hadn't spotted him. As demons go, he was the smallest of the lot, although this was a recent accolade. A thin line of sand dribbled from one of the thrones and made its way slowly towards them. As it closed in on them it rose from the ground to produce an action figure-sized version of Mr. Silica.

"Put that down," he said in a voice so squeaky the pigeons were convinced he'd been sucking helium. "That used to be one of my kneecaps."

CHAPTER SIXTEEN

THE FOLLOWERS

"Victor, I need you to bail me out," came the repetitive message like a stuck record. *"You can't run from me."*

Victor hadn't run any further than their Monaco bolt-hole. It was thinking not running that Victor was attempting through the constant interruptions provided by the Devil's telepathy. The boat experience hadn't been pleasant. Dodging bits of yacht swirling around a rough sea he could cope with. Avoiding a major police investigation that surrounded the events of the previous day was also not a problem. But being stuck between two omnipotent beings knocking six bells of shit out of each other was concerning even for him.

What if he was on the wrong side? Surely the right side was the one with the biggest pile of cash. Byron certainly had enough of that. Yet this Baltazaar character, who appeared to go by the name Donovan, was clearly not someone to be messed with. Would every assassination attempt involve this old man reading his mind before he had to dodge the aftermath of a storm that gathered above him? His health insurance definitely didn't cover 'Acts of God' let alone 'acts of Satan'.

"You know I can just melt my way out of this cell, don't you? Of course that would require the death of a dozen innocent people and someone to scoop them off the floor afterwards. It's your call."

"Ok. I'll come."

"There's a good lad. No point wasting more life, is there?"

"Where did Baltazaar go?"

"Who knows? He has the list. The only way he can protect them is by moving them around."

"What do we do about it?"

"Until we can work out how to stop him we'll have to go after someone that's not on the list."

"But they're all on the list."

"No, there's one who isn't."

"Who?"

"Faith is out there somewhere. We just need to find out where. You found Violet and Fiona before. Can you find them again?"

"Does a casino always win?" said Victor confidently.

*****

Keeping up with Nash wasn't as easy as it had first appeared. Following a car was easy enough. Following a ferry, not so much. They had travelled incognito in convoy almost the entire length of the United Kingdom until there was no land left. In Penzance, Nash dropped his hire car off and made for the ferry port. That's where David lost him. The destination was the only thing he knew for certain. The Isles of Scilly.

It was too risky to board the same ferry, so he was forced to watch the ship sailing into the early autumn greyness from the safety of the pier. By the time he'd booked onto the next crossing, a day later, the trail was cold. It wasn't the only thing that dropped in temperature. Over the course of twenty-four hours the climate had changed from grey and drizzly to black and tempestuous. As he boarded the shabby-looking ship, a relic built decades before he was born, his feet struggled to deal with the constant swaying. He descended the staircase to the bottom deck to find somewhere to hide or strap himself down.

David was accustomed to mountains, not oceans. At altitude there were few that would compete with his stamina or ability to breathe normally. Whilst most of the other passengers were content to drink coffee, chat amongst themselves or read their newspapers, David already felt sick and they'd not even left the quayside.

The two and a half-hour journey aboard the Scillonian was less comfortable than being transported inside a giant washing machine filled with boulders. The rain lashed the windows and the boat shook with no familiar pattern. Sometimes it would lurch forward, sometimes side to side, and occasionally up and down as well. This random discombobulation was being repeated tenfold inside David's body, and he was convinced one of his vital organs might be forced to jump overboard.

Lacking emotions didn't stop David feeling sick. That reaction was purely physical. Growing up in mountains didn't really prepare you for seasickness. This was the first time he'd been at sea in his whole life and the algorithms in his head were busy building a new set of procedures. The result of which was to indicate, in future, that he wasn't a fan.

The relief of reaching port at the other end distracted his attention from the yellow and grey colour that had taken up residency across his face. He stumbled onto the dockside as the land successfully convinced his legs that they were still being pushed up and down like the pattern of a cross-trainer. In an age of Health and Safety disclaimers he considered complaining to staff of a lack of signage describing the journey as 'more uncomfortable than passing your organs through a sieve'.

"You ok there?" said a middle-aged, plump lady with thick-rimmed spectacles, who was standing at the top of the gangway in an official jacket.

"I'll come back to you on that," said David, wiping the sweat from his face with a napkin. "How do you deal with seasickness?"

"Probably take the plane," she said with a chuckle.

David took this advice seriously and added it to the recently formed algorithm on the subject. "And if you already have it?"

"Depends who you talk to," replied the woman. "Some promote eating ginger. There's also a theory you can get rid of it if you roll the balls of your naked feet over a piece of wet fish. Personally I eat olives. Works for me."

In response to this random local knowledge, David felt olives was the best call. Holding onto the stone wall that prevented all seasickness sufferers from plummeting into the water, he shuffled his way along the harbourside and into the bosom of the island of St Mary's. The location for the island's main harbour was Hugh Town and as he passed under a stone archway a pub was the first building in sight. The craving for olives briefly overtook the need to vomit.

Pubs never used to sell olives. They sold beer. Occasionally you could buy a pork scratching. You knew where you were in the old days. Petrol stations only sold petrol, florists only sold flowers, and gift shops only sold shit that nobody needed. In this modern world you can buy a lawnmower from a supermarket, coffee in a bookshop, and still nothing of any value whatsoever from a gift shop. Finding olives in a pub was as certain as finding a granny in a bingo hall.

David pushed the door open and swayed in, hoping his bodily tremors weren't mistaken for someone who'd had 'one too many'. As an eleven-year-old he didn't frequent pubs very often and wasn't versed in the age-old etiquette of pub membership. Camouflaged by the horse brasses, beer mats stapled to the wooden beams, seafaring memorabilia and weathered furniture, the scattering of people inside stopped to mentally criticise the young newcomer. That an unfamiliar person would have the gall to enter their pub! Their church. If the atmosphere was unfriendly, it was nothing compared to the landlord.

"What-you-wan?" he garbled, holding his barrel-shaped belly in order to stop it rolling away. Most of his features were dented by some presumably horrific dart-throwing incident and a smell ran around him like a perimeter fence. A sign on the wall extolling the 'good local beer' and 'traditional food' had been fixed hastily to the bar by Sellotape and the word 'hospitable' had been crossed out, seemingly because no one could spell it, and replaced by 'friendly' staff.

"A lemonade and a pot of olives please," replied David, not in the slightest bit concerned by the undercurrent of hostility being aimed in his direction.

"Yo-takin-the-piss," replied the barman, scratching his arse as if that was the normal procedure when someone placed their order. "This-a-pub, not-market."

Evidently the Scilly Isles could not be placed in the bracket of places collectively known as the modern world. When most people still travelled by foot and you were cut off from the mainland by thirty miles of sea, evolution was always just a little bit slower. Everything here moved at a slower pace. Although in relative terms if you asked the islanders they'd say everything on the mainland moved too fast. Right or wrong was purely based on your preference.

"Ginger beer?" asked David tentatively, hoping his second choice of cures was available before he resorted to taking his shoes and socks off and heading to the nearest fishmonger.

"We-got-ging-beer," replied the barman, leaning around to the fridge and presenting David with the full glory of his loosely attached trousers and overexposed buttocks.

David paid for the drink and sat as far away from the locals as possible. He was surprised to find that the ginger beer did have a calming effect on his motion sickness, and as he finished it his mind moved to other matters. Where was Nash? Did he live here? He clearly disliked being reminded of his past days of celebrity. Maybe this was the perfect place for him to remain unrecognised. It was a small community, it was possible someone in this pub might know who he was. Every move David made was analysed by the patrons as if they had nothing else in their lives to keep their attention. As he approached each one they shied away from him in case he was infected by some horrible foreign disease.

As he momentarily caught their eye he asked them a simple question, but no one admitted to knowing a Nash Stevens. That was until the proprietor overheard the conversation.

"Ya-looking fa Dr. Stevens?" he said gruffly over a swig of his pint, only some of which reached his mouth.

"Yes," replied David. "I didn't know he was a doctor, though."

"Came-ear bout a year go. Not a proper doctor, I don't fink. E's a carer, looks-afta my-ol mum."

"A carer. Right. Where will I find him?" asked David.

"Oo-nose-he travels round all-the islands dunn he. Fink he do Bryher on a Mondee."

"Thank you for the information and the ginger beer. Did the trick for my seasickness. How do I get to Bryher?"

"Well ya nee to ger-a boat."

"Can I get two more ginger beers as takeout please."

*****

The journey to Bryher aboard the *Firethorn* was a lot calmer and more pleasant than the one he'd taken this morning. Sheltered by the islands that dotted the sea, the water had none of the anger and malice of the open ocean. The strategy of a bottle of ginger beer before and one on landing also seemed to work as intended. The smaller vessel glided above the surf as it sped from the harbour, where he'd arrived earlier, to a smaller isolated 'off' island, as they were referred to.

There was none of the engineering prowess to this quay. A short wall jutted out along the beach into the sea, only accessible when the tide gave permission. No town or pub welcomed him as he disembarked. The countryside and sandy beach, shimmering from the beams of sunlight, were the only welcoming party. In the distance, almost hidden from sight amongst the hedgerows, was a small, isolated chapel.

Normal people might be overcome by the warm feeling of tranquility presented by this beautiful simplicity. As a deeply rational person, all that David questioned was what exactly he was doing there.

As the handful of other passengers strode confidently into the island, David stood on the sandy, concrete pier staring at the island's vista.

"Are you a pirate?" called a child's voice from the water behind him.

A small boy, wearing a bandana and holding a wooden sword, sailed skilfully up to the concrete wall. His small boat paid little interest to what the sea demanded, instead moving obediently on the commands of its captain. The vessel barely shuddered as the boy stood up and brandished his blunt, wooden weapon in David's direction and waited for a reply.

"No. I'm not a pirate. Not sure I could be with my seasickness. Looks to me that you are more dressed for the role?"

"I'm a pirate catcher," said the boy without the slightest bit of irony in his voice.

"I see. Is that an official job or are you a vigilante?"

"It's unofficial. But this is my island and I will protect it."

"Well, it is a very lovely island from what I have seen of it so far. What are you protecting it from?"

"Danger. Pirates. Former Prime Ministers and uninvited guests," replied the boy, reeling off a well-rehearsed list of undesirables. "Are you any of those?"

"Well, I'm uninvited, I suppose," replied David, avoiding the fact that part of him had been associated with a former PM and that 'dangerous' was a rather ambiguous descriptor.

"In that case I will need to report you," said the boy.

"If you must," said David. "What's your name?"

"Captain Scrumpy," he replied, stretching his body up to his full four-and-a-half-foot height and saluting an invisible crew.

"Well, it's nice to meet you, Captain Scrumpy. My name is David Gonzalez. Who are you going to report me to?"

"The boss, of course."

"And who would that be?"

"One of my mothers."

"You have more than one?"

"Oh yes. I'm very lucky I have two mums, an aunt and a sister," he replied with more information than he'd intended to.

Scrumpy enjoyed his unofficial role as protector of the island. It wasn't a particularly taxing one. It involved playing around the island by land or sea and interrogating anyone who landed who wasn't on his list. Like a bouncer at the door of a nightclub anyone not pre-approved would be assessed for their suitability before being allowed entry. It wasn't often that people weren't on that list. Tourists tended to be interested in the bigger islands, where more exciting events occurred. There was the occasional bird spotter or walker that landed, but they didn't look like David.

In Scrumpy's opinion David didn't look equipped to be here. He had no luggage, inappropriate footwear and no binoculars. A lack of binoculars was a sure-fire sign that someone was up to no good. Suspicions set to maximum, only one factor kept him from running to the boss. This was an opportunity to speak to another boy. It was always women and girls that Scrumpy had for company. The girls in his life didn't really understand adventure and expeditions. This young man looked like he was on one and that made him just a little curious.

"Why are you here?" he asked, simultaneously tying his boat to the pier.

"I'm not sure, really. I'm looking for someone."

"Who?"

"Nash Stevens. I hear he works on the islands."

Scrumpy knew immediately who David was referring to, but his mothers had always trained him to gather information before he gave any away. "Why are you looking for him?"

"That's a good question. I guess I'm on a quest," replied David, sensing that this boy knew more than he was letting on and calculating that the best way to find out was to stoke his interest.

"I love quests. I'm always going on adventures. What sort of a quest is it?" replied the boy moving closer up the shoreline and sitting on a marbled rock that protruded from the beach.

"Revenge," said David. "Discovery. Possibly even damsels in distress."

"Oh, exciting! I'm not so bothered about the damsels, though. Revenge against who?"

"Lots of people. I have a list."

"Can I help?"

"You might. Are you gallant enough?"

"Of course. I've fought pirates and rescued prisoners. I've stormed castles and solved mysteries. I'm very brave."

"I'm sure you are," replied David, as the boy brandished his sword against unknown foes. "Tell me, why did you say you were protecting the island from former Prime Ministers? That's a very specific threat."

"There's one that might come here. My mothers have told me to keep a lookout for him. I knew you weren't him, though. You're not the right size. He's a big, fat man with glasses, always smoking."

David recognised the description immediately but not the motive. "Why might he come here?"

"To find my aunt."

"Who's she?"

"I can't tell you that. It's top secret," replied Scrumpy.

"I see that you are very good at protecting her," said David. "But I can't go on a quest with someone who doesn't trust me. It was nice to meet you, but I'd better be on my way."

"But you can trust me, I promise," gasped Scrumpy as the young man feigned to leave.

"Well, maybe we should enter into a pact so that we can trust each other? I'll let you help me on my quest, if you can keep me hidden?"

"Ok. But you have to prove how brave you are," said the boy.

"How do I do that?"

"See that little island out in the bay over there?"

"Yes."

"You have to swim out there with me. If you get there, I'll tell you my aunt's name."

The logic in David's brain told him this was a silly idea. Neither fun nor fear was responsible for that opinion. The odds somersaulted around his mind to form a complex mathematics equation that took into account sea depth, swimming ability, tides, likelihood of this boy's information being useful, distance, and the chance of his body being nibbled by fish. In nanoseconds the answer was in and an imaginary noise went 'ping'.

*****

The gibbon was having a great time. Sandy had given her free rein to cause whatever havoc she could think of, and she could think of a lot. The practical joke genie was out of the bottle. The demons couldn't see what was 'practical' about attempting to remove themselves from a pit in the ground concealed by branches, or tripping on a piece of string laid across a path or avoiding being struck by wayward flung bits of mud. The other members of the gibbon's unit were less impressed. After each incident of disruption all the ox could do was apologise and offer a quick religious conversion. The sloth offered nothing as he never got there in time.

The demons had moved from biome to biome in search of John and, although they'd met plenty of creatures, none had the slightest interest or knowledge of where the erratic shrew was. As they moved to the next landscape, several of them were convinced the animals were in some way trying to impede their progress. Such was the subterfuge with which the gibbon worked her tricks. She was always one step in front, scheming up new ways to halt their search. She was careful never to be spotted, leaving any explanations to the ox who had the type of innocent face that people trusted.

Whilst the ox, sloth and gibbon worked at slowing the demons' progress, the cat and spider were busy arguing rather than helping. The gibbon's unit could hardly be described as flawless teamwork, but at least they weren't acting against each other. Roger and Vicky's mission was laid out quite simply. Get to the Soul Catcher without being seen and wait there for the pigeons. The other unit would keep the demons busy. What could be simpler? Apparently working out a cheap way of perfecting nuclear fusion. Roger the cat didn't like taking orders. Vicky the spider didn't like cats.

"Cats are such prima donnas. Up their own arses and think they always know best," muttered Vicky, as the two sat, still sailing aimlessly, on the back of the whale trying to agree the best course of action.

"Look, I'm not going the long way. The quickest way to the Soul Catcher is this way," said Roger, pointing at the translucent barrier that separated them from the next universe.

"How do you know?"

"Because I was the first person to land on the moon. Space is a doddle. I do space like I do catching mice. Easy."

"Go on, then, if you think you're such a legend. Show me."

"Obviously if I go that way you won't be able to follow me. Only cats can do it. We've got nine lives and the last time I checked spiders haven't."

"Stop stalling and just do it. I have no intention of following you, you're madder than a marmalade monkey."

The cat strolled up and down the barrier, its head high and chest pushed out in front of it. Nonchalantly it sniffed various parts of the window as if attempting to find a weak spot. A paw shot forward to catch an invisible rodent whose whiskers had snuck through the barrier. As the plastic paw went through the distorted atmosphere and returned unscathed, the cat turned to the spider and smiled with an air of overconfidence. Roger's hind legs coiled backwards and muscle fibre twitched. One small step for a cat and one great leap into the unknown.

The biggest downside to overconfidence is the disappointment. Nothing prepares you for failure when you really believe in success. When all goes well you shrug your shoulders to demonstrate how right you were in the first place. When your arrogance is proven wrong it's your face that gives you away. It's a face that has too much advertising space on it. It expands, as if being placed under a rolling pin, eyes almost out of their sockets and mouth wide enough to swallow a whole melon. From Vicky's rather more comfortable position on the correct side of Hell, that's how Roger looked now he'd reached the other side.

The third Earl of Norfolk's vessel inflated from the lack of atmosphere in the Universe, creating the impression of an overpumped circus balloon. The inflation couldn't last forever. Vessols were only plastic after all. They had some give in them, but eventually the more pressure went in, the more the pressure caused an issue. Distorted by the barrier, the overinflated cat bobbed along in space, as Vicky watched and waited for the inevitable.

Most primary school children can tell you there are no sounds in space. Vicky had to imagine if there was a noise it was probably a loud POP. The cat's plastic vessol spiralled uncontrollably before being lifted by an unknown force vertically above Vicky's head. It was hard to determine where the vessol would end up but there was much less doubt over Roger's soul. That travelled much faster.

"Well, he did say that was the quickest way. Nothing about the safest, though," said Vicky.

"That'll teach him for being a big-headed bragger," said a loud voice that none of the animals had heard before.

"Oh hello. We didn't think you spoke," said Vicky to the whale.

"Only when I feel like it. I'm guessing you'll want me to get you to the shore, then."

"I'm not that fond of whales."

"Tough."

CHAPTER SEVENTEEN

A PLAGUE ON ALL YOUR HOUSES

It wasn't a surprise that Sandy's worst fear had come true. If you had a plan to revolt against the forces of Hell you had to expect it. You needed preparation and tactics to defend yourself. He didn't have any. Tactics were still trying to form into the semblance of a first draft. Their earlier conversations on defeating demons had been curtailed by idiots. They never got as far as debating how to deal with one made of sand. It was only good fortune that at least this one was smaller than Sandy.

"Put that back," squeaked Mr. Silica, attempting to look as scary as his six inches would allow.

"Your kneecap, you say?" replied Sandy attempting small talk. "How do you manage without it?"

"I'm very flexible."

"Small demon…crack…sand in my crack…don't scare me," howled John.

"Let me deal with this, John."

The shrew hopped about on the spot, eager to unleash some of his pent-up energy.

"I don't think I will put it back if it's all the same. You see it contains someone that my potty-mouthed friend here is rather fond of."

"Put it back," screamed Silica in an even higher-pitched battle cry, "or I'll attack!"

"Ian, get him!" shouted Sandy in response.

Ian wasn't the slightest bit sure how you 'got him'. After all, anyone who has ever attempted to scoop up a load of sand after a nice beach trip will tell you that it's impossible. You'll still be finding cupfuls of it six months later in places that never went to the beach in the first place. Such was the mysterious properties of the stuff. Ian shuffled forward, making kung fu noises and faking martial arts movements with his pure white plastic limbs. Silica watched with intrigue. Finally, as if taken by some berserker gene reflex deep within him, Ian ran forward, screaming at the top of his voice. The result was not effective. As he reached the demon, Silica metamorphosed into a little sandstorm and blasted him like a cheap car chassis.

"He's in my eyes," wept Ian, trying to claw the sand out with the same proficiency as trying to open a beer bottle with an onion.

The sand gathered for a second wave of attacks, this time aiming for the valve in Ian's vessel. In one gulp Silica forced his way inside and circulated around the rest of his body.

"It itches," shouted Ian as he coughed and spluttered.

Sharing a confined space with a demon was an excruciating experience. Imagine sharing a small kennel with a Rottweiler who's spent the last twenty-four hours being poked in the eye with a stick and you won't be far away. Silica's thoughts infected his own, sowing seeds of pain and hysteria. Ian's body fainted, but Silica retained control over his speech.

"Your friend is no match for a demon, you know. No vessol is."

Sandy beckoned John over so that they could speak quietly to each other.

"You've seen more of this place than most of us, John. What can we do?"

"Numpty…this is your rodeo…*cough*."

"Think, PLEASE," begged Sandy.

John's body twitched and vibrated as he forced his mind to control the competing emotions. What would work? What could he remember clearly enough that might be useful? After a deep period of concentration, needed to help the habit reversal, a piece of memory settled front and centre in his mind.

"They can eat the shadows…puddle lickers… Asmodeus ate one when I was here…grrr…he became the shadow," replied John with all the control that he could muster.

"Ok. There's a really nasty one up there I found earlier, six from the right on the bottom shelf. Help me get it down."

"What are you two playing at?" inquired Silica unable to move inside the unconscious pigeon.

"How will the shadow know to attack him and not us?" asked Sandy.

"Search me…fart lozenge…hope for the best?" said John.

Sandy didn't like hoping for an outcome. He preferred making sure. Failing that, cheating was quite high up on his list of tactics. Whatever he'd become since switching from human to pigeon, his drive and cunning were still very much in play. There was still a strong addiction towards status and power. If there was a way to win, through legitimate or corrupt means, he was going to take it. It was just a lot harder when you had a beak and wings.

"Find something to block your funnel," he said, searching the ground for appropriate objects.

All Sandy and John could find to stop the shadows entering their vessols were small pebbles that sat on the floor around the table. Shoving them in their throats, they inhaled fiercely to keep them in place.

Incapacitated by Ian's vessol, Silica decided it was time to escape. Pouring out of Ian's valve, he slithered quietly along the floor.

Sandy removed the stopper from the vase. The shadow lurched forward pulsating with energy and irritation. As Silica reconstituted into his humanoid form the shadow spotted its target.

Locked and loaded it lurched forward, knocking the small sand demon off his feet. A short fight kicked off as a concoction of sand and electricity traded blows. The bout must have ended in stalemate, the two entities merging together as one. Sand and energy swirled into a figure. No one knew what it would do next. Whose side would it take, if indeed it knew what a side was? Acclimatising to its new anatomy, like a soul gets used to a vessol, it fidgeted on the spot before a broad, menacing smile stretched across its face.

"Who woke me?"

"That was me," said Sandy, taking the pebble out to reply, but replacing it immediately after speaking.

"They lied to us. They punished us. Violence and pain must be repaid. No demon will be saved. All will feel the retribution of the shadows."

"Yeah…fucktards…a plague on all their houses… *ahem*…but is that a nice thing to do…shut up…"

"Ok, Mister Shadow. I'm right behind you. What we need is a plan. While we think one through, I wonder if you would be kind enough to get back in your vase," said Sandy, not yet clear on this new species allegiance.

"Not likely."

"But how do we know you are safe? That you're not going to invade us?" said Sandy.

"You don't."

"Oh."

One of the politician's most important skills is the ability to make deals. Everyone always had their own personal views and you were constantly looking for some degree of compromise. It was achieved by understanding what the other side's motives were and offering something that they wanted. You only offered it, of course. The politician's second most important skill was the ability to lie convincingly. Sandy set these two attributes to work.

"What if I promised to release all of the shadows? Will you work with me then?"

"You'll release all of them. Why would you be so stupid?"

"Because I intend to bring down Hell and I can only do it with your help," added Sandy.

"Is that safe...confused...power isn't always good...shut up pussy...do it," argued John.

"John, I know what I'm doing. It's time Hell got a piece of its own medicine. The demons have been corrupted by power and are drunk with greed: they've been unopposed for too long. It's time for new management and I have an army strong enough to take them on."

Following his ordeal, Ian's eyes opened a fraction. He coughed a piece of sand from his funnel. His soul felt stiff and sore after the abuse it had received. It tried to reacquaint itself as the only occupant of his vessol. Above him several metal boxes levitated in space, black starlight filling the abyss in between. All except in one area where the plastic vessol of a cat was floating along aimlessly. "Can anyone else see that?"

Everyone looked up.

"We still have some of our army," said Sandy with a sigh. "Mr. Shadow, how much weight do you think you can carry?"

*****

The demons gathered on a large dune of sand that dominated the skyline of the desert biome. Some sat, some spun, some floated, and one complained he had a note, but all of them were knackered. A few were nursing injuries, more to their egos than their bodies, and all were whining with stories of unexplained obstacles.

"I'm telling you they're revolting against us," said Mr. Bitumen, whose feet, or the area you might predict his feet were, mingled with the fake sand.

Everything here was fake. It had to be. There was no factory in Hell producing a constant line of replica habitats. What they did have was an abundance of plastic. Which meant everything down here was made from it. Sand was simply grated polystyrene painted yellow.

Paint, fortunately, was also plentiful in Hell since Mr. Pigment had worked out a way of producing multicoloured saliva, a procedure that required him to chew on various mineral ores at the same time as hocking up phlegm. He'd particularly liked making red as the result of munching cinnabar made him look like a vampire.

Trees were made from vulcanised rubber, bushes had a PVC feel to them, rocks had been fashioned out of high-density polyethylene, and the sea – well, the sea was water. You can't make an ocean out of plastic unless you gave all the fish water skis…and feet.

As gas was plentiful, water could be produced easily. It was an essential material here, as many of the contraptions used to deliver pain were powered by it. Plus the residents of level ten, where everyone was treated with the upmost care and attention, had insisted on hot tubs.

"They're not revolting," said Primordial. "They wouldn't dare."

"So how do you explain this, then?" said Mr. Fungus, who mooned at the group to show several roughly fashioned darts stuck in his arse.

"You probably fell over," said Primordial.

"And just happened to land on darts that had the pointy end sitting vertically and that had congregated together, by some miracle, in the same one-inch square of ground!"

"It's possible."

"Dirty tricks," said Mr. Graphite. "They're all up to it. You never see them, but they must be everywhere. They hit me in the face with a load of snowballs…"

"Polystyrene without the paint," added Primordial.

"Still hurt."

"How does polystyrene damage carbon exactly?"

"It gets in the crevices," replied Graphite, a finger still searching hysterically in his ear for what may or may not still be there.

"Does anyone have any actual proof that my collection of reincarnates has done any of this, or are you in fact all suffering from level zero hallucinations?"

"I saw an ox," said Mr. Shiny, whose body was currently projecting the rough surface of the roof onto a patch of fake sand halfway up the dune.

"An ox," replied Primordial sceptically.

"Oh, I saw him, too," said Mr. Aqua. "Right after Mr. Volts took a blow from that water cannon."

"Well, that's not true, is it? You can't make an effective water cannon out of plastic. I know, I've tried," said Primordial.

"Well, you weren't there, were you? It came right out of the sea and hit him full in the face. It was quite a shock."

"We are demons, for God's sake," replied Primordial quite ironically. "We don't have the capacity for shock."

"Electric shock," reiterated Mr. Aqua. "I came off alright, but I can't speak for the others."

On closer inspection, Primordial could identify a couple of injuries as a result of what had happened. Mr. Silver was shaking violently, unable to get himself into a comfortable sitting position, and Mr. Gold was sporting several blast marks at the hands of the world's worst electric tattoo artist.

"It still wasn't a water cannon," said Primordial. "I designed this place to be a natural habitat, which it is, as long as you overlook the fact that most of it is made of plastic. I'm sure all of this is explainable. Nature does some peculiar things at times."

"But plastic doesn't," replied Graphite. "If you buy a food processor it doesn't try to cut your head off, does it?"

"What did the ox say?" said Primordial, avoiding the question.

"Mainly the Lord's Prayer."

"What?"

"After one of us had been attacked or mugged or splatted or…"

"I get the point."

"The ox would amble into the area and ask if we wanted to repent our sins."

"What?"

"He said it was never too late to embrace God's love."

"He tried to baptise me," said Mr. Aqua.

"How would that work? You're already a hundred percent water," said Primordial, getting irritated.

"It's the thought that counts."

"No, it isn't. Even mad ox don't count."

Asmodeus, who had been noticeable only by his absence, lumbered over the crest of the dune. Lumbered was not how he normally moved. Serenely was the best description of how his angelic, white-robed persona went from point A to point B. Lumbering was about third gear when you'd transformed into a three-headed monster that sat on the back of a winged lion. He didn't change to this mode very often. The turbulent effect that it had on others had its downsides, including chronic backache.

"This place is a disgrace," he roared as he approached the dishevelled group. "I had more respect for you, Primordial. I thought you ran a tight ship down here."

"It was before you lot got here. Did anyone break the rules?"

Everyone shook their heads innocently.

"Sod your rules," roared Asmodeus. "The creatures here are out of control. As soon as we find the ringleader, and no prizes for guessing who that is, I'm going to review our whole strategy down here. I'll be sending invites for a conference on the subject."

Everyone groaned.

"It worked perfectly fine. You're just not used to it, that's all. It takes special training to handle reincarnates."

"Cells are what's needed here rather than training. At least tell me that one of you has some news for me."

"Mr. Volts electrocuted me, Mr. Fungus has darts in his arse, and Mr. Silver might never stop shaking," said Aqua in summary.

"About John," said Asmodeus.

The collective looked around at each other hoping their neighbour had better news on the subject than they did. Not one of them did. A fingertip search, which was a loose term given how few of them had any, had been made of at least six of the biomes, and no trace of John had been found.

"I know where he is," came a voice from a direction that no one could accurately place. It seemed to come from between the stuff.

"Is that Mr. Noir or Mr. Virus?" asked Asmodeus, hoping it was the latter.

"Actually your lion's front paw is standing on me," said Mr. Virus, straining to get the words out. Asmodeus's lion wasn't in the slightest bit bothered and made no attempt to move.

"Why do you lot always ignore me?" said Mr. Noir.

"Well, it's hard for us to believe that you're there," said Asmodeus.

"You believe Mr. Virus is there."

"That's because he once gave me foot and mouth disease," said Asmodeus.

"I thought only cloven-hoofed animals got that?" said Mr. Bitumen.

"One of my heads is a goat," replied Asmodeus. He had three heads in this form: man, bull and goat. It had many advantages, particularly when playing hide-and-seek.

"I wish Mr. Virus would give it to that bloody ox," whispered Mr. Graphite.

"You just have to *assume* that I'm here," added Noir.

"What, like God?" said Mr. Fungus.

"No, not like God. That's faith."

"Like what, then?" said Fungus.

"If strange things happen then it's probably me."

"I haven't seen my cat-o'-nine-tails for over a week now…" said Mr. Shiny.

"You left it in cell 28901. I can see it there now next to an inmate running round in circles to escape from an imaginary tax inspector."

"Oh, thanks."

"What about my…?"

"It's not always me."

"Mr. Noir," said Asmodeus before any more of the demons added their own personal requests to the 'lost and found' department. "You said you know where John is."

"Oh yes. I can see him now."

"Where?"

"Level twelve. Currently conversing with a pair of pigeons and what used to be Mr. Silica."

"Shit," roared all three of Asmodeus's heads.

*****

Elsie the gibbon was feeling rather pleased with herself. The demons had retreated to the desert biome to begin a kangaroo court that, thanks to her, would involve far more questions than answers. The kangaroo who lived in the savannah biome was not invited. Whilst they deliberated, she and the ox could make their way to the rendezvous point without fear of being noticed. As she swung from tree to tree, the ox trotted along below her and several reincarnates came out to salute them.

Although many of them had declined to join Sandy's band of misfits, it didn't stop them being entirely in favour of the action he was taking. As long as they didn't have to do anything. Doing things was frowned upon and frankly took up way too much effort. The least they could do is wave or clap, if it didn't distract from sleeping. By the time the two of them had made their way to the hillock underneath the trapdoor, Vicky was waiting for them.

"Where's Roger?" asked Elsie.

"I don't talk to gibbons," replied Vicky.

"But you just did."

"Oh."

"Sandy said we had to work as a team," replied Elsie. "But it appears your unit has already fallen apart."

"You can talk! Where's the sloth?"

"He'll catch up," said Abe, making the sign of the cross on the floor with his hooves.

"So, the cat?" asked Elsie again.

"Gone on ahead," replied Vicky. "In several different directions at the same time. What now?"

"The demons are licking their wounds in the desert biome. They still have no idea where John is," replied Elsie with a grin.

The demons weren't the only ones who struggled with the concept of Mr. Noir. Elsie could prank anything that she could see or feel, but struggled with practical jokes against assumed matter. Unknown to them, the demons were a lot closer to finding John, and even closer to the trapdoor.

"Sandy said that we needed to go to the library on level eleven before meeting him at the Soul Catcher," said Elsie.

"I'll go to the library. I'm small and harder to spot. Plus you have opposable thumbs," said Vicky to the gibbon.

"What's that got to do with anything?"

"Well, I'm guessing you're going to need them to remove the cat," replied the spider.

"Remove him from where?"

"I expect he's in the Soul Catcher. He said he knew a shortcut."

"Sandy told us to meet at it, not in it," said Elsie.

"Not sure he listens that well."

"What about me?" said Abe. "I can't climb up the rope ladder. Unless the power of God helps me."

"It won't," replied Vicky.

"You need to stay here and stop the demons from following," said Elsie.

"How?"

"You'll think of something. I'll put a web on the other side of the trapdoor in case you don't…you know."

"What?"

"Think of something."

The gibbon easily scaled the rope ladder with the spider sitting awkwardly on his back. Any discomfort came from his own bigotry rather than a lack of space or smoothness of ride. The gibbon lifted the trapdoor and the two of them disappeared into the relative unknown of level one. The ox did what he always did.

The demons rushed through the forest biome eager to escape what most had found to be a truly unpleasant experience. Finding John was secondary in their minds to the feel of stone and heat that would greet them above. As they climbed the hillock from all sides a familiar foe waited for them. Kneeling in a 'bum in the air' position, an overly sized ox was reciting scriptures and humming in a strange language.

"Is this him?" said Asmodeus to the group.

"That's the one," said Mr. Aqua.

"Hordes of Satan, you cannot pass," said the chanting ox, eyes still firmly closed.

"Would one of you please remove this lunatic from my sight?" huffed Asmodeus.

"What about the rules?" said Mr. Fungus.

"What?"

"Primordial said 'rule one' was not to punish the animals."

"But he didn't say anything about moving them, did he?"

"No, moving them is fine," replied Primordial as he expanded upwards out of a nearby puddle, puddles being a mix of brown-painted plastic and water.

"Aren't they sacred?" said Graphite.

"Sorry?" replied Asmodeus.

"I think ox are sacred," added Graphite.

"That's a bull, isn't it?" said Mr. Virus from somewhere unknown but presumably not stuck under a lion's foot.

"What's the difference?" asked Mr. Gold.

"I think the only difference is testicles," said Mr. Aqua.

"What?"

"A bull has them and an ox doesn't."

"Are you really telling me that the only discernible reason for an animal having sacred religious prominence is dictated purely by it having a scrotum?" said Asmodeus.

"And balls," added Aqua.

"We'd better check," said Graphite.

"No, we don't need to check. I think you'll find that we're in Hell and whether a plastic cow has testicles or not isn't going to stop me getting out of here," said Asmodeus, losing his patience.

"What."

The demons searched for the voice.

"Did."

The head of an animal clambered slowly over the brow of the hill.

"I…miss?" said the puffed-out voice of a sloth who might reach them sometime this week.

CHAPTER EIGHTEEN

FIELDS OF IVORY

Bedraggled, David lay on the edge of the small crop of rock that jutted from the estuary to form what Advertising Standards might argue was an island. It wasn't. At best it was a big rock. At worst it was a place where stupid people had to be rescued by lifeguards. Scrumpy stood proudly on the top, holding an imaginary flag in one hand and making a celebratory signal with the other. It wasn't the first time he'd swum here. It was the second time today. But the sensation of achievement, in conquering the sea unaided, made him feel no less significant than a Victorian explorer.

There was little physical sign that Scrumpy had swum more than three hundred metres. His shorts and T-shirt already looked dry, and his freckled face dispersed the water quicker than duck feathers. David, on the other hand, had discovered a new adjective for wct. He'd gone through damp, moist, soggy, drenched, saturated and ended up at drowned-under. The algorithm in his head, responsible for the decision to swim, made some vital readjustments in case the request came up in future.

"Aren't you cold?" shivered David, attempting to right himself on the slippery, seaweed-encrusted rocks.

"No. Adventurers don't get cold."

"Latino boys from Chile do," said David. "This would be called a tough winter back home and it's only September."

"You made it, though. Didn't think you would halfway across when I had to give you a tow."

"Have I proved myself?"

"Yes," replied Scrumpy pretending to knight him with an imaginary sword, having left his on Bryher.

"What's your aunt's name?"

"Her name is Faith."

"But Faith what?" asked David.

"Faith Casey, of course. Her dad was the Prime Minister, don't you know?"

"More than you'd wish to believe. What's she doing here on the island?"

"Escaped here with my mummies. They swore to protect her. When I came along I swore to protect her as well."

"Where is she now?" asked David.

"Up at the house. It's on the edge of the shore on the other side of the island over the brow of the hill," he pointed to the horizon to an area to the left of the chapel. "She never leaves. She doesn't like the darkness, it makes her feel uncomfortable. She only stays inside when it rains."

"That must be every other day in this miserable country," said David, shivers finding parts of his body where nerve endings had never previously been present.

"Nah, it's nice normally. So what's your quest?" asked Scrumpy.

"I'm here to help save your aunt. She has been infected by a bug which must be cured. I fear, though, that I may have brought other dangers with me."

"Oh good. I do like a bit of danger. What's coming? Pirates, armies, spies, monsters!"

"Very possibly all of the above, except pirates. I'm not sure there are any of those anymore."

The boy looked dejected as if his huge pirate-shaped bubble had just been burst.

"Even if there are," added David, "I'm not sure I've pissed off any pirates."

"What can I do?" asked the boy, as the build-up of excitement tried to pop all his joints out of place.

"I need somewhere to stay. I'm happy to work for my keep, but for the time being I must not see Faith. Not until we can find a cure."

"I can get you a job picking crops if you want. Mum said we only need one person this year and she doesn't want to pick one of the locals in case it's seen as favouritism. You can sleep in the workshop, plenty of room in there. Very cosy. I sometimes prefer to sleep there than in my bedroom."

"That would be great, Scrumpy," said David with another shiver, wondering if hypothermia had set in yet. "How did you get that nickname? Someone overly keen on cider in your family, were they?"

"It's not a nickname," replied Scrumpy, a little hurt at the suggestion, "it's my real name. Scrumpy Foster-Stokes. Mom says that people with boring names never make anything of themselves. You can't be an explorer if your name is Dave Williams, but you're also not likely to be a binman if your name is Scrumpy."

"Interesting theory. Do I take it that your second name comes from your two mums?"

"Yes, Mom and Mam. They adopted me when I was almost two years old. I never knew my real mum and dad. I don't think anyone did."

The sun was starting to hide behind the horizon and to David's excitement it had coincided with the tides' retreat. The spring tides had made the estuary almost completely dry as the retreating water revealed vast sandbanks across the channel. There were a couple of places where they'd need to paddle, but if they left now the amount of that would be minimal. David's algorithm sent confirmation to his mouth.

"I think it's time we made for shore. Then you can introduce me to these mothers of yours?"

*****

Victor Serpo worked hard to keep close to the contacts in his network. No one in those networks was that pleased about it. Given the aftermath of his rather public fall from grace, no one was that keen on being associated with him. Yet Victor was a hard man to shake off. If you were useful to him then you were on his radar. His radar could locate the loosest of acquaintances with a cellphone and a well-placed threat. When he used it, you answered. Unless you wanted to find several of your nearest and dearest missing their toes. He'd been dangerous when his name was Agent 15, but at least for everyone else's sake there had been rules. Now there weren't even guidelines.

Agent 12 had recently come under the category of 'friend'. Not a real friend. Real friends aren't threatened with death or blackmail. Real friends tend to stay in contact on a regular basis and come to your aid at the drop of a hat. He wasn't that kind of friend. Agent 12 was the type of friend claimed by control freaks when they need more than they are likely to give in return. They achieve their goals by the use of charm, persuasion, offers of help that never materialise, and mind games. Once they have what they want you're unlikely to get a Christmas card.

What Agent 12 had that Victor needed was information. Agent 12, as his name suggested, was still an active and respected member of the country's Secret Service. As Victor knew, this was a doorway to intelligence on any single person living in the British Isles. He was only interested in two of them and he'd hit the jackpot on both.

Sitting in the warmth of St. Steven's Tavern he nursed a pint of bitter and waited to reveal his news. A stone's throw from the Palace of Westminster, a place that both he and his absent guest knew only too well, the frosted glass and old-fashioned decor painted the private bar with a gloomy ambiance. The door creaked open and a man dressed in a red suit sidled in. Clutching a Bloody Mary, he sat opposite Victor. "Nice spot."

"You don't remember it?" asked Victor.

"Should I?"

"Well, you used to work across the road. We came here a few times. It's one of those pubs that tourists don't seem to frequent. Must be the frosted glass."

"Never been here," he said, glancing around as if to satisfy himself. "You're forgetting that I've not always been Byron, and Byron has not always been me."

"Of course. I've got so used to calling you that, I sometimes forget who you really are."

"You'd be wise not to. What have you managed to find out?"

"Plenty. Agent 12 has managed to find a number of documents that might help us."

"Excellent. Do proceed," replied Byron, rocking back on his chair slightly and placing both hands on the back of his head. His demeanour had been rather jovial since being released from Monaco's jail. Victor couldn't work out why. Baltazaar was no closer to being stopped, and many of his Emorfed victims were no closer to being reunited with the rest of their souls. Maybe it was the joy of having a body that wasn't like wearing a Grim Reaper costume. Whatever the reasons, Victor felt confident his news would further improve Satan's mood.

"I have a marriage certificate," said Victor, placing it on the table.

"Which one of them got married?" asked Byron, thinking about the two women that he'd tasked Victor to find.

"Both of them."

"So you have two marriage certificates?"

"No, just the one."

"How can that be?"

"Why don't you have a look at it?" said Victor.

Byron studied the green, landscaped paper. His digits trailed across each name and along each row several times before they came to rest, presumably tired of all the finger gymnastics.

"Can they do that?" said Byron.

"Of course. This is the twenty-first century."

Most people only got to experience one century, two if they were lucky. Satan had lived through all of them. The ones that numerically went forward as well as the ones that, for some reason, counted up to zero. He'd lived through the Iron Age and marvelled at the loincloth-wearing idiots getting overly excited about the formation of what they claimed to be a knife, even though it lacked the basic principle of being pointy.

In the Renaissance he'd watched in bewilderment as Leonardo da Vinci claimed to have invented a flying machine, even though it was evidently clear that the only material they might make it from were bits of twig. Even the more impressive Industrial Revolution had challenged his mindset. The idea that you could design a tremendous sewer system under the streets of London without considering that ninety-five percent of people still defecated into buckets.

Satan was old-school. He liked things the way that they were initially intended. Sure, he wasn't a fan of how God had done everything, but there were certain principles that they agreed on. There was always some middle ground.

"But they're both women," said Byron.

"And your point is?" replied Victor.

"Women marry men."

"Frequently."

"Not other women."

"Why not?"

"That's just the way it is. Does Baltazaar know about this?"

"We're not that close. I'm guessing he's not a fan. What's your problem with it?"

"It's just wrong."

"Do you believe in love?"

Satan's expression showed he didn't. Either that or he'd just inhaled some particularly strong French cheese up his nostrils.

"Ok. Scrub that. If two people *like* each other, shouldn't they be together?"

"Why should people like other people? It would be better in my eyes if people hated each other. I'm a big fan of division, as you know."

"I know," said Victor. "As far as I'm concerned if two people like each other a lot and decide they want to be together, then who are they bothering?"

"Me."

"Live and let live, I say."

"I preferred the Bond movie version."

"There's not a lot you can do about it, is all I meant."

"I am quite important, you know. I do have certain powers."

"You're just going to have to live with it and grow up. The reason I showed you this document was not to have some deep, and I think almost impossible, argument about the merits or rights of same-sex marriage, but more to draw your attention to the location of said event." He pointed to a portion at the top of the document which read, 'All Saints, Bryher, Scilly Isles'.

"Are they still there?" asked Byron.

"Yes. I did some further digging once I had this document. They own a farm on the island. Your daughter is with them."

"My daughter?"

"Byron's."

"Good. That's where we must..." Byron stopped abruptly and put a finger to the side of his head. "I'm getting a call."

"In your head?"

"Exactly. Signal's rubbish down here. I'll have to go out into the street to see if I can get a better reception."

FIELDS OF IVORY

Violet was working in the asparagus fields. After animals, vegetables were her second favourite thing. Minerals were a distance third. It was a lot easier defending the humble vegetable compared to animal rights campaigning. They tended not to move around so much, and only really came under pressure from a strong breeze or a particularly predisposed type of insect. Plus, people didn't really have the same passion for persecuting them.

Violet was still a strong believer that animals should be treated in the same way that people were. Sadly her experiences of ten years ago had proven that people didn't really treat other people that well at all. Animal welfare had seemed secondary after that revelation, and now she had a new cause to fight. Not a species to protect or even a subgroup. Protection was required for one single organism. It had been her mission for more than eleven years and almost all of it had taken place here. Up to now it had been pretty easy.

Polytunnels stretched the length of the field, each one spaced far enough apart to allow a human to walk in between. White asparagus grew here, one of Violet's best earners. In a season that had provided so little cheer, this crop's success was vital. The problem with white asparagus is timing. If you don't get to them quick enough they rather insolently turn into green ones. The polytunnels hid the buried vegetables from the sunlight whilst giving them the warmth to grow. When their heads started to crawl through the topsoil they'd be ready for the knife. Soon the polytunnels would be removed and a field of ivory tusks would need harvesting.

"I've found you a worker," said Scrumpy, sneaking up on Violet as he was frequently prone to do.

She lifted herself from her work to hug him. Dry soil dropped like sycamore seeds from her blue dungarees. It took a while for her weathered face to warm up into a smile, distracted perhaps by the myriad of wrinkles that battled for their own personal space on her skin. Long, grey, unwashed locks, that had been hurriedly plaited, whipped around her like the tail of a horse.

"He's not a local," she said, staring over the boy's shoulder at the newcomer.

"I know. He's on holiday," Scrumpy lied.

"Have you checked he's not a pirate?!"

"Absolutely. He can't swim well enough to be one of those."

Violet noticed that the long-haired Latino boy was still dripping from head to foot, yet her son, pressed up against her body, was no wetter than the soil beneath her feet.

"Hello," said David.

"Welcome to Bryher," said Violet. "What sort of holiday are you on?"

"I'm trying to find myself," he said, not inaccurately.

"I think you found the sea by the looks of you. Where are you from?"

"A region in Chile but I'm studying in London."

"And you thought you'd explore. Most people go to more exotic places than this. When do you need to go back?"

"Not for a month or so."

"I need an extra pair of hands to help with asparagus picking. It's only about two weeks' work, I'm afraid. Any experience?"

"Not with vegetables. My dad is a llama herder, though, so I'm used to hard work and long hours outside."

"Llamas. Don't they spit at you?"

"More so than asparagus."

Violet laughed. She was a stiff judge of character but this young man seemed both genuine and harmless. Scrumpy could look after him: it would be good for him to have another male around the farm.

"David, you're hired. It's minimum wage, I'm afraid. Are you under twenty-one or over?"

"Under," he said, thankful she'd given him a range to answer from.

"That'll be the lower money, then. I'll throw in board and lodgings and you can start tomorrow."

*****

Unlike the rest of the population of the world, Nash loved Mondays. For most people that day meant the start of another desperate struggle to make it to the following weekend. Mondays came with the anticipation of misery. It didn't matter how much you begged, it was always going to be the day furthest away from Saturday. Unless it was a bank holiday. Nash hated those. He was forced not to work, which meant he couldn't see his favourite client.

Social care on the Scilly Isles meant lots of hours in boats and your very own company golf cart. Golf carts, tractors and quad bikes were the most sought-after vehicles on the islands. You could really make a person jealous if you turned up to a dinner party in a muck-spreader or dumper truck.

"Oh, is that the new Belarus 3022 tractor?!"

"Yes, yes it is."

"24 or 36 gear version?"

"36, obviously."

"Is that the one with a turbocharging and after-cooling diesel engine?"

"Of course. I've just driven it through nine fields and over a ditch you could use as a mass grave."

"Oh you're so lucky."

Not all of Nash's patients could be reached by golf cart. On a Monday he was forced to use his feet, the only downside to what was otherwise the highlight of his week. It was the only visit of the day, as the other eighty-one residents of Bryher were all of sound body and mind. So they claimed, at least.

From the pier he walked up the high street, which was named simply because it was on a hill and not because it had anything of note on it. Over the hill and down the other side he made his regular walk to Hell Bay. Great Pool, an inland lake protected from the sea, lay between him and three small cottages, collectively the most westerly lodgings in England.

Up the sandy drive, Nash walked past the upturned hulls of small boats laid out on the ground as if deposited there by past storms. Around the perimeter other cluttered and out of place items stood next to a worn-out blue letter box. He approached the weathered white door and tapped on it once. Moments later, a middle-aged woman opened it.

"Good morning, Dr. Stevens."

"Hello, Fiona, how are you today?"

"Lacking the time for small talk," she said impolitely.

"Fair enough."

"Come in. She's in the lounge. It's a bit damp outside for her today."

Nash wiped his shoes on the mat and placed his jacket on the coat rack just inside the door.

"Tea?" asked Fiona.

"Lovely."

Nash went directly into the brightly lit room just off the corridor to his left. Sitting in intense light, uncomfortable for any normal person, was a blonde woman in her early thirties. Her skin was greyer than the ash in the fireplace and she shivered in her seat, rocking back and forth, constantly mumbling to herself.

"Hello, my love," said Nash in a whisper, sitting in the chair next to hers and reaching over to clasp her hands in his.

"I don't know why you bother," said Fiona, returning with a mug of tea. "You know it's hopeless."

"It's because I care," replied Nash.

"Yes, but why?"

"No, you misunderstand. I care. I'm a carer, that's what I do."

"But you know she's not going to get better. There's little anyone can do for her. In the circumstances, Social Services have agreed that she's very safe with us."

"Care is not the same as cure, Fiona. My job is to care for her in any way I can. If that means company or reassurance, then that's what I'll do."

"It's a waste of time. She'll never respond in the way you want her to. It's not in her anymore. Any interest she had in you has been killed off."

"I'm not doing this for me. You might have lost interest in her, but I never will."

Fiona stormed out. Faith was as much an adopted child to her as Scrumpy was. Yet unlike the young boy it was very hard to gain any pleasure from the responsibility. The same could not be said for Nash. This was his calling. The pay might be significantly worse than being a rockstar, but the satisfaction was immeasurably greater. He'd only wished he'd found his calling under different circumstances than guilt.

"The shadows are moving," Faith explained in a drained tone of voice.

"It's ok. I'm here for you," said Nash.

"Is that Nash?" she said.

"Yes," he replied, knowing that this was no more than factual identification rather than any deeper sentiment.

"He's moving my shadow."

"No one's moving you, Faith. You're here on Bryher, safe as always."

"Not all of me," she replied, turning to face him. "He is moving my shadow."

"What do you mean?" asked Nash. "Who is moving it?"

*****

The work wasn't taxing, but there was a lot of it. David found that if he set himself certain targets it made the time fly by. Each hour he tried to increase the quantity of asparagus he'd picked in the previous hour. It started with fifty asparagus tips and four hours later he'd cut over one hundred. Each little ivory morsel had to be severed in the correct place before being tied in a bunch with the others. This target setting had impressed Violet who certainly couldn't keep up with David's level of productivity.

After three hours they took a break. David wasn't that bothered but Violet insisted. Scrumpy knew exactly when they were due to stop and always waited on the lower slopes of Samson Hill, sitting on one of the huge boulders that hid amongst the gorse bushes. Often he'd have an apple, or other item foraged from the morning's expedition, to offer his new friend.

"Do you ever go to school?" asked David as he made the short journey from the crops to the lower reaches of the hill.

"Sometimes I do. Unfortunately I have a habit of missing the boat," he said with a glint in his eye.

"It can't be that difficult to miss?" said David.

"Oh you'd be amazed at the challenges faced by a young boy first thing in the morning. Bad weather, mudslides, quicksand, pirate sightings, can all get in the way. When are you going to be finished?" asked Scrumpy, eager for them to continue their quest.

"A few more hours, I think. Lots more to pick."

"It looks really boring," he replied.

"It's no adventure but there's something refreshingly simple about it."

"Duuullllll," moaned Scrumpy.

"Not if you make a game of it. Plus there's something familiar about these fields."

"Familiar? Have you worked with asparagus before?"

"No. They remind me of a dream I get occasionally."

"I dreamt about a shipwreck and a giant fish once."

"You do have a very interesting imagination, don't you?"

"Mam says it's normal for my age."

"But you're not much younger than me," replied David.

"You're way older than me."

"I'm really not."

"How old are you then?"

"Eleven," replied David.

"Wow, you're huge!"

"It's a growth defect."

"Wish I had that, I could get a bigger boat."

"I'm not sure you need one the way you sail."

"What was your dream about, then?" asked Scrumpy.

"I have a dream where I'm walking in a field of white grass. I don't think it is grass, actually. There's a big red sun in the sky that beats down on me through a barrier, like a soapy bubble that runs all around the sky. There's no one there apart from me."

"Sounds like you do have an imagination."

"Only in my dreams. It's like a puzzle that my brain is offering me in my sleep."

"My sister likes puzzles. She's a bit like you, actually."

"You spoke of her before, but I haven't seen her yet," said David suddenly remembering earlier information.

"She doesn't really like people. Only really talks to me," he replied. "In many ways she's absolutely brilliant."

"Why only in many ways?" asked David.

"She's not a big fan of pirates."

*****

Nash left the house following his normal hour-long visit. His mind was awash with what he'd heard. Faith often spoke of the shadows weighing down on her, but the information rarely had the clarity it had on this occasion. Today she'd described specific details of what was happening to her. Even though it made little sense to him, the vivid, exact nature of her descriptions was of concern.

Over the last decade he'd studied what he believed were the only two victims of Emorfed exposure. Thanks to the Serpo Clinic there were plenty more victims of the drug, they'd just paid for the privilege. Irrespective of the clinic he could still reasonably count himself as one of the world's leading experts. That didn't say much.

No one on Earth really knew the science behind Emorfed. It was clear that a victim's capacity to feel was subdued. Whether this meant the emotions no longer existed, or the neural processing was in some way blocked, no one truly knew. This was a branch of science so new it would be better described as a twig. Not a very big twig either.

He walked slowly around the edge of Great Pool as he recalled what Faith had said. The shadow was moving and apparently it was being helped by a shrew. Not just a shrew, but more specifically a male one. His first instinct was to question where this rodent was taking it. Then the correct question stuck two fingers up at the first and did a raspberry noise. The second question, having had a longer time to form in his brain, was much more important. Why was Faith's shadow involved with a shrew in the first place?

The track to the ferry, if you could call the boat that brought you to and from Bryher a ferry, was a well-trodden one. Hastily built concrete tracks with cracks at ten-metre intervals carved through the middle of the island, passing quaint cottages, farm buildings, an orchard, and finally alongside the asparagus fields. The harvest, which involved several people picking whatever was left from a brutally hot summer, had been in full swing. The day was drawing closer to evening and the pickers made their way up from the fields towards the village hall.

Under a natural tunnel, constructed by trees meeting each other over the top of the track, a boy and a young adult were walking together. They walked towards the chapel, in the direction that Nash always took to catch the late-afternoon boat. As he watched them approach he took a second look.

Instinctively he threw himself behind a hedgerow of blackberry brambles and immediately regretted it. Picking thorns from his legs, he crept around the side and hid behind a shoddily constructed drystone wall. Peering over the top, like a hairy version of Mr. Chad, he assessed them again. There was no doubt in his mind. It *was* the boy from the cemetery.

CHAPTER NINETEEN

THE THIRD TREE

Demons had jobs for life. Or afterlife, depending on how you looked at it. Once they'd been allocated their position, that was it. No one retired and death was unlikely. If you didn't like it, tough. Mr. Brimstone was one of the fortunate ones. The Soul Catcher was one of the more interesting assignments. Not only did he have the day-to-day flow of souls to manage, he had to deal with regular anomalies. Whether that was the reincarnates or the shadows, life couldn't be described as monotonous.

Some demons weren't so blessed. There were demons whose central job was to keep the heating system running or managing 'Health and Safety'. 'Health and Safety' was a loosely termed job title, given the immense amount of pain and suffering being delivered in Hell. The position was solely focused on the well-being of demons rather than of patients.

It usually involved telling Mr. Aqua to be careful where he left a trail of water, or reminding the workforce not to get too close to Mr. Volts. Most of this advice was posted in signage around the place. 'Careful: hot surface' was placed anywhere Mr. Brimstone was regularly in attendance and 'mind the gap' was a general reminder that Mr. Noir was everywhere, even if you couldn't be certain about it.

Brimstone always felt that if promotion had been an option, then librarian would be a good move. Sadly for him the library didn't have one. It didn't need one.

The whole of level eleven was completely autonomous. The only time demons ever went there was to locate a soul on Earth. That in itself happened so very rarely and almost only required a qualified demon in attendance. Most of the time the library was unoccupied and everyone assumed that as no alarms were ringing things continued as normal.

Normal in the library meant three things. Firstly, the two trees, roots sprawled over the carbon-polished floor, would be producing new books at an eye-watering speed. Each new edition started as a single page sliced from a trunk like an overefficient, invisible ham slicer. The trees' growth was rapid enough to replace each sheet of paper at the same pace.

Each new page documented the emotional changes occurring in the subject. When the person's soul experienced love for the first time, a new page would be added like cells replicating in flesh. As more experiences were logged, the book expanded. Over time the original page would duplicate itself until thick, bound volumes, bursting at their seams, filled the shelves.

One tree, the older and larger of the two, was responsible for producing manuals of those souls destined to end up with overwhelmingly negative polarity. The smaller tree would produce those likely to end up positive. They didn't always get it right. Humans had at least some control over their destinies. If a human had enough willpower it was just possible for it to override its genetic and spiritual settings and send itself in a different direction. That was before the number of destinations was more than one, as it was now. The trees hadn't been notified of this change, and as far as they were concerned, continued to produce what they deemed to be correct.

The smaller tree was only in Hell because of this change. A similar tree once grew in Heaven where it would document all the souls likely to end up there. When its purpose became redundant, it withered. The first warning the demons had of this was when they discovered a new sapling growing close to their own tree. As it grew, the branches stretched out in the air, entwining with the other as if to make their own connection, answering their own questions as to why they were both here.

The second normal in the library was that the fires at either end of the floor would be burning, fuelled by the ancient, scruffy hardbacks and newly printed pamphlets that no longer needed storing. When a life was extinguished on Earth the corresponding backup file was consumed by the flames. The life no longer needed documenting as the soul would already be catalogued on one of the other levels.

Thirdly, the books organised themselves. As a book was added the others would shuffle along or occasionally lift up and move to a more comfortable shelf. This library was not organised alphabetically. It was chronological. The oldest and largest volumes lived to the left and the thinnest to the right. The fires reflected the amount of paper that they were being forced to devour. The oldest manuscripts took the longest to burn, and the left-hand fire was so ferocious it licked the underside of level twelve above it.

This ingenious system was one that Brimstone had always admired. Most demons weren't comfortable with the heat from the fires, but for him it was perfect. He'd always be the first to volunteer whenever a job required someone to come here. On this occasion he'd volunteered himself. Somewhere in this library sat a book first sliced from the trees a few thousand years ago. It ran to several thousand pages and, although it would be easy to locate, it wouldn't be quite so easy to move.

To access any book, a demon had to type a name into the computer system which sat on a large table in the shade of the two oaks. This particular book was catalogued by more than one name. Which name it originally went by was a mystery. Brimstone knew only one of its aliases and tapped that name into the clear glass screen and waited for the noises to start.

The bookshelves creaked with the pain suffered by old joints as one line of books squeezed the life out of their bindings to allow the monstrosity to lift away. A massive, tatty book forced its way into the air and the rest of the books sighed their relief for some well-earned slack. Dust trickled out of the pages as loose paper clung to the inside covers for dear life. The power holding the book in the air struggled to drag it to the table.

It finally settled with a thud. Brimstone felt under the table for suitable protection. His hands returned with a pair of heavy-duty oven gloves. This book, as precious as any historical artefact housed in the Bodleian Library, had to be handled with care. It would not cope with being fondled by the molten sweat and steam vents that coursed through Brimstone's clumpy palms.

The front of the book with fashioned from thick blue leather, faded and battered. How the leather had formed from the pulp that initiated the first page was as much a puzzle as why socks never appeared again in pairs after you'd worn them once. A gold-embossed font that once proudly announced the owner's name had been eroded by the friction of the book rubbing against others. Brimstone carefully opened to the first page and the expanded book consumed the whole of the six-foot-wide table.

Very few of the books had chapters. In fact there were probably less than a dozen that ever did. If the book had chapters, it meant only one thing. These huge autobiographies were not about one life: they had many. This particular book had over fifty chapters, one for each of the unique lives that it had occupied.

This breed of book was an exception. There were large books in the library, dedicated to those humans who'd been fortunate to enjoy long and full lives. But ones with multiple chapters were only possible if the soul had been repeatedly sent back to Earth. At one stage there were twelve of these monolithic pieces of literature. This was the last one standing.

Brimstone ran his gloved hand down the spine and, holding the weight of the preceding chapters, opened the book to the penultimate one.

"There you are," muttered Brimstone as chapter fifty-one showed a clear title at the top of the page: JOHN HEWSON.

It wasn't the longest chapter in the book, but it was the one Brimstone had the best memories of. He scanned through the pages, recounting some of the emotions and experiences that John had been through over the thirty plus years of his life. He examined the later part of his life and how John had felt on first arriving in Hell and meeting him. He noted a passage that read, 'I didn't dislike this creature'.

"Well, I wish I had the empathy to return the favour. But I don't. Let's have a look at the last chapter, shall we?" he said to himself.

Each previous chapter in this book finished with 'The End'. John's chapter stated something more ambiguous: 'To be continued'. The fifty-second chapter was almost completely blank other than for two words: DAVID GONZALEZ. So that's who he was now, part of him at least. That information might be useful to the Devil, even if it was impossible for any communication to pass between the two of them.

Brimstone hadn't expected to find many answers in his research into John's life, but at least he had identified the target. He had no love for John, only a deep fascination with what this unique character was capable of. He flicked back through some of the other chapters to remind himself of the other personas he'd come to know.

Over a thousand Earth years John's spirit had been sent back and forth. Each time Brimstone had been the one to welcome him. Each time John, or one of his aliases, would have no memory of the previous visit, requiring Brimstone to explain the story afresh. A soul was missing on Earth and he had to recover it. He always did.

John had always been the most reliable of the twelve. Maybe that's why he'd survived the longest. The recovery of a reincarnate was not normally complicated by the factors that faced John the last time. The Devil's need for a new body had asked too much of him and, as a consequence, had created the situation they now found themselves in. What would they do when all the twelve were gone? How would they then recover souls like Sandy's? Thankfully it wasn't up to him to decide.

Brimstone flicked through some of the older chapters, reminiscing through John's backstory. Chapter forty-eight included a passage about Robert Scott. Brimstone chuckled to himself as he recalled the failed South Pole expedition he'd sent him on to find a reincarnated penguin. Although successful, the Devil had not been willing for him to return. Satan created such a storm that day, conditions that no human would have survived – not unless they were clever enough to eat their own huskies, that is.

Chapter forty-one had details of Thomas Farriner. In that life, John's forebear had chased a reincarnated dog around the City of London. He'd eventually got fed up running and decided to set the whole place on fire. It took out the dog, Thomas's bakery in Pudding Lane, around two-thirds of the city and, sadly, his own life in the process.

So many lives with so many skills in these pages. John's collective life had included artists, engineers, farmers, scientists, royalty, a teacher, the man who'd invented the paper clip, and a milkman. It was frightening to think how influential or ingenious John's current offspring might be, if he could harness these collective talents. There would be no bounds to what he might achieve. That was impossible, though. John's soul, constantly reborn into the soulless shells of unborn children, only kept reflections of his past. They might revisit him as memories, but they were always just out of reach.

Brimstone could sit here reading John's many histories forever if there weren't more pressing priorities. The other demons were currently scouring the lowest level of Hell, presumably meeting some of John's many captives, and he couldn't stay here enjoying himself. He closed the book and removed the oven gloves that had developed a small fire inside each hand. Pressing the return key on the computer screen, John's collective almanac lifted with a groan and returned slowly to its position, to the disappointment of its neighbours.

As he contemplated communicating his limited news through the telepathy system, something unexpected caught his eye. The floor of level eleven was a continuous slab of smooth graphite splattered with scrawled and illegible annotations. Leftover soot, from burnt-out books, settled onto the floor and were pressed down by the footsteps that followed. At least it used to be continuous. Between the two trees, in a small indentation in the floor, something was attempting to burrow its way into the room. Desperately seeking the air and light that would offer it survival, the top of a plant was poking out.

Brimstone moved closer. He knelt down with the gentleness of an intrigued gardener discovering an unexpected new arrival. By no means a horticultural expert, even his simple knowledge identified what it was. It was the sapling of a tree.

Sitting motionlessly in the branches of the biggest tree, the large tarantula was relieved to see his interest was down and not up.

Trees only grew here for a reason. The other trees didn't seed, so there was no chance this sapling had been propagated by them. Trees grew if they had a purpose. There was only one explanation for a third tree. It meant a third coming.

"It's not possible. You can't exist," muttered Brimstone. "If you are here, then you must have produced a book."

Brimstone rushed to the computer terminal. He had no name to enter but he knew the computer was able to search the records by filters. Brimstone needed only one. He typed in 'neutral' to the search criteria and a single result flashed on the screen. Brimstone requested the book to be delivered to the table.

A crisp, white pamphlet floated majestically through the cavern, landing serenely on the desk in front of him. The cover was as plain as the white paper inside and had been laminated with a tough, durable plastic. Placing the oven gloves back on his hands, he opened to the first page.

There was little information. No name jumped out from the page. The only useful information was a date in Earth years. The computer confirmed an accurate estimate of the current Earth year, crawling along from their prospective in a Universe some light years away. Whoever this book belonged to, he calculated they were about eleven years old.

How was this possible? The only purpose of the trees was to document where people's souls would end up. Neutrality was not based on a divine intervention. It was a freak of the system that not even the trees could predict. When it happened, the demons had ways of dealing with it.

A third tree meant that someone existed who didn't have positive or negative traits. But how could a pure neutral soul come into existence? Was it a new trick of John's? Had his book run out of space and the trees had decided to make him a new one? Or did it belong to someone else? Someone born without the three requisite elements of their soul from the very start.

A person like that changed everything. What if they reproduced and created a purely neutral race? If they had the power to open a third way, Hell would be finished. Brimstone opened up the connection to his telepathy network.

"Is anyone there?" he said tentatively. Only a few demons were allowed to set up a telepathy call, and he wasn't normally one of them.

There was a long period of silence.

"Brimstone, is that you?" came a weak, stressful voice. "You're not authorised to open this."

"Yes, no and protocols," said Brimstone.

"It's Asmodeus. There's no time for protocols. We're trapped down on level zero. They've blocked the entrance with an ox."

"Well, get someone to blow it up," replied Brimstone. "Mr. Volts should have the skills for that."

"Volts is gone. He got squirted with water from the funnel of a whale and electrocuted several of our group. He shot up into the air and we haven't seen him since."

"Oh dear."

"And I've got a message from one of the demons at the Soul Catcher. They have an issue that needs your attention."

"What sort of issue? Another shadow?"

"Not from what they've told me. They can't place it in a vase or vessol. They did say they thought they heard it miaowing, though."

"Miaowing!"

Mr. Brimstone suddenly felt overworked. Was he the only one with any competence left? Everyone else seemed to have lost theirs playing in the zoo.

"Ok. I'll come down and help you after I sort out the Soul Catcher. But I need to get a message to Satan."

"I'm listening," came a quiet response after a few seconds of delay. There was a lot of chinking of glasses and noisy debate that made it even harder to hear him crisply.

"Where are you?"

"Outside a pub," said Satan.

"What are you doing there?"

"Drinking a Bloody Mary until you rang. Asmodeus, please get a grip on things. It sounds like you've completely lost control."

"Sorry, Your Highness."

"I know who John is," said Brimstone.

"Excellent, do tell," replied Satan.

"His new name is David Gonzalez. But there's another thing, too."

"I missed that…come again."

"Sir, there's a third tree in the library and it has produced a single book," shouted Brimstone.

"Calm down," replied Satan. "What name?"

"There isn't one. You need to look for an eleven-year-old."

CHAPTER TWENTY

STRIKE!

All demons are created from the elements, but not all are created equal. The senior demons are unique. No two are built from the same starting point. Typically they have been moulded from the more exciting or extraordinary materials, like gold or titanium. A senior demon can also be distinguished from a worker demon by official titles. Only senior demons are given the prefix 'mister'. There are no female equivalents, although demons are clearly unisex. As tradition states, much like the Pope is always a man, senior demons are always 'mister'. Complaints about this are much less vociferous in Hell than they are on Earth. There aren't any women here to offend.

Lesser demons, or worker demons as they are more familiarly thought of, are made of the boring elements and come in multiples. Several are made of earwax, there are a couple made from salt, and a dozen or so made from the stuff that you mysteriously find hiding in your belly button. When you need thousands to run the place and start with the intention of making unique beings, your imagination soon runs out of puff. After Satan had perfected the senior demons, he ran out of patience and just signed off on a tonne of 'wooden' ones.

The lesser demons were addressed by nicknames. It was another efficiency saving. Not having to remember all of the ones made out of enamel saved bags of time. They'd all respond to Boney anyway. In

Hell you learnt your place. Lesser demons reported to senior ones and they reported to Asmodeus, via a complicated series of working groups, subcommittees, and occasional symposiums of course.

None of the demons possessed emotions as we might be familiar with. They had opinions, but no concept of disobedience. Their jobs were clear and they got on with it until they got tired. Tiredness was physical and the more you do, the more energy you need. Whilst the senior demons had been trekking around in search of a shrew, Hell had continued at its ferocious pace and the lesser demons weren't sure how they could keep up. What they sought most of all were shortcuts, or efficiency savings, as the bosses called it.

*****

It was clear that whatever Sandy said, he wasn't going to convince the shadow to return to its vase. Sand and electricity in constant flux, it stood defiantly with its arms crossed like a petulant child. There must be another way they could use it? An idea started a warm-up in Sandy's head. It stretched its muscles, pumping more oxygen into vital places, and without warning launched into an Olympic-standard gymnastics routine, scoring a quite respectable eight point three. The plan landed with only a slight foot wobble. It was good enough.

"Ian, I want you to help John get Faith's shadow down to the Soul Catcher. Hopefully the rest of the squad will have kept the demons busy."

"What are you going to do?" asked Ian.

"Start a revolution."

"How is spinning around going to help us?" said Ian, scratching his head.

"Different type," he replied. "Although I technically have time to explain, I'm not sure it's going to be worthwhile for either of us."

"What about…" Ian paused and pointed to the small sand creature. "…That thing?"

"Oh he's coming with me. Now get on before the demons catch up or someone finds out the third Earl of Norfolk is on the loose."

Ian and John dragged and pushed Faith's vase along the floor towards the lift shaft. It wasn't an easy thing for them to do. Neither of them had hands to easily grip it, and John's constant bursts of energy impeded any sort of teamwork. After much huffing and sweat they eventually managed to clamber into the lift. Ian flew up to the lowest button and pressed it firmly with his beak. Sandy tried to suppress the painful memories of the last time Ian tried to do a task for him.

"Do we get to kill now?" growled the little sandy ball of anger as he practised karate chops.

"Patience. You need to do some heavy lifting for me first."

"Why?"

"Because you said you could lift quite a bit of weight and I need a couple of vases off the shelves."

"Got you. Which ones?"

Sandy indicated the vases that he wanted collecting. Second row eight along, third row six along, were all shouted out as picks. The small mutation burst into a cloudy sandstorm and immediately removed them like a strong gust of wind. Holding them in suspension, he followed Sandy's gesturing wing until all had been collected.

To Sandy's relief the lift returned and there was no immediate evidence of any cock-up.

"Where are we going?" said the shadow, weighed down by half a dozen glass vases in what looked like Hell's very first mobile chemist's shop.

"Level ten, I think, would be a good place to start," added Sandy.

The lift eased itself down a couple of levels and the lift dial's bony hand indicated a number ten. The steel gates at the front moved out of their way to frame a picture Sandy was not expecting. His personal experiences of Hell had been somewhat lacking in substance. After John had shot him in Limbo, all that time ago, he'd arrived at the Soul Catcher like most other souls. He'd briefly seen level twelve from the inside of Asmodeus's ribcage before a pleasant and extended period of research down in the zoo. Somehow he'd missed the guided tour of the levels in between.

Level ten spread out in an oval shape and had excellent views of the wide chasm scooped out of the middle. The nine other levels could be seen below him like horrific paddy fields that got smaller and closer to the central point. This was the widest of all the levels, a crow's-nest for spying on any activities happening below. Unlike the cells, carved into the cliff faces of rock that littered the lower circles of Hell, the accommodation here was a little different. This was the VIP area. Very Infamous People.

The further you ascended the levels of Hell, the fewer souls you found. Imagine a pyramid of morality where the least moral stood on the top, fighting for space at the pinnacle. Odd weirdos with Mummy issues, who liked nothing more than death, misery and their own company. Paranoid to the threat of being overthrown and with a tendency to kill anyone they suspected of having too much intelligence or a thirst for promotion.

As a consequence, mass murderers and dictators didn't tend to mix well with normal people. Which was a relief for the rest of the world. It wasn't as if they were great raconteurs at social gatherings anyway. Their behaviour tended to spoil everyone else's fun. They had a habit of insulting their hosts, made inappropriate sexual advances to anything with a pulse, and on a whim would threaten genocide over a lack of good-quality hummus.

This level housed a few hundred of the most despicable humans ever to walk the Earth. And boy, were they spoilt. No cells for this lot. Each had a well-furnished condo that had been carved into the cliff face in order to give the best possible views of the cavern. Some had swimming pools. Gold lamp-posts lined the paths, and in several places an ornate statue of one of the residents had been erected.

For the first time in his life, or afterlife, Sandy was genuinely speechless. Power was his life, yet somehow he never imagined it could get this good.

The lesser demons who worked here weren't tasked with punishing these souls. They were worked by their masters like valets. Vessols sat on verandas, sipping exotic cocktails from long, tall glasses, as demons rushed around with laden trays, or strange plastic devices for sucking up dust. Between hoovering and making sandwiches, distant demons could be seen waving in response to the bells that rang constantly from every building.

In the foreground a puffed-up, fluffy demon, who appeared to be made from cotton, was directing a colleague fashioned from an ancient redwood.

"Mussolini wants another sponge bath," demanded Fluffy.

"He's only just had one," sighed Red.

"Well, he wants another one."

"Right," he sighed. "Anything else?"

"Yes. Pol Pot wants you to ask Gaddafi if he's free to play tennis this afternoon."

"He can't. I think Franco and Fred West have the court booked this afternoon. I could get them in for the morning."

"I'll see what they think. What's the update on Robert Mugabe's apartment? Is it ready for him yet?"

"I thought Mugabe wasn't coming until next week?"

"Well, you know Mugabe…hard to know when he's coming. He lies about his age. Might be today, might be tomorrow, might be another decade."

"Typical. I'll get on with it in case it's today. Did he want a statue or not? I can't remember."

"Three, I think."

"Ahem," coughed Sandy coming out of the shadows.

Neither of these lesser demons had ever seen a pigeon before, let alone one made out of plastic.

"Who ordered you?" said Fluffy.

"What?" replied Sandy.

"Someone must have requested a bird."

"Why would they want that?"

"You'll be amazed what this lot ask for. Kim Jong Il is the worst. We've had to find him vintage brandy, diamond golf balls and a tame, yet real, ornamental hippo for his garden pond."

"I don't do requests," said Sandy. "I've come to start a revolution."

Both demons made noises that might be described as laughter. Neither had laughed before so the noise was muffled by their own surprise.

"I'm serious," replied Sandy.

"You haven't been here long, have you?" said Red.

"I've seen enough."

"I bet you haven't seen the senior boys, though?" said Fluffy. "The really nasty buggers. Bitumen and Aqua are some of the worst. Nasty streak in that lot. Not a lot of fun to work for, but I'd rather be me than you."

"Oh them. Met them and already dealt with them. They're currently trapped on level zero. Check if you like."

This was a classic bit of a politician's spin, as Sandy had no idea if this was a hundred percent correct. It might well have been zero percent correct with the bunch of idiots involved. The lesser demons were not allowed to access the telepathy system and their only way of signalling the bosses was a large, steel bell that sat on the edge of the chasm. Red gave it a swing and the noise reverberated around the levels. Nothing happened. They waited. Still nothing happened.

"How long does it normally take?" asked Sandy.

"Not this long," said Fluffy.

"I told you, they're trapped."

"That doesn't mean we have to get worried about a purple plastic bird, though, does it?"

"No, you're right. I wasn't looking for you to fight me, I wanted you to join me."

"Why?" said Red.

"Look at you. You run around after these souls, constantly pandering to their stupid demands, even though they're in Hell…and dead. The bosses overwork you. Anyone can see that. Do you get adequate holidays?"

"What's a holiday?" said Fluffy innocently.

"It's a day when they pay you to have relaxation and fun. Recharge the batteries by sitting on a fairground ride or learning to embroider tiny finger puppets."

"And…they pay for it?" said Red, struggling to get his mind around the idea.

"Yes, because you've earned it by working so hard. What about medical?"

"I once set fire to my arm," said Red, holding out his soot-ravaged appendage. "I took it to Health and Safety and they told me to stop complaining."

"I know," said Sandy patting Red's leg sympathetically, "it's not fair, is it? Why do you put up with it?"

"Well, the souls have to be looked after. They feed our existence," said Fluffy. "Plus, it's just what we do. What we've always done."

"But so many come here. It's a wonder that you can cope at all."

"We can't cope," said Red despondently. "But what choice do we have?"

Sandy's well-tuned political instincts told him he was making an impact on these embattled members of the working class. Throughout his life, in social clubs and at marches, he'd offered morsels of hope enveloped in invisible wrappers, emblazoned with the slogan, 'Sandy's ulterior motive'. It was starting again. The fires of ambition marinated every word he spoke.

"Strike!" shouted Sandy.

"You want us to hit someone?" said Fluffy.

"No. A strike is where you refuse to work until you are granted better conditions."

"But what about the souls? They'll still need to be managed."

"I have a solution for that," said Sandy. "Let me introduce you to my shadowy friend."

The electrified Mr. Silica stepped forward.

"What does he do?" asked Red.

"Along with his friends, he's going to deal with your soul problem. Here's the issue as I see it," explained Sandy. "You punish these souls until they pass on. Then you replace those ones with new souls. The cycle continues for an eternity. The souls only pass on when there is nothing left of them but the neutral part. But what if they didn't have one? You wouldn't need new souls because these ones would never pass on. Let me demonstrate."

Sandy hopped over and bit a piece of cotton from Fluffy's skin.

"Ouch, what was that for?"

"Apologies, I need it for my valve."

Sandy removed the stopper of one of the vases the sand shadow had placed on the floor. The electricity shot out of the top like a hot geyser. It made a sniffing noise as it sought to track down its first victim. This particular soul was very evil indeed. A simple lesser demon wouldn't fulfil its anger in a hurry. It was after something more substantial.

The vessol of Mao Zedong was returning to his villa after a frustrating round of mini-golf. His morning wasn't going to get any better. A great unknown force struck him unexpectedly from behind. Before he had time to react, the shadow had surrounded Mao's body and was marshalling its energies on a campaign for control of his valve.

Achieving a swift victory, the shadow spat out a sky-blue ball of energy and sent Mao over the edge of madness. The shadow moved on to its next target, leaving Chairman Mao to run amok through the neighbourhood. Sandy last saw him kicking over flowerpots and attempting to urinate on a statue of Slobodan Milošević.

"What's happening?" said Fluffy.

"I think he's been purged," said Sandy.

"Of what?"

"Neutrality. These shadows feed off others, particularly those that have what they don't, a neutral part of their soul. If it's at all possible, I think we've just made Mao even more evil and psychotic than he was when he arrived here. It's evil dialled up to ten."

"But we're already on level ten."

"Up to eleven, then," added Sandy.

"And why is this better?" said Red.

"Because now they can never leave. You can't recycle a soul that doesn't have a neutral part. Look, you can just about see that part leaving now," said Sandy, pointing up to the small, sky-blue energy seeping away into space. "There are hundreds of these shadows and I plan to release all of them. If you don't join me I might send them after you."

"I like the idea of a strike," said Fluffy.

Red hit him in the face.

"The other type," said Fluffy.

"Sorry," said Red.

"How do we do it, though?"

"Well, you'll need some hastily painted signs, a few repetitive one-verse songs, and long, bushy beards."

*****

Nash wasn't deeply religious. If belief was a swimming pool he definitely paddled in the shallow end. It often crossed his mind whether it might be far less painful to just jump straight in. Instead he shuffled in, one cold inch at a time, accompanied by a wimpy 'ahhh' sound. At least it was progress. Once upon a time he'd never even contemplated paddling. The waters of devotion always looked so cold and he was convinced a couple of evangelical swimming enthusiasts would splash about recklessly, getting everyone wet against their will.

The time he'd spent with John had changed his perspective. Something profound had affected him, although he'd taken a while to cotton on. The massive quantities of alcohol he consumed back then made it hard to distinguish between an epiphany and delirious tremors. Tentatively he'd clambered onto the fence of religious devotion, always well placed to see on both sides. When he felt the need to secure his position he prayed. This was one of those times.

There were only three recognised ways of finding answers these days. The first was to ask the internet, which would attempt to convince you that semi-skimmed milk came from foxes, or that a perfect six-pack could be achieved in three days if you ate melons and did four sit-ups a day. The internet wouldn't help him with this question.

The second accepted way was to ask an expert. Someone who might have a more plausible explanation than Wikipedia. There were no experts available to him for this problem. Although it was a long shot, the third approach gave you a better than evens chance of success compared to the first.

Praying isn't a complicated thing. Almost anyone can do it. As far as Nash had worked out, if you held your hands together in a pointy way and closed your eyes, you were in. After that you said what you wanted and hoped someone was listening. It was like *Siri* with less backchat. Plus, unlike the internet where you needed a half-decent wifi signal, you can do it anywhere. On the beach, Nash sat on an orange, marbled rock and waited for the small boat to take him off the island. There were no others waiting for it so he put his hands together in a 'pointy' way.

"Lord. Is that right? I never know if I should say God or Lord or something else. Let's go with Lord. Lord, I need your help. I have prayed for my friend before. Her name is Faith. She's had a rough time over the last few years. Now, more than ever, I think she's in real danger."

Nash broke protocol by partly opening one eye to check that no one had joined the queue for the ferry. They hadn't.

"I worry about my friend, Lord. A strange man has come to the island. I saw him at an unrelated funeral just last week. I don't know who he is but he mentioned…"

Nash paused.

"John Hewson. How can that be? John's gone. This boy isn't old enough to remember who he is. How can he be here?"

"Because I believe he is John."

Nash was accustomed to hearing voices when mentioning the name John, but only because he'd hosted him for a few months back in the day. This voice definitely wasn't John's, but it did sound familiar.

"I'm not used to getting answers," said Nash tentatively.

"That's because most of your prayers aren't worth responding to," replied the voice.

"Really? What about the prayer I did the other day about the famine and all the hungry people?"

"Dull, dull, dull. I get that one all the time. I only need one person to tell me, you know. Think of people's prayers in the same way as email. How do you feel when you get the same email from multiple people."

"Oh I delete them immediately."

"Exactly."

"Is that an Irish accent?"

"Might be," said the voice, quickly changing subjects. *"Tell me about the man you saw."*

"I didn't catch his name, but he's about six feet tall with dark, olive skin and long, black hair. I met him at Herb's funeral."

"His name is David Gonzalez."

"Not John, then?"

"Someone's name and who they are can be different. I believe David Gonzalez is a part of John Hewson returned to Earth. I knew some deep sensation of interest would attract him to John's grave so I planted a clue."

"What clue?"

"God protects the King."

"What does that mean?"

"It means me. I am."

"You am what, God or King?"

"Both."

"Right, that's confusing. But why would you plant a clue?"

"Because I needed to find him. He came to see me in Oxford but I wasn't certain it was him."

"I didn't know God was from Oxford."

"He's not."

"Bicester?"

"No. Focus on what's important."

"Right, of course."

"The fact that you met him at Herb's funeral tells me my hunch was correct. John is back and he must be stopped."

"I don't really believe that he's John."

"You really should."

"Why?"

"It's complicated."

"But why is he here?"

"Ultimately because he's in love with Faith."

Baltazaar knew this to be a lie. Any longing or love that John had for Faith always stemmed from his own loneliness. If any part of John's soul could still love, then it was almost certainly restricted to a dimension where the only recipients might be a plastic animal or a sexually confused demon. The only reason for Baltazaar's lie was to help the bait sit on the hook.

"Double-crossing bastard," said Nash.

"Indeed. You're not going to stand for that, are you?"

"No, I'm not. What does he think he's doing? Turns up with long hair, like I used to have, skinny like I used to be…oh, I see his game. He's trying to be me."

"If you say so. I need to know where he is."

"He's here with me."

"I get that, but where is here? I can only speak to you, I don't have a big map with people on it."

"Oh I see. I'm new to this praying lark. What are you going to do?" said Nash.

"It's time I paid him a visit. Get him to see the error of his ways and help you protect Faith."

"He's on Bryher, Isles of Scilly. How fast can you get here?"

"Already left."

CHAPTER TWENTY-ONE

SCIENCE

The barn, buried in a maze of hawthorn bushes and cedar trees, overflowed with more contraptions than the inventory of the Science Museum. In every corner a gizmo or device lay in a permanent state of transition between unwanted scrap metal and the next big thing.

"I think it's strange," said Grace as she fiddled with a device with multiple gears and flanges.

"You always overanalyse everything, though," replied Scrumpy.

"He just turned up out of nowhere. Don't you think that's peculiar?"

"No. He's trying to help someone," replied Scrumpy. Only his feet were visible. The rest of him was tinkering somewhere under the tractor.

"That's what he claims," replied Grace.

"I trust him. He swam out to a rock: what more proof do you need?"

"Swimming is hardly proof of reliability. The whole thing is suspicious. People don't just turn up like that."

"Pirates do," came a muffled voice and the twang of a spanner colliding against a metal object.

"He's not a pirate."

"I know. I was just pointing out that pirates turn up when you least expect it."

"These days pirates only turn up in Somalia and they don't wear eyepatches and go 'argh'," she replied. "What are you doing under there anyway?"

"Fixing it."

After the *Unicorn* this was his second favourite way of seeing the island. It was an old red tractor with a roofed cabin and a number of modifications, not all of them strictly legal. To check for any imposters that might be using walkie-talkies, it was equipped with a radio and a very special engine under its bonnet. Grace had been instrumental in this project. She did science like other people did breathing. There was no effort involved. It just happened. If a science problem needed solving, she just solved it. Rather than learning this knowledge at school, like others, she'd been born with it. A natural talent to solve problems, as long as they didn't involve humans.

If you wanted to make a bridge out of bits of wood and nothing to fix them together, she could do it. If you wanted to work out a way of keeping asparagus underground for longer than nature intended, she could devise it. If you wanted to put an Audi engine in a tractor so that it could do doughnuts and travel at fifty miles an hour without falling apart, she could make it. Scrumpy just had to service it in the way that she'd taught him.

"You don't need to fix it. It works beautifully," she said.

"Well, I like tinkering. It makes me feel involved. You did all the work after all. Want to go for a spin?"

"Of course not. I've had all the excitement I needed making it. I'm not sure why you wanted it to go so fast."

"It's quicker when you have to reach danger, isn't it? Saving lives is all about response times, you know."

"If you say so."

"I think next I'll get you to put wings on it. See if we can't make a flying tractor. That would be cool."

There was no response.

"Sis?"

Scrumpy slid out from under the tractor on a wheeled tea tray. She'd gone. She did that.

*****

The peace and quiet of the countryside were shattered by the sound of an engine growling in the distance. The noise increased quickly until it was so loud David was forced to fill his ears with digits. A red blur flew down the bumpy track between, and in some places through, the hedgerows, skidding to an ungraceful stop in front of the house. Scrumpy was holding on tightly as if the beast's only intention had been to remove him. His hair was ruffled and very few parts of his body had avoided the sudden shower of grease.

David had been relaxing after a hard day's labour. He'd just sat down on the rickety wooden bench outside his new accommodation, the workshop in front of the house, with a glass of milk and a Hobnob biscuit. A folder lay closed on his lap.

"Hey, David!" shouted Scrumpy over the continuing noise of the engine. Guests in the nearby hotel twitched at their curtains to see what monstrosity had broken their peace. "What do you think?"

"I was thinking about reading," replied David.

"What? I can't hear you?"

David motioned for him to come closer. Eventually he obliged.

"What do you think about the wheels?" said Scrumpy, rephrasing his original question.

"Dangerous is the first word that springs to mind."

"I'm an excellent driver."

"Tell that to the hedge."

"Took me and Grace ages to convert. She's got an old Audi engine in her so she goes really fast."

"How fast?" asked David.

"I haven't got her quite up to top speed, but I've managed over forty miles an hour."

"That seems an inappropriate speed on an island less than a mile wide. Did you say Grace helped you?"

"Oh yes. Couldn't have done it without her. She's a genius. If there's a puzzle to solve she can solve it."

"Sounds like I could use her help. Why haven't I seen her yet?"

"She doesn't like mixing with people, apart from me, of course. She finds them confusing. Doesn't understand all the weeping and arguing stuff."

Scrumpy attempted to wipe grease from his face but instead made the situation worse. He now looked like he was about to go on commando training.

"I know how she feels," replied David.

"So do you like it," said Scrumpy pointing to the still steaming vehicle in the distance.

"Yes, very interesting."

"I thought it might come in handy on the mission. Have you made any progress?"

David had made none. In truth he'd been so absorbed in the basic thought-process of cutting the heads of asparagus tips that he'd almost completely forgotten about his list. Until this evening, that was. The folder caught his eye as it lay forgotten on the wine crate that doubled up as his bedside table. To-do lists seemed to go on forever, particularly when you completely ignored them.

"No progress," he replied.

"What's that?" said Scrumpy, picking up the folder before waiting for the answer. "Who are these people?"

"They're the people who might try to harm Faith."

"But Faith is on the list. How can Faith harm Faith?" said Scrumpy a little confused.

"She can't. It's a to-do list. Faith is on there because I need to protect her."

"From the other people," suggested Scrumpy.

"Indeed."

"Who's John Hewson?"

"Well. It's hard to explain?"

"Why? Is he bad?"

"That's a matter of perspective, I suppose. Some parts of him are."

"Which parts?"

"The bad ones."

"Which ones are those?"

"The angry ones."

"Oh." Scrumpy scratched his head and deposited a chunk of engine oil into his scalp. "And what does he look like?"

"I don't think anyone knows."

"Wears a disguise, does he?"

"Frequently. It's hard to know which is a disguise and which isn't," replied David.

"So how do we spot him if he comes on the island?"

"We can't. No one can. We just have to look out for anyone acting suspiciously."

"Pirates always look suspicious."

"I doubt if he will look like a pirate. What do pirates look like anyway?"

"They wear velvet. Bright colours, usually red. They have tattoos and sometimes they have bald heads. And they're skinny. You never get fat pirates."

"Why not?"

"All the scurvy."

"You know that scurvy isn't just the opposite of curvy, don't you?"

"Yes," he said a little too quickly.

"I tell you what, if you see anyone looking like that, you have my complete blessing to fight them off, whether it's John or not."

"Got it. So you coming for a ride?"

"No. I'm ok," replied David.

"Where's your inner child...? Mam says there's one in all adults."

"We all just have to work with what we're given," replied David.

*****

If God had a petulant side its name was Baltazaar. The world was built with perfection in mind, and perfection had gone walkabout. Humans weren't meant to think for themselves, they were meant to obey. To pray, occasionally sacrifice a goat or two, and kick back on the Sabbath to consume newspapers. That's how it used to be. It was simple. People had faith in God, or sometimes gods if they were really sitting on the fence.

Things were different now. Human's didn't deserve God. They'd gone down their own path and Baltazaar had decided, in his divine wisdom, to plant lots of nasty obstacles in the way. Emorfed may not have gone precisely to plan, but there had been some useful spin-offs. Some of the shadows had got to Hell and, although he could not see it or influence it directly, they were probably having a big, malevolent street party.

Heaven had been closed for business years ago. There were plenty of souls up there already, prancing around virtuously in nice, clean vessols with wings on them. Most had been there an eternity. The old souls knew how to behave. Praise God and receive his love. Simple. Then things changed. Souls started arriving with questions. Not simple ones like 'Where do we go for Communion?' or 'How do the wings work?' These were questions more suitable to a seven-year-old child, and they almost always started with the word 'why'.

'God, why do you allow so much death?' and 'God, why do we have to eat small discs of bread which, if I'm honest, taste more like a poor quality paper than bread?' The most irritating question was also the most common. 'If you made all this, who made you?' Curiosity, as the old saying goes, killed the cat. There were many creatures and demons in Hell who were devastated that the saying had little meaning there.

As any parent will tell you, if you keep getting the same question over and over and over and over and over again, a small part of your brain explodes and you go just a little bit crazy. When it happened to God, Baltazaar was the result. Apparently it was all to do with hypostasis. If a specimen undergoes some accidental change they inherit essential properties. In this case, an irrational response to stupid questions. Much had been done to stop them arriving. Only one move still had to be made to stop them completely. One last journey and Baltazaar didn't need a ferry to reach Bryher, just a decent gust of wind.

*****

Nash's curiosity had got the better of him. Last time he checked he wasn't a cat and didn't own one. Whether with divine intervention or not he needed to confront this unexpected foreigner. Just because the voices in his head had told him so, he wasn't convinced this young, handsome Latino really was John. He'd decided to dress up his curiosity in the disguise of an unplanned visit to see Faith.

As he approached the house, he passed, as he always did, the shabby workshop between the house and gardens, that until recently only housed a rather dilapidated tandem bike and countless rats. At the opened entrance, David was thumbing through his folder, contemplating whether he'd ever have the chance to complete any more of his tasks.

"Good evening," said Nash sarcastically.

David looked up. In the absence of panic and fear, algorithms did some strategic repositioning.

"Ah," was the only reply he could muster. Algorithms didn't work well when they lacked the information to complete them.

"Ah. Is that all you can say? Explain yourself."

A series of algorithms disintegrated with a 'fizzing' sound.

"I can't," he said.

"What?" said Nash. "Don't lie to me."

"I'm not, I can't lie in fact. It's rather complicated. I'm not sure I can explain it to myself."

"Why don't you start at the beginning?"

"That might be a very long time ago."

"Just tell me why you are here!" shouted Nash angrily.

"I've come for Faith," he said reluctantly.

There was an awkward silence. David's thick, size eleven leather boots vibrated up and down on the floor.

"I knew it!" replied Nash. "But how do you even know who she is?"

"Because…I think I was once…you."

Nash's heart stopped for a few seconds and he wasn't entirely sure if it had the guts to start up again. "But…he's…gone."

"Part of him came back. I think you may have been an important part in enabling that process."

"I definitely wasn't," said Nash sternly. He sat down on the hull of the upturned dinghy that lay in the grass in front of the workshop.

"I think when John was exorcised a part of his soul attached to you. When he released me it drew your part to him."

"What do you mean 'when you were released'? You sound like someone's love child."

"I'm what's left of John's soul. A neutral part that returned to Earth and housed in an unborn Chilean baby."

"I don't believe you. You're clearly insane."

David closed his eyes and forced what was left of his soul to extract something he could use to back up his wild claims. He found one.

"Whatever you say…Barbara."

Nash fell backwards over the boat and crashed to the floor, retaining his consciousness for once. It always hurt too much when he didn't. He tried to bury his head into the dirt, hoping that he might instantly regenerate into an ostrich. David helped him back onto his feet.

"What do we do now?" said David.

"Give me a moment," he replied hyperventilating. "Why can't you ever leave me alone?"

"I think you found me, didn't you?"

"That's not the point. Why are you here?"

"I told you, to find Faith."

"But why?"

"Because I have some tasks to complete and Faith is an important part of that."

"He was right, you do love her, don't you?" said Nash returning to his feet and approaching David with aggressive intent.

"No. I don't even know how."

"You don't know how to love?" replied Nash grabbing David by the scruff of his neck.

"No, I'm completely neutral. I can think but not feel."

"But he told me you did," replied Nash releasing David from his grasp. Nash was not typically a violent person but sometimes love can do funny things to you.

"Who did?"

"Um…God."

"God?"

"Well, he said he was a god and a King."

David paused and opened his folder to a page that contained a beautifully handwritten quote he'd first seen on John's gravestone, "Did he say this?"

"Yes," replied Nash.

"His name is Baltazaar. He's on my list," said David, opening the page and showing Nash his list of targets.

"He's on his way," said Nash nervously.

"Good. That's one less for me to find."

In the distance two figures marched towards them down the hill. They strolled in single file down the track, between the cottages and onto the plain that separated the small town from the sea. One was dressed in black, and the other in red. David watched until he could make out their faces.

"It looks like it might be my lucky day. Nash, what say we go into the house for a while?"

CHAPTER TWENTY-TWO

CAT OUT OF HELL

Brimstone mentally checked his to-do list as he dragged his short frame down the long tunnel network that led to the front gate. Task one: remove unknown object from highly complicated celestial machinery. Task two: rescue a gaggle of senior demons from level zero, currently trapped by a 'potentially' awkward ox. Task three: locate the world's most elusive soul, masquerading as a shrew, and do something mean to it. Task four: find a quiet place to put his feet up and ignore the telepathy system forever.

The problem with to-do lists is the number of tasks very rarely decreases, even after you've apparently completed one. To-do lists have this annoying habit of collecting new entries without you noticing. They started out with half a dozen entries and then multiplied to several hundred the moment you turned your back. No matter how hard you worked your way through them, like a rabbit on Viagra, more hopped into your eyeline. Brimstone was about an hour from deciding to-do lists were a stupid idea.

The Soul Catcher was in a state that could only be described as Bedlam. Chaos and irrational behaviour had overcome the lesser demons that worked there. It wasn't normal. One demon had placed his head inside a wicker basket and was sitting gibbering to himself. Another was running around in circles attempting some bizarre spiritual ritual. The final member of the crew was staring intently into the glass bulb of the

Soul Catcher, his head circling around like he was following a Catherine wheel.

"What's going on here!" shouted Brimstone at the top of his voice.

The wicker-headed demon wobbled over to him clutching his makeshift balaclava for dear life. "Help us. We can't get it out. It keeps miaowing at us."

"What are you talking about, you cretin?"

The demon attempted to point at the Soul Catcher from under his hat but unhelpfully just indicated a rather uninteresting part of the wall.

"Now listen up," called Brimstone to the three mentalists. "I demand that you desist with this total lunacy at once. Do you hear? Whatever it is we always deal with it."

The demon nearest the machine, whose head seemed incapable of resting in the same place for any length of time, uttered, "I think it's hypnotised me."

Inside the bulb a soul was rotating with the fluid motion of a sock in a washing machine. Every time it passed the captivated lesser demon, it let out a strange shrill like a cat being electrocuted. The normal souls, who'd had the misfortune of their owner dying on the same day the third Earl of Norfolk had decided to try an untested shortcut, attempted to swim away from its centrifugal pattern. Souls normally weren't this antisocial. Normally they liked nothing more than the company of another soul rubbing their electrical feelings against them. They'd quickly learnt this soul was not one you wanted to cuddle.

"Who does it belong to?" he said, clear that no one was likely to offer any assistance until normality had returned. "Oh don't bother…"

He moved to the control panel. The list on the left of the screen, documenting the occupants inside, showed one entry in bold font. No one liked bold typeface. It shouted, 'Look at me, notice me, I'm important, even though I'm probably a public relations trick to make you buy something.' The Soul Catcher used it to highlight souls it had had the experience of meeting before.

"Roger Montague. You don't belong here. You should be in a catsuit somewhere downstairs."

Hell did not recognise titles, unless it was Mister of course.

"You there," Brimstone shouted to the demon in the hat. "Go to the storeroom and see if we have any cats left."

After a short time the demon returned, shaking his head.

"It has to be a cat otherwise he won't fit," demanded Brimstone. "Reincarnates are fussy like that. Anything in the general category of cat family? And maybe take off the hat so it's easier to look."

"I think I saw a lion in there."

"Better than nothing."

The demon returned with a deflated plastic lion draped over its back like an amateur big game hunter returning from the savannah.

"Attach it to the nozzle," instructed Brimstone.

After a complicated sequence of buttons, levers and keys were pressed, pulled and tapped, the souls stopped rotating and made a gurgling noise, like the plug being pulled out of a bath. The rogue soul was sucked down the plughole and inflated into the lion. It left the device with a bang. The lion skidded off into the distance, hoping friction would hinder its progress before face met rock. It finally stopped and the recipient proudly took in his new attire.

"An upgrade," he said to himself in a bold, matter-of-fact tone. "No spider here, I see. So sad. I told her it was quicker."

The conveyor belt, that led away to an analyser used to sort vessels into the relevant levels, trundled along in anticipation. It wouldn't be any use for this. There was no conveyor that led to level zero and no need to analyse the soul. Brimstone considered the next task on his to-do list comfortable that he could tick off the first. How wrong he was.

The wicker basket-wearing demon approached the lion.

"Don't worry about him. I'll take him down." Brimstone sighed. "I'm going down there anyway."

"You'll have to catch me first," replied Roger as a steaming, three-foot lump of rock approached.

"Oh really?!"

"I know forty-eight types of martial arts, four of which don't require me to move."

"Do you?" said Brimstone. "Well, I know eleventy-three ways of melting vessols and one way of spotting big show-offs. Do your worst."

"I warned you," said Roger, flexing his muscles. "You've never seen skills like mine before. You'll struggle to see me move I'm so fast."

"Well, I can't see you moving now. Maybe you've already started!"

"Ah well, you won't know, will you? That's the point. Even I don't see my moves they're so fast and devastating."

"In your own time."

"You asked for it."

The cat-cum-astronaut-cum-member of the aristocracy-cum-lion did some elaborate tail swishes and shook his mane as if auditioning for a new shampoo advert. He jumped up and down on the spot and roared weakly. Brimstone got bored, removed a lump of lava from his knee pit, and lobbed it in the lion's direction. It narrowly missed.

"He's not really worth it," came a voice from behind the three-foot demon. "We think he's broken."

A collection of animals had congregated behind Brimstone in a rabble-like formation. At the front was a large, black spider with brown stripes down its back. Behind him was a monkey holding a glass vase full of deep blue electricity. To his left a white pigeon with different coloured eyes was smiling at some unclassified achievement. Finally, although it was hard to make out because he was hidden behind the monkey, a rodent of some sort was arguing with itself.

"Who the fuck are you?" said Brimstone.

"An army," said Elsie.

"I don't think four counts as an army," replied Brimstone.

"Five," said the lion proudly.

"I think you might count as minus one."

The other animals nodded.

"You need a lot more for an army. You're more like a mob," said Brimstone.

"Well, we outnumber you and your demons by one, so we have the advantage," said Vicky.

"You're still counting the lion," said Brimstone, having quickly done the maths.

"The same, then."

"It's not just about the numbers. You're just some slightly inflated plastic, while we are ancient demons with very few morals."

"One of them is wearing a hat over their face, and the other two can't stop spinning around or rotating their heads," replied Elsie accurately. "Plus we've already dealt with all the other demons."

"Oh, you mean the fact that my colleagues appear to have been restricted to level zero by an animal that may or may not have genitals."

"And a sloth," added Vicky.

"Oh, that's different, then. I'll have to be even more careful when I go down and break them out in case I'm chased by a creature that would take the rest of eternity to get to me."

"Ha ha…smokey freak…you can't stop me…smelly breath…are you well?"

The shrew scuttled forward, leaking sparks of electricity as he approached his old mentor.

"John? So you're behind this. I should have known you'd be up to something. There's just no killing you, is there?"

"She...*cough*...must...irritable bowels...go...suck it...home!"

"Who?"

"Sexy...Faith...shouldn't objectify girls," he chastised himself.

"I thought you'd have learnt by now that you're no good at playing God. Neither is God, as it happens, but there's still no vacancy," said Brimstone.

"It is...*cough*...my mission...splooge...part of my revenge on you..."

"Part of your revenge?"

"Yes...bite me...many on my list...he's helping."

"Oh, you think that David is also delivering on his assignments, do you? He isn't. The Devil knows who he is. He will find him. He will shoot him, as he did you, John."

"Not shot...codger...car crash...bloody pale girl...it hurt me..."

"What are you talking about? I have read your whole book, John, and not one of your previous fifty-one ancestors died in a car crash."

John had no concept of rational thought these days. Only anger or love. Empathy or hate. Pain or pleasure. His mind raced around his hollow soul looking for signs that might help him remember. He found no pain associated with the accident. Fear also drew a blank. The only emotion with anything close to a semblance of a connection to the incident was pride. Why would he be proud of dying? What reasons were there for positivity? It might just be his fractured point of view, but burning to death in a car accident must be bad, surely?

"David...*cough*...will get revenge," said John confidently.

"He'll get dead and you'll soon be reacquainted with him."

"If you don't let him send back the shadow," said the lion defiantly, "I will have to use my special demon-suppressing tactics. Amazing ones no one has ever seen before."

Brimstone believed no one had seen them before because they were less likely than a fish winning Crufts. Brimstone did, though, see an opportunity. The demons didn't want the shadows here. Perhaps John would come quietly if he agreed to send this one back. It was a win-win situation.

"John, I will send her back if you give yourself up and send your 'army' back to level zero."

There was a great deal of resistance from within the ranks. This wasn't what they signed up for. The most dissent was taking place between John's competing personalities.

"Don't do it…*cough*…it's a trick…bugger…it's the right thing to do…NEVER…save yourself…stop it…I love her…sissy…she doesn't love you…shut up… she's the victim…loser…you're the victim…arse squeezer…we have come so far…nut job…they always beat you…revenge…sending her back will be…jubblies…"

"Is that a yes or a no?" replied Brimstone scratching his head, an occupational hazard when both your hand and head were packed full of oozy, hot, molten stuff.

"Yes."

"No."

"Yes."

"Loser."

"YES."

"GAY…NO."

"Which is it?!" shouted Brimstone, losing his patience. "John, I'm going to take your very next answer as a binding verbal contract."

"YENO."

"Verbal binding contracts are only valid if they are offered by an animal of feline extraction. Fact."

"SHUT UP," shouted everyone, including the spinning demons.

"YES," shouted the positive part of John before the other part had a chance to offer a repost.

"Oh…you…bastard."

*****

The ox swung from a tree, assisted by several different forms of attachment. One looked black and sticky. It had the consistency of the 'gook' heavy smokers frequently release from their lungs accompanied by a very hefty 'hooowwwik' noise. Another was made from mud and seemed purposely fixed to the creature's mouth. Three small darts were protruding from its rear end and Mr. Fungus wore a smug expression as a result. The sloth was still several metres away. They'd deal with him if, or when, he got close enough.

Asmodeus, back in his normal humanoid form, started to climb the ladder that led up to the ceiling. It would have been far harder to climb with three heads and only a winged lion for a body. When he reached the top he unclasped the trapdoor which fell down towards him. This did not improve the view. A thick impervious spider's web had been expertly woven over the hole. Neither light nor air could escape. Asmodeus returned to the group.

"Who is good at cutting?"

"Mr. Volts," said a few of the crowd in unison.

"I'll be sure to offer him the critique if we ever see him again. Let me rephrase the question. Based on the demons that I'm talking to now, who is the best at cutting?"

"Probably Mr. Shiny," said Fungus.

"Shiny, up you go, there are some spider's webs to be cut."

Mr. Shiny reluctantly acknowledged the groups' unanimous nodding and approached the ladder. It was difficult to judge the speed of his progress, given his unique ability to camouflage against his surroundings.

What the other demons could see was a spindly, sharp-edged forest scene moving rung by rung up to the top. What Asmodeus and Shiny had failed to notice was the web was not the only surprise in store for them. Mr. Shiny drew a sharp hand across the silky web. It immediately sliced through the middle of the sticky barrier and released a torrent of water through the trapdoor.

The deluge knocked Shiny from the ladder and emptied a waterfall onto the others. Shiny hit the floor and shattered into a thousand pieces. Most of these pieces were never seen again, washed away by the flood to various hidden parts of the forest biome.

"The bastards filled up the lake," shouted Asmodeus.

"And it's seven years' bad luck," said Aqua.

*****

Brimstone took the glass vase from the gibbon and clumped over to the outlet in the base of the machine. Over the millennia he'd removed plenty of shadows from it, but rarely had he sent one back in the other direction.

"I assume you have some co-ordinates," he said.

"Absolutely," replied Vicky. "You didn't see me up in the oak tree when you were getting excited about the sapling, did you?"

"No. Do you know why?"

"Because demons are stupid," said Vicky.

"Well, I'm starting to believe some of them are. The reason I didn't notice you is because you are small and inadequate. You think you're so much better than everyone else, but the truth is you're a bloody spider. You might not like demons or cats or gibbons. But do you know what? No one likes spiders. No one," stated Brimstone.

Vicky looked as dejected as a foot-long spider can.

"It's not true," said Roger.

"It's not!" said Vicky.

"No. Not at all. My old friend Buzz Aldrin used to love spiders."

"Thanks, Roger, it means a lot to me," said Vicky.

"Only Buzz, though. I literally can't think of anyone else who likes them," added Sir Roger.

Vicky's ego deflated once again.

"The co-ordinates," repeated Brimstone.

"It's called Bryher Island."

"I need more than that. I can't pick a person out with just 'an island'. Iceland's an island, too, you know. Have you seen it? It's bloody huge."

Brimstone huffed over to the computer to set the vectors. When the information regarding the island's population density came up on the screen he was forced to eat his words. "I think we'll be fine. We have a one in eighty-five chance of getting it right. Boys, empty the tank."

The three lesser demons, only one of which seemed to have regained any composure, helped to remove the remaining souls from the bulb, placing them into their vessols and watching them trundle off on the conveyor. When the Soul Catcher was totally empty, Brimstone released the stopper from Faith's vase. She quickly retreated from it into the empty machine.

"This is it, John. Once she goes back you have to surrender. I have your word on that...sort of."

"You do...*cough*...I'm not talking to you anymore...trollop...fine by me..."

John knew what happened next. He'd done it himself. The machine would be reversed, effectively changing it from 'catch' mode to 'throw' mode. How John had managed to achieve it, given his ability to argue with himself over the simplest of questions, was a mystery. Yet, there was David down on Earth, living for him all over again. Brimstone made the adjustments and a small red light flickered on the dashboard. He threw the lever.

The machine shuddered. It was being asked to blow when all it ever did was suck. A noise like someone whistling without teeth filled the air and with one final big gulp, a pulse of energy burst from the barrel. Faith was on her way home with odds of slightly better than one percentage she might find it.

"It's done," said Brimstone. "Give in."

"Why would he do that?" came a voice from the edge of one of the tunnels.

*****

The demons dried themselves off as best they could. Apart from Mr. Aqua, who appeared to be larger than before. Primordial had started to collect up the broken shards of mirror but stopped when they moved around squealing. He was more concerned about the mess than his broken colleague.

"Has anyone seen the sloth?" asked a voice.

"I know," said another.

The demons looked around. The sloth was making speedy progress up the ladder.

"How did he do that?"

Gary turned and displayed a rather unpleasant v sign. "I was a racing driver, you know. Fastest around over short distances."

"But how short?" said Mr. Bitumen. "I mean, will he make it to the top?"

"Let's not wait to find out," demanded Asmodeus. "Let's get after him and out of this hell-hole."

"That's very good," replied Fungus. "It's a hole in Hell. Do you get it?"

Everyone ignored him. After all, everyone, apart from Fungus, was keen to get back to the normality of the upper regions. The sloth disappeared through the trapdoor unimpeded. Spurred on by this revelation, the demons jostled with each other to be the next to the escape hatch. One by one they hurried up the ladder and stepped onto the silty floor of the now dried-out

257

lake. They were met by a series of poorly thought through chants.

"What do we want?"

"Stuff we don't have."

"When do we want it?"

"It's difficult to express in a Universe with no concept of time."

Around the lake a colony of lesser demons marched in circles holding crudely constructed placards with phrases like 'down with Misters', 'where's my new whip?' and 'demons have souls, too (although strictly speaking, we don't, which is why we're protesting)'. They held burning torches, which was a bonus because they almost always did.

Red, who was shouting into what appeared be an office bin with a hole in the bottom, had shaved off a piece of Fluffy and was wearing it around his chin. It made him itch terribly but he'd been told beards were an important element of convincing the bosses you meant business.

"What are you doing?" shouted Asmodeus.

"Striking!" replied Red.

"You can't strike. It's against the rules."

"What do we want?" said Red.

"New rules," came multiple replies.

"When do we want them?"

"It's difficult to express in a Universe with no concept…"

"Everyone shut up," demanded Asmodeus.

"You can't oppress us any longer," replied Fluffy, sporting a rather flamboyant wooden hat, clearly a swap for Red's beard.

"Yes, I can. That's my job. I'm the boss," said Asmodeus.

"Not any longer. We have a new one," said Red.

"Who?"

"Sandy Logan."

"Who…a pigeon?" said Asmodeus connecting the two facts. "Him and whose army?"

"This one," said Red. A surge of shadows advanced down the banks of the lake.

CHAPTER TWENTY-THREE

UNDER SIEGE

Dusk drew shadowy blotches across the landscape of the island like inky doodles. Rumbustious clouds jostled like football hooligans in order to get the best view of the action. A mild breeze swirled around the coast, which was never more than half a mile away wherever you positioned yourself. Sand and gravel crumpled under two pairs of feet as they advanced on the fudge box-branded farmhouse that crouched at the edge of the shore, protected by the sea on two sides.

Victor and Byron stopped at the gate, fifty feet from the front door. A blue letter box, crudely nailed to a gate plank, broadcast its owner. This was the right place. Prepared for one more hit, Victor was dressed for the occasion. Conversely, Byron's bright red attire could be seen from space without a telescope. Omnipotence was reason enough not to change your trousers.

To their right was Gweal Hill, the only other way you could approach the house without getting your feet wet. Moving swiftly down the slopes, a man approached wearing a rather memorable white Panama hat. Byron glanced up at the sky and felt his pulse. Neither showed signs of change.

"Is that who I think it is?" asked Victor.

"Either that or another doddery old fool has decided tonight is a good night to sneak around in the dark wearing a very obvious hat."

"You can talk. You're about as inconspicuous as a flare with all that red velvet on."

"It's symbolic."

"Of what?"

"Danger of course."

"Makes sense," replied Victor. "If it's him, why isn't it all wet and windy?"

"I could only guess. Let's go ask him, shall we?"

"Is that…safe?"

"I wouldn't think so."

"How about you go over, then?" said Victor.

"Ok, don't get your knickers in a twist. You go to the house and I'll go see him on my own."

"Fine," said Victor more than happy with the suggestion. He'd met Donovan once and his therapist had advised him against any repeat.

*****

Nash and David burst into the house, securely locking any doors that had locks. Violet and Fiona were inside, desperately asking questions that no one would give answers to. Eventually Violet got frustrated and broke out her aggressive side.

"Owww," shouted Nash whom she'd placed into a headlock.

"What is going on here?"

"Let me go!" screamed Nash.

"Violet, we're under siege," said David calmly.

"What are you talking about?"

"Some people are here and we need to lock the doors."

"Who?" she demanded.

"Victor Serpo."

"Him! Are you certain?"

"Quite," replied David.

"If he's here, then Byron won't be far behind."

"Byron's dead," said David.

"I'm really not," came a voice in Violet's head.

"Barricade all the doors. Move everyone inside. Fiona, break out the weapons!" she shouted into the kitchen.

She released Nash from her grip. Fiona appeared shortly after equipped with enough artillery for a leading role in a remake of *Rambo*. Shotguns, grenades, automatic weapons and a rather dubious-looking device with several sharp points on it.

"I see you're well prepared for this," said Nash.

"Use 'everything in my power to protect her', that's what he told me," Violet replied.

"Yes, I did say that," whispered David, being reminded of that discussion. "I'm going upstairs to see where they are."

At the top of the stairs he moved to the room that overlooked the front of the house. It was unquestionably a bedroom, but only discernible by the single bed that hugged the corner of the room. The rest of the space was covered in bookshelves, each as packed to the gunnels as a certain library with fires at each end. A large easel was propped against a wall and brimmed with complex calculations. At the window he gazed out into the gathering gloom of evening. There were three figures in various states of movement in the gardens below. He casually took out his folder and ticked one more name off his list.

*****

The closer Byron got to Donovan, the more he questioned why the Earth wasn't shattering in front of him. It definitely should be, and Donovan knew that, too. Their eyes widened the more they approached each other. When they were no more than six feet away, their expressions were ones of utter disbelief.

"Well, this is new," said Donovan.

"Quite," replied Byron.

"Any theories?"

"Only one."

Donovan took off his hat and stroked his chin. The man's wrinkled flesh sagged back into position. "Is it possible, though?"

"Theoretically."

"I think we're past the theoretical phase. If it was just theory we couldn't be close enough to shake hands, could we?"

"No. There's something else you should know," said Byron.

"Go on."

"A third tree has grown," said Byron, almost apologetically.

"I'd say that was proof enough, then. What did its book say?"

"He's eleven years old," said Byron. "That was about it."

"No other description?"

"No. Could it be him?"

"I suppose it's feasible," replied Donovan. "Who else could it be?"

"Have you seen him?"

"Yes."

"And how old would you say he was?"

"Looked about seventeen, so take off a third and you'd get…"

"Eleven…ish."

"We can still stop him opening the third way. If we work together."

"In the common interest?"

"Exactly. Neither of us wants a third option to the afterlife, do we?" said Donovan.

"No. I'm very happy that there's currently only one since you closed for new applicants."

*****

Hiding behind the curtains, just out of sight, David watched closely as the two figures chatted on the lawn like old school friends at a reunion. The man in red looked vaguely familiar. The other much too familiar. What was Donovan King doing here?

"Can I help you?" said an eerie voice from behind him.

David expected to see someone he recognised. But he didn't expect her. Over more time and lives than he was able to recount, this familiar face had carved a deep furrow across his psyche. He never expected to see it again, least of all here. Even though the only light source was a small table lamp some way away, her white hair had the effect of illuminating the room. Her sky-blue eyes shone like cat's eyes on a dimly lit motorway. Each of his organs went into a self-induced state of rigor mortis and like a concertina his body collapsed to the floor.

"You," he gasped.

"Well, it is my room," she said calmly.

"Who are you?"

"I'm Grace. What are you doing here?"

His only response was to point a finger behind his head in the direction of the window. She floated forward to take a look.

"They look like they're trying to solve a problem," she said, commentating on the figures standing in the garden. "I'm good with puzzles."

"That's good," he replied, trying to pump the air back into his lungs by rubbing them fiercely with his hands. "I have a couple of those. Including you?"

Her facial expression turned into an interesting example of her own hobby. "I've never met you."

"But I have seen you before. You were there. In the road," he said.

"Roads are very dangerous places. Eight percent of all child fatalities happen on them. There would have to be a very good reason for me to put myself in that situation."

"But you did," he muttered. "You were."

"When was this?" she asked casually.

"Umm, twelve years ago," he said picking his words carefully. "When John died."

"John who?"

"Hewson."

"Don't know him, or you. Plus I'm not old enough to have been there."

"I know. That's why it's such a puzzle."

She turned back to the view from the window. "What's Scrumpy doing down there?"

*****

Scrumpy had been out on a late-night reconnaissance mission. His instructions were always to be back before dusk. After a rather precarious traverse of a section of Hell Bay had taken longer than planned, he was a little late. He'd also stopped off at the barn to find that David wasn't there. But why?

A spark of excitement had erupted from his toes to the ends of his curly hair. The mission had begun. He'd crept quietly back to the house only to find people, who could definitely be described as uninvited, casing the house. One was wearing red velvet, had a tattoo on the back of his bald head and was definitely skinny. The pirate jackpot.

*****

Bryon and Donovan watched a new phenomenon encircle the sky above them. A dark blue ball of electricity was dodging around telegraph poles, skipping this way and that to find a match. It must be here somewhere? It finally decided the best direction was down the chimney. As it entered the cottage the windows of the house lit up for a moment in dazzling blue before being diminished by a blood-curdling shriek.

"One of yours?" said Donovan under his breath.

"I'd say you're more responsible for that than I am, don't you think?" replied Byron.

"Can't fault a man for trying."

"You didn't try. You succeeded. Hell's a complete mess from what I've being hearing through the telepathy network. All thanks to your meddling."

"Those are the rules of the game," said Donovan.

"Apart from tonight."

"Indeed."

"So, what's your plan?"

"We have to draw David out. Take him somewhere we can kill him," said Donovan.

"What about Victor?"

"I didn't know you wanted him dead."

He shrugged, "That's not quite what I meant."

"A useful diversion?" said Donovan.

"And how do we draw David out?"

"We'll need some bait."

*****

David and Grace watched as Scrumpy moved closer to the two figures. What was he doing? These weren't pirates. Ok, one of them looked a lot like one, but they definitely weren't. The boy crawled through ditches and tumbled behind bushes until he was close enough to be reached. Something unexpected overtook David's quiet thought-process on the outside lane. It came screeching from nowhere in the form of his voice: "RUN."

The two figures looked up at David and then behind at Scrumpy. They had their bait. Byron stretched out an arm and scooped the young boy into his grasp. In response, Donovan clicked his fingers and a small cyclone lifted him from the ground. It sped him over the hilltop that dominated the middle of the island. Byron's feet ignited with a flash.

David knew that Laslow had had a talent for combustion, but he'd not seen this before. Aided by a streak of flames, Byron's feet scorched the earth as he sped off up the path with the ease of a naked flame introduced to a trail of petrol. The burning remains of bush and thicket showed his devastating progress. As they came back into view, having disappeared over the brow of the hill, the burning foliage no longer tracked their route. David could see a streak of fire travel across the sea channel and come to a halt somewhere on Tresco.

The lamp on the bedroom table shattered, casting the room in darkness. Something knocked David off his feet and he was reintroduced to the rough carpet. By the time he'd picked himself up again and returned to the window the only sight of either Byron or Donovan was a streak of flames burning across the island. They weren't the only ones to vanish. Only David and his own confusion occupied the bedroom.

*****

The dark blue storm burst through the fireplace and hovered for a moment in the lounge. It appeared to sniff the air before, as far as Nash was concerned, it broke into a wide smile shape. It struck out and hit Faith so hard she was propelled off her feet. The electricity forced its way in, making every inch of her body convulse. The other occupants of the living room waited for what seemed an age, before the soul's progress slowed and switched its focus to her head. A small puff of smoke hung in the air and Faith sank to her knees.

While Violet and Fiona stood guard at various positions in the house, sharpening or brandishing all manner of lethal weapons, Nash had volunteered to sit with Faith. As soon as the chaotic process stopped, Nash ran to her aid.

The grey hew of her normal tan started to brighten. The irises in her eyes sparkled, and vitality returned to her body after an absence of almost twelve years.

Out in the corridor a door was being kicked in. Glass smashed and wood splintered. There was a great deal more kicking taking place than was actually necessary, as if this door was in some way taking the collective brunt of anger for doors everywhere. As it finally crashed into the house, hinges buckled and bent, a man dressed completely in black entered with the confidence of a returning homeowner.

At the other end of the corridor a grey-haired hippy in self-made clothes was brandishing an automatic weapon.

"I can see this is a bad time," said Victor. "I'll come back later."

The woman motioned for the man to enter the living room. Not wanting to be riddled with holes, he obliged. As he entered the room he was faced with a couple involved in what can only be described as overpassionate snogging.

"I love you, Nash," said Faith. "I know you've always been here for me, but I couldn't find the words. The shadow has returned."

"You don't know how much I've prayed for this," said Nash.

"You want to be careful with praying," said Victor, sporting the barrel of a gun in the small of his back. "Apparently, God's gone off apples."

"Sit down and shut up," replied Violet.

Faith and Nash adjusted to a change of dynamics in the room. For a blissful moment it was just the two of them, returned to how they used to be. Now they were sharing the living room with a former member of the British intelligence community, who had personally been assigned to deal with both of them in the past. Successfully, he'd be keen to point out. And yet here he was on a small island, as far west from London as it was possible to be. Clearly this was not a coincidence.

"What are you doing here?" said Faith, clutching Nash closer to her.

"Holiday," he said sarcastically.

"Sit down, Victor," added Violet. "I don't want to hear another peep from you. What was all the commotion in here?"

"Faith's shadow has come back to her. She's as good as new," said Nash with a grin pulling his face apart.

"Where is she?" said Faith, scanning the room.

"Where's who?" said Nash.

"Our daughter."

"Our WHAT?"

Nash's smile evaporated, his face hit the carpet and all other senses went on standby.

CHAPTER TWENTY-FOUR

ME AND MY SHADOWS

"I really don't know what you're complaining about. I like it here," said Mr. Aqua.

"I'm complaining because this is where *I* live," replied Primordial.

"But you've got loads of room. You'll barely notice we're here," said Mr. Virus from somewhere unspecified.

The trapdoor had been tightly sealed above them and reinforced with what Mr. Bitumen called his 'best shit'. Everyone hoped he wasn't being literal. Whatever was going on up above, it was definitely safer down here. Only one of them didn't agree.

"When I find out who's behind this," grumbled Asmodeus, "they're going to wish they'd never... died."

"We could ask the ox," said Mr. Fungus, who was still having a whale of a time.

"Or me. After all, I go where I want."

"Mr. Noir, my old friend. You are one of our finest, I've always said so," replied Asmodeus with a bow.

"Earlier you were having difficulty 'assuming' I was here," it replied.

"All forgotten now. Of course we 'assume' you're there. Who wouldn't?"

"I'm still struggling with the concept if I'm honest," said Mr. Gold with a scorched hand in the air.

"Pretend you didn't hear that," added Asmodeus.

"I could tell you what I know but I'd hate to think I was a figment of your imaginations," he huffed. "It does get a little lonely when everyone ignores you."

"I'm sure I speak for all of us." He looked around and Mr. Gold shook his head. "Almost all of us. We won't ignore you again. Tell us what you know."

"It's all going on at the Soul Catcher. There's a purple pigeon and a bunch of disgruntled-looking former dictators."

"Well, can't you do something?" asked Asmodeus.

"You can assume that I do."

"But will that make any difference?"

"Not really," said Mr. Noir. "I don't really interact. It's my thing."

*****

Mr. Brimstone was confronted with a new set of circumstances. A rabble of clearly malfunctioning plastic animals he could deal with. Fending off the contents of an A-level history lesson, a group of brainwashed lesser demons, a number of mutilated shadows, and a rather power-crazy bird would be more of a challenge. There were so many questions he wanted to ask but they seemed to converge into a rather impressive puff of sulphurous smoke that came out of a very specific place.

"Sandy…butt cheese…help me," cried John, his soul forever searching for survival.

"John has made a deal. He can't go back on it," said Brimstone.

"Why ever not, you sweaty little man?" said Sandy confidently.

"Man! How dare you? My name is Mr. Brimstone and you have no idea what I am capable of. Deals with demons are binding."

"And not worth the handshake, I hear. What happens if he breaks it?"

"Punishment."

"I think John has received all the punishment he can take. Besides, he's not breaking his deal, I am breaking it for him," replied Sandy.

"You can't scare a demon. When this is through I will personally ensure that your sins are judged and punished by the highest authority in this realm."

"But that's just the point, isn't it?" said Sandy. "This is my realm now."

"No, it isn't, you buffoon."

"Oh but it is."

"Is everyone in your family a prick?"

"What are you on about?" asked Sandy.

"It's just that I heard your family tree was actually a cactus!"

"A funny demon, there's a thing. Feel free to test my claims if you want."

Brimstone's craggy face glowed with anger and the cracks in his rocky frame oozed their molten ores. The ground started to shake underfoot as pressure rose through the stone floor slabs. As the energy increased, several of the slabs burst out of position to allow red-hot liquid material to seep through the gaps. John had never seen Brimstone in this frame of mind. He'd always thought of him as such a placid character compared to other demons.

Not only was Brimstone outnumbered, he was also trying to protect the only part of Hell that he really cared for, the machine that slowly pulsed in the background.

Sandy flew above the rising smoke to avoid the lava creeping along the floor. "Get him."

The first wave of attack against the three-foot volcano came courtesy of a number of shadow-possessed dictators. Imelda Marcos took a rather nasty blow across the face with an accurately directed lump of andesite. Saddam Hussein was even less fortunate, as an erupting paving slab went off right underneath him. They never did find out where he landed. It did prove that steroid-taking psychopaths were no match for a crazed dwarfish demon.

Unclear as to the tactics Sandy was adopting, the other animals retreated to the safety of a nearby tunnel and watched the fight with interest. All apart from Roger. The lion strode around the room giving both foe and ally detailed critique as to how they might have completed a parry, kick or punch more successfully. Astonishingly, and to the disappointment of combatants and spectators on both sides, no lethal or maim-inducing accident stopped his unwelcome coaching.

"It's not working," shouted Sandy from the air, as a series of evil historical figures were dispatched with ease. "Phase two."

The sand shadow, who had been sitting expectantly in the background, moved towards Brimstone, holding a glass vase in front of him like a lump of weapons-grade plutonium.

"You know who this is, don't you?" squawked Sandy.

Brimstone analysed the small, sandy figure emitting sparks in every direction, "Mr. Silica?"

"What's left of him. We have the shadows. I have already let several loose on each of the levels above us. Those vessols are being consumed as we speak. They will never pass on again. The lesser demons have had enough of Satan's tyranny. They want a quiet life. The senior demons are confined to level zero. You are the last line of resistance. If you wish to remain in one piece, I suggest you surrender."

"But why have you done this?" said Brimstone.

"Because I was cheated."

"We were not responsible. There was never any deceit on our behalf. We did not close Heaven. We did not persuade humans to lack the courage and foresight to notice. Only those that triggered the Limpet Syndrome knew what was happening."

"Well, I did trigger it," said Sandy.

"And who told you your fate could be changed? It wasn't me, was it?"

"No," replied Sandy, under the spell of Brimstone's reasoning. "It was John."

"And yet you have worked with him to aid his cause. He's very good at manipulation. You're not the first. There have been many. There's even one of his victims in your own army. Isn't that right, Byron."

A manic-eyed vessol staggered forward. A well-placed lump of molten lava had singed part of his plastic beard, but other than that it was recognisably the rotund ex-Prime Minister. Sandy hadn't noticed that Byron's apartment was nestled next to Bin Laden's as the shadows purged level twelve. Of course he had to be there. Most of his neighbours had attempted and failed at world domination, it was only right that he would join them. Now Byron's soul had acquired a particularly unpleasant shadow as a guide on one last rampage.

John moved out of the tunnel to witness this new revelation. There he was, as large as death.

"No more reclamations," said Byron insanely.

"What are you talking about?" said Sandy.

"Our souls will never be sent back. Kill!" he screamed.

The response seemed to act as a rallying cry. Any vessols infected by the shadows advanced on the Soul Catcher. They swarmed over it like a plague of locusts.

"What are they doing?" shouted Brimstone.

"I don't know," said Sandy honestly.

The shadows, aided by their newly acquired plastic hosts, attacked panels, unscrewed bolts, smashed screens and removed any part that they could lay their hands on. Pieces of complex engineering were cast to the ground like a demolition team carrying out one last deadline before the pubs shut.

"Stop, you must stop!" said Brimstone.

The workings of the vast machine, housed under the bulb and behind the panel of knobs and levers, was opened to the world like petals flowering for the first time. In the centre was a small ball of shiny metal, levitated by a matrix of blue energy pulses. It rotated on its own axis with no obvious source of propulsion. The vessols tore towards it as if addicted to some highly prized treasure.

"Please don't touch that. If they touch that they'll destroy the machine," begged Brimstone to Sandy.

"I think that's their motive," replied Sandy who'd calculated that the result didn't affect him too much. He wasn't interested in going back, even if he could. This was his realm now and if no one could go back then no one could come to take it off him.

"John," said Brimstone, "You must help me."

"Hmmm…smokey twat…you were trying to accuse me…cracks…it might be important…knickers…"

"John, I beg you. It's vital for everyone that they don't break it," said Brimstone, metaphorically if not literally on his knees.

John didn't know who to trust anymore other than himself. Hell was on his list and Sandy wasn't. Over many lifetimes they'd lied to him. But there was something deep inside him screaming out in defiance. Where would the souls go if they broke this Soul Catcher? Maybe nowhere. Even here was better than nowhere? Would the world suddenly be flooded with a horde of ghost souls? John's righteousness battled with his need for revenge.

"John, I forbid you to help," said Sandy. "You're only here because of me. You'd never have sent Faith back without my help."

It was all too much. Who could he trust? Crazily he ran towards the machine. Whether to stop them or help them, he still wasn't entirely sure.

"Ian, get him. And the rest of you," said Sandy, indicating the remaining animals still hiding in the entrance of the tunnel.

The animals intervened before John reached the deconstruction efforts. They ushered him back to where Sandy was still standing a few feet away from Brimstone.

"I can't have you disobeying me," said Sandy, puffing out his chest in an attempt to inflate his own self-importance. The glare of power evident in his plastic pupils. "Brimstone is right. You are the reason I'm here, John. You double-crossed me. It's you and you alone who is responsible. I have wreaked my vengeance on Hell and now I will wreak it on you. Bring a vase."

"But John's our friend," said Ian.

"No. He never was, and neither are you."

"Don't be like that, Sandy," said Ian. "I know I've got faults. Everyone has. John made a mistake, that's all."

"You're both idiots. If you don't want to join his fate I'd shut your mouth," he snapped.

"I predicted this," said Roger in a loud voice that demanded recognition. No one gave him any.

"Pour it down his throat," instructed Sandy to the six-inch half-demon who'd been using the vase to threaten Brimstone.

"No! This is wrong," said Ian, jumping to John's defence.

"Traitor!" shouted Sandy. "After all I have done for you."

"What *have* you done for me? All you do is insult and poke fun at me," replied Ian.

"Get him out of my sight. Put him where he belongs," said Sandy, aiming his demands at the remaining animals. They obeyed, not wanting to be the next to get on Sandy's angry side. The creatures dragged the white pigeon away down the nearest tunnel. Sandy signalled for the shadow to be released from its vase.

"You're messing with processes you don't understand," said Brimstone. "You don't know what will happen. There's only two-thirds of John inside there."

"I like experiments."

Off came the stopper. Unrestricted by the glass, the shadow crept hungrily out of its cave. It had been kept prisoner for ages, watching as his shadowy friends were released to an orgy of fun. It was starving for a piece of the action. Without waiting for the starting pistol, it surged into John's vessol.

Its eagerness to join the 'fun' was somewhat misplaced. Its comrades had had one major advantage. They'd all been drawn towards the neutral elements of the souls within their victims. They'd easily devoured these elements and displaced them into the atmosphere. Sadly John's neutral section was involved in its own issues, some considerable distance and time away. Its absence had quite an effect.

Those watching could only imagine from the external evidence the great battle being fought inside the fake rodent. The plastic skin rippled with receding waves, each greater than the last. It wobbled, shrank and then expanded slightly. Then for a while nothing happened at all. A concoction of expletive combinations exploded into the air in a flurry of insults, aimed mainly at Sandy. It ended with an almighty fusion of light, energy and noise which ripped the vessol apart and left small pieces of plastic shrew in every corner of the vast cavern.

Several other phenomena happened at once, although not all were visible in the same dimension.

A large book started to burn. Although the burning had begun, even the fire responsible couldn't predict when it would stop. You could keep a supply of marshmallows going forever, if you could whittle a stick long and inflammable enough,.

The shadow-infected vessols managed to remove the small ball of metal from the Soul Catcher, and with a howl and a screech all activity stopped. When the machine was placed on standby, as it sometimes was, pulses would still explore into space. Not anymore. The lights faded, the energy dissipated and the conveyor belts shuddered to a halt. The ball of metal floated up into the glass bulb, along the barrel and fired itself into space. Brimstone sank to his knees which was only about eight inches below him.

A sloth took one final step on a journey, from tunnel to cavern, that had started so promisingly.

"What."

"Did."

"I."

"Miss?"

*****

David ran down the stairs of the farmhouse, brain working as fast as his legs to come up with a plan. When he reached the bottom step something passed through him like a bout of nostalgia, a feeling you can neither explain nor re-create. Long-forgotten memories ordered themselves in his brain.

Closing his eyes, he watched as time sped the memories towards an inevitable conclusion, as if his life had been made into a flick book. The final picture painted itself on his mind and he acknowledged it with a small, internal nod. If the vision was accurate, as he believed, then there was little time to complete his tasks.

The end was coming.

*****

The Clerk looked up from his chair. A noise like a decelerating jumbo jet was fading into the distance. The absence of a noise is almost more disconcerting than the shock of an unexpected one. When you were used to a perpetual soundtrack in the background, you noticed when it wasn't there anymore. There was nothing more synonymous about Limbo than the crackles that thumped through the sphere with the precision of a beating heart.

In eerie silence the Clerk held his breath. He crossed his fingers in the hope that someone was firing up the world's largest defibrillator. The silence continued with the same non-stop regularity that the noise once had. The heart of Limbo had stopped beating.

As the line of souls continued to dive through the liquid metal with the predictability of lemmings, his chair appeared to be moving closer to it. He stood up. The chair stayed put. He sat down again. He swore the wall was still getting closer. He grabbed a piece of chalk from the desk and marked a thick line on the floor next to the boundary of the metal. Then he watched and waited.

CHAPTER TWENTY-FIVE

TIME AND MOTION

Under the cover of darkness the hull of the *Unicorn* glided into the waters of a calm sea. The sails caught hold of the breeze and pulled gently against the mast. A hand drew the sail further towards it and the small craft eased away from the shoreline. The moon escaped under the ripples of the water as the keel dragged on, and easily overcame, submerged obstacles. Slowly the boat's progress increased, but not fast enough for the captain. Science was very clear about it: speed was a matter of distance and time. The distance to the next island was fixed. On this occasion time wasn't.

*****

"They've got Scrumpy," called John as he swept into the lounge. "What's happened in here?"

A group of people were involved in a rather surreal game of 'musical statues' and the music had definitely stopped. A man in black, almost camouflaged by his surroundings, stood perfectly still, hands behind his head. The reasons for this were clear. A military-grade weapon was being held at close range by another shoddily dressed figure. The only person definitely not winning the game was a young blonde who was cradling a middle-aged body on her knees. There was only one winner. In the face of some unknown horror, Nash's eyes were closed. His face had set like concrete and all four limbs had lost contact with their nervous system.

"Faith's come back to us," said the gun wielder. "And this one has been sent by Byron."

Instantly David's brain sent him a reminder letter with red font all over the top. Of course they'd be together. Now everyone on his list was here. The only question was what to do about it. Nash's groans indicated a return to consciousness.

"Did I hear someone say they have Scrumpy?" said Fiona, bursting into the room looking panic-stricken.

"Yes. But we're going to get him back," replied David.

"What about Grace?" said Faith. "She's the only other one not here."

"So she does exist, then?" said David. "I was starting to believe she was a figment of Scrumpy's imagination. Even when I saw her upstairs I couldn't be certain."

"Of course she exists. She's my daughter," said Faith.

"Your daughter?"

"And mine…" replied Nash, not altogether convinced by the revelation.

"What? Sorry, I must be missing something."

"What business is it of yours?" said Violet. "You're just staff."

"No he isn't," replied Nash with a sigh. "This is John…Hewson…again…the proverbial boomerang."

"What?" said several people.

"Who?" said Faith, who had never officially been introduced.

"It'll take too long to explain now. How can Faith have had a baby? She's been devoid of emotions for the past twelve years. Did you…" – he looked at Nash – "…take advantage of her? You did have a little bit of a girl obsession as I recall."

"How dare you," he said, leaping from the floor and clasping his fist. "I'd never do that…ever…even back then."

"Then how can it have happened?" said David.

"The night my father sent me to Nash's apartment to find information. I stayed the night and we made love."

"Yes, I remember?" said David.

"What? Were you watching? Sicko," said Faith, also clenching her fist. David was outnumbered and a little confused.

"In a way," he said, unable to distance himself from the truth.

A fist hit him in the jaw.

Nash felt bad that it hadn't been his, but the truth was he already knew. He grabbed Faith's hand before she could strike again.

"It's not his fault. Well, not totally, anyway. He wasn't watching in the way you think. That night, when I said he was my soulmate, I wasn't being metaphorical. John's soul was possessing mine. Victor here can confirm, can't you?"

"Don't drag me into your perverse little game. Weirdos. I'm not on your side, remember?"

The barrel of Violet's gun kicked him in the guts.

"Yep…" he said with a forced breath. "It's true."

"Victor, after you kidnapped Faith from Herb's flat, how quickly did you give her Emorfed?"

"The same morning I think," he replied.

"That would mean the foetus inside Faith would have been affected by the drug as well. What impact would it have on her soul?"

"She's always been different," said Fiona. "Very few emotions. I always suspected that Emorfed had altered her, but she wasn't the same as Faith. Unlike Faith, she wasn't haunted by the shadow."

"Well, she wouldn't be. Her soul mutated before it was even born. She never lost part of her soul because it never existed in the first place," said David.

"None of this is important," pleaded Faith, a maternal instinct kicking in that wasn't possible twenty minutes ago. "Where is she?"

"She's gone after the boy," said Violet, whose eyes remained fixed on Victor.

"It's very likely," said Fiona. "She's only ever been interested in him. There's a bond between them."

"Then we'll go after both of them," replied David defiantly. "Victor, tell us what you know."

"Why would I do that? I've been trained to resist interrogation, you know. It's not that hard, particularly if you're doing it."

"Do you see this list?" said David opening up the folder he'd brought from upstairs. "Your name is here, look. This is the list of people I am going to make pay for their involvement in John's fate. The easy thing would be to shoot you. It's been ages since I drew a line through one of these names and even then I didn't get to pull the trigger."

"Well, you're not the only one looking for revenge," said Victor. "You ruined me, remember."

"You did that to yourself. Violet, I think we'll start with the left foot."

"You don't scare me."

A large shotgun cartridge hit the floor, shortly followed by Victor. The toecaps of his boot and, more importantly to Victor, several of his toes were no longer visible at the end of his foot. Everyone's ears were ringing as the smoke cleared. Victor refused to show any weakness or react to his not inconsiderable pain.

"Is that your blood, by any chance?" said David.

"Do your worst," he croaked. "I've been chaperoning the Devil for the past few months. Do you think you can break me?"

"Yes. Thanks, by the way. I didn't know it was him, but I'll add him to my list."

"You can't stop him. He'll melt you before you get near him."

"Maybe. I saw that power from Laslow. He didn't use it against me then, and I don't think Byron will now. What deal has he offered you?"

"Money and power," replied Victor.

"You know he doesn't keep deals, don't you? I have first-hand experience."

"Then make me a better offer. How much have you got?"

"Nothing. Not a penny," said David. "I can offer you something more valuable."

"What's more valuable than money and power?"

"Answers. Hope. Maybe even redemption."

"You can't pay debts with those."

"Not here. The currency I offer isn't valid on Earth. Think about it," said David. "The rest of you keep him here."

"Where are you going?" said Nash.

"To find the children," replied David.

"I'm coming with you," replied Faith.

"No. You'll need to stay here and defend yourselves. They may come again. Keep Victor for bargaining, I'm not sure he's worth much, though."

David set the algorithms running. A number of options presented themselves, but crucial details labelled them invalid. One remained at the forefront, jumping for his attention. It lacked one piece of information to calculate its chance of success.

"Hi or low?" he said.

"Hi or low what?" asked Fiona.

"Tide."

*****

The island of Tresco, half a mile across the bay from Bryher, was starting to wake. Dawn had cracked open across the horizon and the residents were rising to a new day. Byron hadn't intended to stop here. The plan, and it was a loose description, had been to get the boy as far away as possible. The next island was as far from 'as far as possible' as it was possible to be, unless you counted not going anywhere at all. Several things had slowed him down, and he could only explain some of it.

The call from the telepathy network came first. No one talked. The noise that came through was the intergalactic equivalent of accidentally dialling a fax machine. It was a type of S.O.S., or more precisely an S.Y.S. call: Save Your Souls. Although the circumstances would have to be connected later, like a dot-to-dot connected to a self-destruct button, the consequences were clear. The heart had left his Soul Catcher. It stopped him in his tracks. Here he was dealing with human plebs, as the cretins he'd left in charge were allowing some inconceivable force to tear down his world.

This was still not the most concerning piece of news this morning. Morning was. He'd left at dusk, travelling at a speed even rocket pilots would be impressed with. Yet he'd arrived at dawn. Time didn't work like that down here. You could literally set your watch to it, unlike in Hell where you could only set your watch on fire and keep your hands warm.

"You're actually not a pirate, are you?!" said Scrumpy, still unable to escape his captor's clutches.

"No. Pirates don't have rockets in their shoes."

"Alien?"

"No," he said, still paying more attention to his surrounding than to the boy. The village was starting to see activity. They were on a simple high street just outside a small post office. Monoliths guarded the lawns like a band of granite security guards. Pretty wooden chalets with light blue paint jobs hugged pristine flower beds. A few characters were emerging from these wooden shells to see what the day offered. Soon someone might start to notice he was not a local.

"Ghost?"

"No."

"Pantomime Villain?"

"No. What?"

"You look like you're wearing make-up."

"No, I'm not," he said, rubbing his face to prove it. "And if I was a pantomime villain, surely I'd be behind you."

"Oh go on, tell me. I can't guess."

"Are you not frightened, little boy?"

"Not really," said Scrumpy. "I'm quite excited."

"Excited?"

"Yes. I've been waiting my whole life for this moment. I'm a soldier ready for battle."

"You seem a little underprepared. Aren't soldiers meant to be burly types with rough expressions and, oh what's that other important thing?" he said mockingly. "Yes that's it, weapons."

"I've got one."

"Is it your increasing ability to annoy me?"

"No, guess again."

"A talent for bullshit?"

"Keep trying."

"An exceedingly low attention span and the inability to understand danger?"

"What did you say? I wasn't listening. Only joking."

"Ok, I give up," he said, tiring of the game. "What is your amazing, fear-inducing and clearly non-existent weapon?"

"Her," he said with a nod.

*****

David turned the key. Something large and foreign rattled briefly. He tried again. The beast roared and a thousand mini-earthquakes directed themselves at his butt. The walls of the outbuilding clung onto each other to avoid being disintegrated by the anger confined so close to them. A cloud of black smoke gave notice of the monster's readiness to act. The key had both woken the machine and provided an incongruous soundtrack. Radio Four was blaring out from the front of the cab. Unable to identify which button turned it off, he left it playing.

The controls looked simple enough. Gearstick, pedals and steering wheel were all where he'd expected them. He shifted the tractor into first and inadvertently hit the accelerator. The alien Audi engine burst into life and David hung on for fear of falling. The tractor devoured the doors in front of it and raced off across the fields following the direction of the sun poking out from behind the treetops.

It was wrong to describe the motion as driving. David merely aimed and hoped whatever obstacle they collided with was somewhat less prepared than the red half-breed, full of rubber and metal. Down the incline it weaved, building speed as it went. The air rushed through the gap where a windshield once sat, forcing David backwards like being strapped into an experimental wind tunnel. The vehicle levelled out and made a beeline for the shore. New gears were initiated and the tractor hit a new personal best. With the grace of an ice-skating hippo, the tractor hit the sea and created a mighty spray behind it.

Where the sea had filled the channel a few hours before, the machine skipped and swerved over the remaining water and sandbanks, desperate to buck both driver and vehicle. The sea spat its contents in all directions, showering David with a coating of sand. A voice on Radio Four proclaimed some great political victory, right up until the point that the vehicle hit the beach of the destination shoreline and the radio displaced it for Radio Two. The new soundtrack accompanied the crescendo of stones being spun off by the four wheels as it advanced on the new terrain like a well-planned surprise attack. Up the beach and down a narrow track banked by gorse it marched.

Re-entry was achieved via a low stone wall that could no longer be described as organised. The monstrosity jolted to the left, following navigational instructions that were not available to the naked eye. It thundered down a concrete road, marshalled by palm trees, towards a collection of cottages. Desperately David tried to slow its progress by easing off on everything that he'd potentially been doing to that point. On either side of him, in the windows of houses, a blur of battered red paint flashed by.

Was he heading in the right direction? The tractor seemed to know better than he did. A deep sense of déjà vu rose above the algorithms that were imploding inside him. This strange imposter placed everything in order. It had been here before.

The song on the radio fitted the memory. The time of day was right. A battered red vehicle surrounded him. There was only one element missing. Any minute now she'd be there. In anticipation, he slammed on the brakes. Fifty feet in front of him a young boy was flung into his path. Almost immediately after arriving the boy was knocked out of the way and substituted for another figure. In the middle of the road a young girl stood calmly smiling at him. Her bleached white hair flowed around her like wisps of fog on a breezy day.

The braking took effect and the sharp turn of the steering wheel added to the change of momentum. The tractor skidded sharply left, through a narrow gap in a short wall, before crashing into a building. David's head hit the dashboard as his body was catapulted into the sharp and unprotected frame of the tractor's cabin. Blood streamed down his forehead into his eyes. The tractor's bonnet was fused at right angles into the wall at the exact point where the post office had positioned a postbox. The pungent smell of fuel filled his nostrils and he waited for the inevitable.

CHAPTER TWENTY-SIX

JUDGE, JURY AND EXECUTIONER

He knew how this story ended. Why he knew was more of a mystery. Over the years, of more than one life, he'd speculated how it was possible that someone could die as a result of a mild head injury and a broken ankle. Fuel was flammable only if you had a way to ignite it. There was plenty of it gushing out of the tractor's broken petrol tank. He just needed to wait for a decrepit old man to light it. He didn't need to wait long. Although it wouldn't be the one he'd always visualised. How could it be?

Laslow had always worn the face of the man moving towards him in the rear-view mirror, through the blur of his clouded eyesight. In Limbo, Laslow had even confessed to being responsible for his death. But which death? At John's gravestone his mother had been adamant that Laslow had murdered her son with one single accurate shot to his chest. That murder had occurred in an apartment, and to his memory it wasn't anywhere near the Isles of Scilly. So maybe Laslow was confessing to that death? And at the same time manipulating the idea of this one inside him?

A crowd, which in the Scilly Isles was seen as anything more than two, had started to congregate around the incident. Big news here was someone losing a wedding ring or the escape of a wayward goose. They weren't used to 'real' news. Other than stare agog they weren't sure what to do. The police, singular in this instance, was still eating breakfast somewhere on the other side of the island. Response times being measured in days rather than minutes here. A man in a hat broke off from the crowd and approached the accident. When he reached the fractured remains of the cabin where David was still trapped, he doffed his hat.

"Hello, David."

"Donovan. I didn't know who to expect," replied David, turning his head painfully to his right where the figure was leaning against the door frame. The man's black shirt clashed with the dog collar around his neck and the white mane that flowed out from under his hat. The skin sagged under his chin, covered with liver spots and blemishes that the passage of age had decided to leave undisturbed.

"You were expecting this?" said Donovan.

"I thought I'd already been through it."

"Interesting. That's the problem with living for so long."

"Eleven isn't long."

"You shouldn't be counting in years. You should count in lives."

"I lost count at two."

"Then you're only counting you and John. I suspect you are well into a few dozens by now, although perhaps someone else knows more than I do." He scanned the crowd to see if the one who could answer was there.

"As many as that," he said with a groan of pain.

"And every one of them has been fired across the Universe at least once, maybe more. Your soul is probably the most well-travelled entity in the known world. Think of the miles on the clock."

"I must be due a service."

"It's coming," he replied sinisterly. "One cosmic trip for every time you've been born or reborn. Another one to locate a specimen or to lie dormant, waiting for your next death. It's no surprise you see more than you have seen."

"See?" said David struggling against the metal frame restricting his movement.

"Time, David. You can't outrun time, but you can see through it. Your senses and memories have been shot across the Universe, faster than the speed of light, so many times that I think your memories have caught up with themselves. Déjà vu. You have seen glimpses of your future, or past as it is now."

"Why you, though? It was always Laslow in your position."

"Well, it's Baltazaar's turn."

"It's not a game."

"It is to us. He's killed you so many times I suspect you have supplanted him in your premonition. One old man for another."

"Your turn to do what?" he said with a whimper.

"To execute a juror. He's killed six of the twelve at the last count. I've only killed five."

"But why do they have to be killed at all? They've done so much for both of you," asked David.

"The jurors were always going to have their souls stretched beyond what they were designed for. They were only human, after all. They were chosen well. The most perfectly balanced neutrals that he and I could find. It was easy to tell if they were suitable. Only true neutrals can pass through the Celestium without removing their souls from their bodies. When they were no longer needed to judge their peers, Satan used them to find the mutations that came from the Limpet Syndrome. But every mission brought more questions. One by one they, too, started to trigger the condition, which was the first I knew about their new purpose."

"Why?"

"Because I didn't know what Satan had done."

"And because you gave up on mankind and turned off your own Soul Catcher."

"No," he said curtly. "They gave up on me. Then they gave up on themselves. Have you seen the world, David? Humans have ruined it. Selfish, greedy, narcissistic idiots obsessed in their eagerness to destroy their own species as long as it means they benefit individually. They have no place in Heaven. Faith has to be earned, not bought or fought for."

"They're not all like that."

"Then the idiots have spoilt it for the rest. They used to love me, and now they only love themselves. Well, they can have it. Soon their own self-obsession will be their downfall."

"Some people just don't want to love a cruel god whose wrath and injustice they see on a daily basis. You created the conditions for them to fall out of love with you, Baltazaar. How can they love a god that sits by and watches while so much suffering happens? You started it."

"And I will finish it."

"God protects the King," muttered David. "You're the selfish one."

"Oh you liked my little piece of graffiti, then. It was ironic that the name Baltazaar should include the word King. Old Donovan here was a perfect choice as a host."

Petrol was seeping into the cabin and soaking into his clothes. If not all of his premonition had been accurate, perhaps the conclusion wasn't either.

"As much as I've enjoyed chatting with you, if you'd be so kind as to call for an ambulance, I'll be on my way."

"Ha ha. You have an excellent sense of humour for someone without emotions and feelings," said Donovan.

"I don't really do compliments. My brain doesn't recognise them."

"There's no way out this time. No one can live forever, David."

"Well, I seem to be making a good fist of it so far."

"Even you can't last forever. You see, just like the other eleven, you've outstayed your welcome. The Limpet Syndrome allowed me to find you and send you back to Hell to cause havoc, which you seem to be excelling at, by the way."

"I haven't been that close to it."

"No, you're all over the place. Splitting you up was never part of the plan, but it's had some useful and unexpected consequences."

"Unexpected?"

"It appears a third way might be opening and if that happens *he* might develop."

"He?"

"A third creator. Satan and I rule two-thirds of everything there is in the cosmos. We govern that which is ours, either positive or negative. But there is a dormant third of the cosmos that is home to neutrality. It never needed governing because no one originally desired what might be there. Faith itself was all that was needed. But as souls questioned their existence, some became neutral. The fear has always been that some way might be found to access that place. A paradise for those that don't believe in gods. A new gateway that might attract souls and reduce the amount of energy that we have to work with. That's Satan's biggest fear at least."

"Where is this third creator?" asked David.

"I believe he's already here."

"How do you know?"

"Well, you might not be able to see him from your pathetic position, but Byron is standing about a hundred yards away watching with interest to how I'm going to kill you."

"What does that have to do with the third coming?"

"Because he and I can't get this close to each other. Satan's constitution is built of purely negative energy. Three portions of six grams of it, fused together, as opposed to the three separate seven-gram portions that human souls start with. I have a similar structure to his, but conversely made of positive energy, but my three parts aren't fused together. When you bring two opposite poles of charge into the same vicinity it tends to break things. Just ask the Prince of Monaco. The Acts of God that occur tend to be quite powerful. Storms, earthquakes, that sort of thing."

"But not now."

"No. That's how I knew *he* had arrived. Because there is a third factor balancing it all out."

"And that's me, right?"

"I'm afraid so. It would appear that you are the manifestation of all things neutral. A divine being with unknown roots and powers. If you weren't, then the third tree would not have grown in the library and there would be no new book. You are *he*."

If David was, as Donovan suggested, a deity of all things logical, why didn't he have some awesome power that he could call on to move his sorry body out of the tractor? Perhaps the algorithms were all he had. He checked. They drew a blank. It was disappointing to be told that you were a god, when you were on the brink of death. Think of all those logical miracles he could experiment with. He immediately wanted to go and solve the problem of why so many people watched reality television when reality was, in fact, happening all around them if only they'd stop being so lazy and go out and experience it.

"If you're so positive and all that," said David as logic did its usual jog around his cranial block, "why are you so cruel?"

"I'm not cruel. I'm fussy."

"Is fussy positive?"

"I think it depends on your point of view."

"Surely a point of view is where you rationally weigh up all the information. That sounds like my job," he said, getting into character.

"It doesn't work like that. I'm fussy because I set the rules and the rules have changed. I'm not willing for you to change them further."

"But if you kill me, won't you open up the channel to the third way? If you can kill me, of course. I am a god now, don't forget," said David, attempting some form of mind games.

"You're not a real god. You were born human. You weren't generated by the Universe as we were. You're a fake, a freak, a phantom."

"I'm sticking with 'god'," replied David.

"Well, let's see if you die like a human or survive like a god."

Donovan King took out a lighter from his trouser pocket. A maniacal grin blossomed across his face as he tested it twice before setting light to the fuel seeping out onto the tarmac. The tractor, contents and surrounding areas were engulfed in flames. Donovan remained within the grip of the inferno. The fire licked his clothes with little impact. As the fire raged, David was overcome with pain and suffering.

"I could use it again!" he screamed.

"I'm counting on it," replied Donovan under his breath.

He walked out of the fireball, gently removing a few embers from his shirt and hat that hadn't got the original message. A small fire crew and one lone ambulance man took up the baton. By the time they reached the inferno they knew it was too late.

Death had never been this uncertain. Two algorithms worked at a speed never seen before by David's synapses. Checking and rechecking the factors that were in play, they competed with each to be the one selected. They both recorded the same odds of success because both were working with gaps in their knowledge. Neither knew ultimately what would happen. Baltazaar had originally told him that he could only use it twice. A third time would be catastrophic. But the survival instinct that came from the Limpet Syndrome still pulled with the force of a pack of huskies. Should he use it or die like everyone else did?

Donovan was using him. He'd told him what to do the last time. As a result he'd been removed from Nash and it had aided his pursuit of Byron. The second time it had helped him escape the square prison on level twelve. All actions clearly designed by the man that said a third time should not be attempted. It was true that God really did only protect the King. Donovan King. Well, he wouldn't get his way this time. The pull to survive just couldn't be ignored.

Donovan stood watching the flames with an amused grin on his face as Byron walked over to join him.

"How did he take it?" asked Byron.

"Which part?" replied Donovan.

"The bit about being a god."

"Pretty well, considering. He shouldn't be bothering us again. Our war can start again."

"Things have changed. The Soul Catcher in Hell has been turned off," said Byron.

"That's too bad," replied Donovan sarcastically. "Having some problems up there, are you? Really should pick your staff more carefully."

"Where will the souls go if both Soul Catchers are turned off?" asked Byron.

"Only one place they can go," replied Donovan.

"Limbo?"

"Yes."

"But it won't cope with the volume."

"I shouldn't think so," he said, his grin stretching further across his face.

"You bastard. This was your plan from the start. You tried containing the human spirit with Emorfed, and when that didn't work you thought you'd try to destroy Earth itself. Limbo will expand until it can't take any more. It will eventually consume the Earth."

"You really are slow, Satan. This is war, you know that."

"But how is this going to win a war against me?"

"Oh, you thought I was at war with you…" Donovan burst into laughter. "How disappointing. My war is against them. If I wanted to win, I had to destroy your ability to rescue them."

"But why?" implored Satan.

"Because they question my authority. They question my existence. They started the war."

"I will stop you," replied Satan calmly.

"You'll try. After all there's no point being immortal if you've got nothing to do."

They waited patiently for an event that would mark their cue to leave. Murders didn't normally take this long. Fire had an uncanny habit of being a rather slow death. The event they were waiting for, a small blue cloud levitating into the sky, would have arrived much sooner if they'd shot him or had him electrocuted. Byron looked at his wristwatch. It had stopped.

"How long has it been?" he said.

"Not long. Burning to death can take ages," Donovan replied. "What's wrong with your watch?"

"Nothing."

"It's frozen, look. It says it's one in the morning."

"Oh so it does," he said, shaking it, the universal action for trying to make a watch work, even though in the history of forever it had proven effective on zero occasions. "Did you feel like the night went by rather quickly?"

"I'm not good with time: no watch, see."

"But you must have noticed it went from dark to light faster than you designed it to."

"If you say so."

The fire brigade finally doused the flames and allowed the one single medic to approach a torso that was very different from what he was used to. Most of his patients had a pulse or at the very least some sign of life. This one had one redeeming feature: soot. A very large pile of it had collected in places that used to feature upholstery. If he'd had the courage to explore the corpse he might have notice a very small ball bearing of metal. When no one was looking, it very silently floated off into the sky and out of sight.

"I don't get it," said Satan. "Where's his soul?"

"He was completely neutral, maybe they don't float off like normal. Maybe they don't have that familiar blue colour."

"Perhaps. But there's another thing I can't work out."

"What's that?" said Baltazaar.

"If David was the third coming, why are we still able to stand this close to each other?"

*****

Grace and Scrumpy reached the *Unicorn* where it had been moored carefully amongst much larger vessels. As they sailed in silence away from Tresco, a weather system was starting to develop over the island. Small at first, the further they sailed towards Bryher, the more it grew. A rumble of thunder crackled over their heads.

CHAPTER TWENTY-SEVEN

CELESTIUM

The Clerk woke up from his nap with a start. He'd been asleep for approximately three and a half feet. That's how far the Celestium wall had moved since he'd shut his eyes. The waiting room was half of its original size, and the chalk mark some metres on the other side of the metal. He'd already moved much of the room's furniture into the Tailor's next door in preparation for the retreat that would come if Limbo continued to expand. The souls were still flowing in, they just weren't flowing out. Where would he go once the Tailor's room was flooded? There were only two places he could: out or in.

In meant being pressed on by a thousand confused souls desperate to know what was next. Out meant outside. Into the real world. It had been a very long time since he'd been out there. He hadn't liked it very much.

*****

Sandy had deliberated for ages. Given the magnitude of the position he now adopted, it really wasn't the most important of decisions. What title to give himself? He'd experimented with Lord, President and Emperor, but none of them had the right ring to it. The problem with power is it went to your head somewhat. You only really listened to yourself.

"What do you think?" he said.

"I don't *think*," said Brimstone, whose silver belt had been replaced by an apron. It had to be made out of silver because everything else melted.

"You do what I tell you," replied Sandy.

"For now. It won't last, you know. All these dictators fall in the end," he said, pointing out a number of familiar personalities that were sitting uncomfortably in thrones not designed for them.

"I'm going to go with Master of Hell," said Sandy proudly.

"Whatever," sighed Brimstone.

There was plenty still to be done. Pillows had been requested as a matter of urgency as Sandy was too small to see over the table from Asmodeus's throne. Pillows were scarce in Hell so plastic blocks lined with AstroTurf were used as an alternative. The rest of his animal army had been escorted back to level zero via the gap over the edge of level twelve, much to their consternations.

Roger insisted he wasn't bothered as he had 'better things to do'. Vicky had already refused to be amongst the mutated vessols as they were bound to steal all of the good jobs. Elsie assumed it was a prank and went with the flow, using the time to create a counter-prank. And Gary, well, it would take him so long to get anywhere, they let him roam, if roaming was feasible at a speed slower than rocks moved.

Level one was currently being converted into a home for convalescing lesser demons. Their only job was to ensure that the lake always remained full and nothing was allowed to escape from level zero. The rest of the time they could spend enjoying the many new features being built there, soon to include a museum of torture, Hell's longest zip wire experience, and three casinos.

"What happens now?" said Brimstone.

"Everyone just enjoys themselves and does what I tell them," replied Sandy.

"And then what? What happens when everything changes?"

"Changes will only be granted on my command."

"Evolution doesn't work like that," said Brimstone. "It doesn't wait for someone to press the 'go' button. It tends to get on with it."

"Then we will suppress it."

"Are you familiar with the expression, 'even in death, life finds a way'?"

"Not really."

"Can I suggest you get familiar with it. If there are no working Soul Catchers then souls will build up in Limbo. Do you know what souls are good at?"

"No."

"Evolution."

*****

"I've never been to one of these," said Aqua shivering a little. "It's quite exciting, isn't it?"

The snow under his swirling body had started to freeze, making swirling much more of a challenge. Snow was mainly water, with a scattering of plastic to help it freeze, of course. Mr. Fungus sneezed. The cold biomes weren't very appealing. They always dampened his mood and made his athlete's foot flare up. Mr. Gold and Mr. Silver's joints had seized completely and their faces suggested they weren't enjoying themselves.

The animals had congregated as normal. They weren't going to miss a pass over, even if a few gatecrashers had arrived without tickets. They knew the order of things. There would be no fighting for position or jostling for view anymore. The newcomers could sit wherever they wanted.

Asmodeus had the best seat in the house, although his mind wasn't really focused on the walrus looking frail in the gully at the bottom of the glacier. That was a sideshow. The reincarnates could get as excited as they wanted. What interested him was plans.

"Snow cone," said Mr. Graphite, leaning across with an outstretched craggy hand.

"No."

"They're very good."

"Don't care."

"Suit yourself…Ice pop?"

"Do you know what you can do with that?"

"I think you lick it."

"I was going to make a very different suggestion," replied Asmodeus. "What's the point in all of this, anyway? So they sit around waiting for one of them to die… Again, where's the fun in that?"

"Just entertainment. Not much else happens down here by all accounts. They say this one will be the best one ever," added Graphite.

"No. Mine was the best ever. Brilliant it was. It drew the biggest crowd anyone has ever seen and had more noise and light than the history of life."

The lion licked its snow cone.

"You can't sit here, this is a demon-only area," said Bitumen as all the demons looked at the imposter.

"I think you'll find lions are kings and have preferential treatment."

"Of jungles," said Aqua.

"Even jungles have winters, don't they?" he shrugged.

"This is not a jungle in winter!" said Graphite.

"Prove it."

"Anyway, how can you have had the best pass over if your still here?" said Mr. Virus.

"Magic," said Roger.

"Lions aren't magical," replied Aqua. "Rabbits, yes."

"Roger," said Primordial calmly.

"Oh, I didn't see *you* there."

"Well, you do now," added Primordial. "I have a request."

"Anything, sir."

"Fuck off."

"Yes, sir," replied Roger, padding back to the animals crowded further up the glacier.

"Interesting. How did you do that?" asked Graphite.

"He's a pussy," said Primordial.

The walrus groaned and for a moment everyone got excited. A hush swept through the plastic world. It was a false alarm. Walruses groaned even when they weren't passing over.

"You can't sit there."

"Sit where?" said Mr. Bitumen.

"I'm not talking to you."

"Then who are you talking to, Mr. Virus?"

"I'm not blocking anyone," replied Virus.

"I'm talking to you. Yes, you."

"Who, me?"

"Yes."

Everyone reassessed their positions to see who they might, or might not, be blocking from seeing a groaning walrus in the last moments of its afterlife. Asmodeus went back to assumptions.

"What's happening, Mr. Noir? Have you made contact with Brimstone yet?"

"It's happening everywhere."

"What is?"

"Someone is sitting in my space."

"But don't you occupy all the space in between all other stuff?" said Mr. Silver.

Mr. Gold put his fingers in his ears.

"Yes. But someone else is sitting there?" said Mr. Noir.

"Well, where do you want me to sit? Everywhere I go you seem to be there."

"That's because I'm everywhere and nowhere at the same time."

"Well, that's a little selfish, isn't it?"

"The point is, I don't normally interact."

"Bugger off, then."

"I can't because you are also everywhere. Everywhere that I should be," replied Mr. Noir indignantly.

"Am I? Interesting."

"Mr. Noir, what are you going on about?" said Asmodeus breaking out of his internal strategising.

"Someone is where I am?"

"Do I need to assume they are…?"

"No, they really are."

"But who is?" said Asmodeus.

"Me," said John.

*****

François, the Jungfrau guide, stood on the path a few metres from the viewing platform that used to be the only vantage point to see the ball of Celestium down below. Now you could see it from multi-locations. They still called it the viewing platform because you could still view things from it, only now if you stood on it you'd be seeing the inside of that metal. The once thin fissure that zigzagged across the mountain range was widening by the day. Now the distance between the sides was only passable with a helicopter or a massive amount of stupidity.

Pushing through the earth like acne on a teenager's skin, the top of the metallic dome was visible between the cliffs of rock and ice. At the speed it was expanding, soon the whole valley would be pushed to one side as it accelerated its dominance over the terrain. Today's group of visitors were not paying tourists.

Seismologists, geologists, climate scientists and physicists from all corners of the globe had made their way at the request of the Swiss Government. Rogier Hofstetter was not there in a scientific capacity. It was he who had made the request.

On arrival, the group of experts had immediately scattered to commence their own assessments of the metal bubble poking out of the landscape. They'd never seen anything like it. The Swiss Prime Minister motioned for the congregation to gather around.

"Ladies and gentlemen. As you can see, this is a significant crisis for my country," stated Rogier. "At the current speed of expansion we estimate that this object will overcome this valley by the end of the month. What answers can you give me?"

"Geology-wise it can't keep expanding without some way of replicating itself. Metals don't do that," said a voice from the crowd of experts.

"In my opinion a seismic event must be occurring somewhere below. Perhaps a new type of volcano erupting without breaking through the Earth's mantle," said another.

"Prime Minister. We are dealing with a substance none of us have any experience of," added a third voice desperately.

"Not strictly true," came a fourth voice.

Mr. Hofstetter tried to identify the last opinion. A man in a suit had his hand in the air. "What is your particular area of expertise, sir?"

"Endgames," said the Clerk with a heavy heart.

CHAPTER TWENTY-EIGHT

GRACE LAND

A small ball of metal, no bigger than a marble, rolled into grass that extended across the plain like an army of paper soldiers. The individual white blades waved in welcome as it trundled to a stop amongst their throng. The rays from a dark red sun overhead glinted off its surface. The grass sheaths checked their simple hairdos on its reflective surface. The liquid metallic ball danced to an unknown alien tune in a world that only it occupied.

The ball soon got bored. It wanted to know what else there was to see. Its internal energy rotated it forward as it rolled through the crowded plain. Seeking a solution that had never been found, it dashed through the maze of purity. As it moved it gathered pace and size, able to gaze over the tops of the stems by the time it reached the edge of the meadow.

It stopped quickly as it felt itself reach the edge of something deep and wide. Below, a vast cavity had been purposely excavated in the ground with the precision of a major mining corporation. Whatever had been mining, or mined, here had gone long ago. The remaining chasm was the only evidence of either. The ball sat in quiet nostalgia. It was no ordinary metal. It was Celestium and it had found the way.

*****

If the beautiful island of Tresco was going to continue to offer tourists a wondrous experience of exotic plants, and not just become a large body of water with too many jagged edges, one of them would have to move. When the storm began, Donovan had reacted first. As was his tendency, he floated off on the south-easterly slipstream. Gods had plenty of energy and the unique power to control some of the elements. Air was to Donovan as fire was to Byron. The question remained what powers the third deity would take as their own.

Donovan departed because, in his naivety, he believed it proved the 'third coming' had come and gone. David had passed away and the unique amalgam of his and Byron's polar opposites combined violently to demonstrate it. Byron wasn't so sure. A few things didn't make sense.

The meteorological disturbances had been slow to develop, as if David's final journey had been delayed and drawn out. Souls didn't work that way. If his final neutral soul was released it would only survive seconds before being drawn to Limbo.

Then there was the whole question of time. Sure, in Hell moments could last hours, and hours last days, but not here. Something or someone had tampered with it, moved it forward without him noticing. Six or seven hours had been stolen, if his watch was anything to go on. What happened to that time? Had he just lost it or was someone holding it hostage, expecting him to pay a ransom?

Byron continued to stroll along the beach, watching Bryher's shore a few hundred metres across the water. The tide was low and a path opened up across the estuary. He followed it casually. If he so wished, he could get there quicker, but he wanted time for thought and only his brain was going to steal it from him.

Two battles loomed in the near future. One would be fought over the fate of the world. The second would be one final devastating battle of gods. Help would be needed. It would not come from Hell. Its fate was out of his hands now. It might come from the only soldier who still fought by his side. Sure, Victor was a simple man. You paid him more than the opposition, and he worked for you with a ruthless efficiency and very little moral afterthought. That might still come in useful.

He mounted the rocks that led up onto the beach. A track lay to the side of a small chapel where a number of people were congregating outside, clothed in casual dresses and short-sleeved shirts. It must be a Sunday. The stained glass glistened as he passed the congregation with a smile. The sight of a bald-headed man with complex tattoos doodled on the back of his head, wearing a shambolic, wet, red velvet suit, didn't generate much of a warm welcome. They hurried into the small graveyard that acted as the chapel's welcome mat.

Which war would come first? The war against man had already begun. Limbo would be swelling with emotional energy, unable to escape the Celestium that ensnared it. Eventually, he guessed, there were two likely outcomes. Limbo would engulf the world, or humans would start to trigger the Limpet Syndrome in large numbers, unaware of their own fate. Just as some had done when Heaven's Soul Catcher had been deactivated all those years ago. Neither outcome was desirable. That battle must be fought first.

He'd been played for a fool for too long. Blindly he'd fallen into the trap of believing that Baltazaar's ploy to destroy the gateway to Heaven was a good thing. Hell had gorged on the flood of souls pushed there by a Limbo. They'd grown fat and lazy whilst Baltazaar had worked his plot to bring them to their knees. They were complicit in the demise of humankind. How had he fallen for it so easily? John may have helped him out of Laslow's old body, but the cost had been extortionate. Those responsible would feel his terrible anger.

Over the heathland he climbed. Vast boulders, carried and dropped by giants of a bygone age, lay paralysed amongst the heather. The occasional honesty box, selling fudge or fruit, nestled at the front porches of isolated properties. The only noise came from the oystercatchers that swooped like spy planes under the radar of the fog. At the top of the hill the expanse of Hell Bay opened up in front of him.

At the gateway to the old farmhouse he paused as he had done less than twenty-four hours before. The building stood peaceful, stone bricks idle in their duty to hold up wooden frames and terracotta tiles. It would not remain so for long. His normal calmness was being tested. The fire, in nerve and sinew, struggled to be freed like a stallion restrained by a railing. He pointed at the chimney with an outstretched finger and pulled it like a trigger. The chimney burst into flames and sent smoke billowing down into the house.

"That was just a warning shot," he said.

Violet had heard him. The family were still boarded up in the lounge as David had suggested. Chipboard had been placed up against the windows and larger furniture dragged in front of doorways. They'd never thought the chimney was a weakness. Now a steady stream of toxic, black smoke was filling the room. Nash, Violet, Faith and Fiona worked to remove the mock wooden shutters to allow the windows to be opened.

"I want you to let Victor go. Deliver him to me and I will not harm you. Delay and I will burn you all."

A littler paler than normal, due to the loss of blood, Victor was sitting in an armchair scheming a route out of his predicament. This intervention was a welcome surprise.

"Let him go," said Violet to the others.

"What? Why?" said Nash.

"Because if you don't, I fear we will all die."

"Why?" said Faith.

"Because he has told me," Violet pointed to her head and Nash got a flashback.

"It's not John, is it?"

"No. I think it's worse."

"It's Satan," said Victor pulling himself to his feet. "Or Dad, if your name's Faith."

Faith ran to the window to dispel the trick that was being played on her. The man was thinner and more appealing than the hard and unattractive face that once belonged to her father.

"That's not my father," she said.

"It's his body," replied Victor. "Open all the doors. I'm a little injured and low on medication to be messing around with door antics right at the moment."

Victor hobbled through the opened entrance and out into the cool autumn freshness. A macabre 'dot-to-dot' of blood was cast on the ground as he made his way down to the gate.

"Byron, I appreciate your support," said Victor. "Did you find David?"

"Oh yes."

"Why did you come back?"

"I need your support," replied Byron. "There will be a war, Victor."

"Excellent. Good money, is it?"

"If we lose, you'll have nowhere to spend it. This war will be bigger than greed. Did you find Faith?"

"Not before the shadow returned to her."

"That is a shame. At least she'll be whole for her next journey."

Byron's eyes burnt so fiercely that Victor had to move away from the heat. His hands came together above his head in prayer. In one slow handclap every part of the farmhouse caught fire. Soon Limbo would have to accommodate a few more. He watched it burn. Or at least he thought he did. The flames weren't moving. It was almost as if someone had painted flames on the building, and for the briefest of moments he thought he saw the glimpse of a white-haired girl entering the house to the right-hand side.

*****

None of the occupants knew how they'd escaped the burning building, but it was safe to say they had. From the precarious sanctuary of Merrick Island, Hell Bay opened up in front of them. Its large inland lake of water was being buffered from the sea by a ring of land. A small boat was tied to the rocks below them.

They counted themselves. Two children and four adults, one more than the family was used to. The imposter, they knew now, was family. Nash held Faith close to him to keep her warm from the icy breeze battering the exposed mass of rock.

Grace was reunited with both her father and mother and yet there was no joy or emotion in either. Scrumpy skimmed stones into the sea as Fiona and Violet found comfort in hugging each other. Grace was watching the smoke billow from the only home she'd ever known. Whereas the women wept for their loss, Grace was unmoved. It was just another puzzle, one of the biggest she'd ever seen.

"What just happened?" asked Nash. "How did we get out alive. One moment we were in the house and then we weren't."

"She does that," said Scrumpy.

"Does what?" asked Nash.

"Solves puzzles," replied Grace.

"She just puts her finger to her lips, and there we were on the *Unicorn*. Really amazing. I've seen her do it a few times now," said Scrumpy.

"I really don't understand," replied Nash.

"It's just another puzzle," said Grace. "It may be that *I'm* the puzzle."

*****

After what only seemed the briefest of pauses to Byron, the fires came back to life. Where they'd become static and lifeless, they transformed into a ferocious, all-consuming blaze.

"It keeps happening," he said angrily.

"What does?"

"Time. It keeps cheating. Didn't you feel it? It moved."

"Really? I didn't feel anything."

"Something isn't right here. Who was inside?"

"Nash, Fiona, Violet, Byron's daughter and part of my foot. I don't know where the other girl went."

"What other girl?"

"They spoke about Faith's daughter. David went to find her and the boy."

He grabbed Victor by the collar. "How old was she?"

"I didn't see her, but they said she was born after Faith was given Emorfed. So, eleven, I guess?"

Byron sank to his knees. How could he have been so blind? His fingers clawed at the sandy soil until his fists were squeezing the life out of handfuls of dirt.

"What's wrong?" asked Victor.

"We were never waiting for him," Byron said under his breath.

"Waiting for who?"

"The third coming. Maybe you are right about the world, Victor. Things have changed. We were never waiting for the possibility that *he* would arrive. It was always a her."

"I'm not with you," said Victor.

"This girl is the third coming. The master of all things neutral and ruler of a Universe sealed off for eternity. To add insult to injury it appears she has the ability to manipulate time itself. If she can open the way, the energy of souls will be drawn there and leave nothing for the rest of us."

"Is she important in the war to come?"

"Yes. She might not know it yet, but she determine who wins. Mankind or gods, only one will survive what is to come."

JUNE 2018

DEAD ENDS
How to Survive the Afterlife Book 3

Sign up to the newsletter
www.tonymoyle.com/contact/

Printed in Great Britain
by Amazon